DEMON
DERBY

ALSO BY CARRIE HARRIS

Bad Taste in Boys

Bad Hair Day

CARRIE HARRIS

DELACORTE PRESS

randomhouse.com/teens

Educators and librarians, for a variety of teaching tools,
visit us at RHTeachersLibrarians.com

Library of Congress Cataloging-in-Publication Data
Harris, Carrie.
Demon derby / Carrie Harris. — First edition.
pages cm
Summary: Once a true daredevil, South Carolina high school junior
Casey is in remission from cancer when a terrifying encounter at a Halloween
party leads her to become a demon-fighting roller derby girl.
ISBN 978-0-385-74217-7 (hardcover : alk. paper)
ISBN 978-0-307-97420-4 (ebook)
[1. Supernatural—Fiction. 2. Demonology—Fiction. 3. Roller skating—Fiction.
4. Martial arts—Fiction. 5. Cancer—Fiction.] I. Title.
PZ7.H241228Dem 2014
[Fic]—dc23
2012046890

The text of this book is set in 12.25-point Columbus.
Book design by Heather Kelly

Printed in the United States of America

10 9 8 7 6 5 4 3 2 1

First Edition

To my heroes:
Dr. Andy Harris and
the kids of Mott Hospital 7E

1

Once upon a time, whenever I saw a tall building, I wanted to jump off it.

I wasn't suicidal; I'd just always been a thrill seeker. But things changed. Instead of leaping off buildings and other assorted obstacles, I started taking a daily walk.

One day I walked to the Ice Dream Hut for a peanut butter shake, because I figured I deserved a treat. Besides, I thought the creamy frozen goodness might distract me from how crappy things were. At least, that was what I hoped.

On the way home, I found myself standing under a leafless maple across from the high school when the last bell rang. School wasn't something I missed; I'd rather be working on a trick, or on wheels, or maybe training at the dojo. There was a certain rush in mastering a new move. I missed *that*. I missed sitting at lunch with a crew of assorted friends, planning a new freerunning video or talking a little smack. Geometry and American lit and endless memorization of historical factoids I'd never use again? Only a masochist would miss those things. So the longing I felt looking at the squat brick building surprised me more than a little.

Within seconds, the doors flew open, spilling out a deluge of my former classmates. Homeschooling wasn't so bad; my parents generally left me to my own devices, and it kept my compromised immune system away from all the germs. But when the gangly, curly-haired figure of my best friend, Kyle, appeared in the stream of exiting students, I had to swallow a lump in my throat before I shouted his name.

"Hey, Kyle!" I clutched the half-empty foam cup to my chest and waved my hand overhead. "Over here!"

"Casey!" He crossed the full length of the parking lot at an easy jog, his hands clutching the waistband of his cargo shorts. At the end of October, South Carolina was still plenty warm enough for shorts, and I wasn't complaining. Kyle wasn't the intentional-droopy-pants type, more the too-skinny-to-find-clothes-that-fit type. "What are you doing here and why are you bald again?"

He was still shouting. The constant screeching came off as obnoxious but wasn't really his fault. He had permanent hearing loss in his right ear from a bad skateboard spill a couple of years ago. I'd been there. I still had nightmares on occasion that prominently featured his bleeding head.

I ran a hand over my smoothly shaven scalp. "My hair came

back patchy. It was either resort to a comb-over to hide the bald spot or embrace the hairlessness. It doesn't look stupid, does it? If it does, I can pass it off as part of my costume for tonight."

"No way. I told you before; you've got a nice head. *So what's up?*" The question came off insistent this time, and I realized I'd worried him by showing up out of the blue like this. I'd never come to meet him at school before, so he'd probably assumed the worst the moment he saw me.

"Chill, okay? I just happened to be passing by." I fixed him with a mock glare. "Why? Am I intruding on a rendezvous with someone you haven't told me about yet?"

He threw an arm around my neck and pulled me close. It wasn't a romantic hug; we'd never been like that, even though everyone assumed "best friends" really meant "secretly in love with each other." As if. It would have been like making out with my brother, except I didn't have one.

Maybe I imagined the hesitation in his voice before he said, "Nope." But we'd been friends for ten years, so I was pretty good at reading him.

"Come on, spill it." I pushed away and punched him lightly on the shoulder. "If I'm messing with your mojo, I need to know."

He grinned down at me, his mouth opening so wide that it practically cracked his face in half. He had the biggest mouth, like Steven Tyler huge. One time, he put a cue ball in it. "Nothing to spill. I got my favorite lady in the whole world on my arm. And if I had a second-favorite lady, I'd bring her to my first-favorite lady to be preapproved."

"As you should."

"Naturally." He paused again, his face screwing up into an expression of concern that didn't sit well on him. Kyle had been the carefree type until my diagnosis. Now he erred on the side of caution, especially where I was concerned. It was a far cry from the guy who used to race me up streetlights at night for kicks. "Can I walk you home?"

I took a sip of my half-melted drink, shaking my head. "Seriously, Ky. Why are you trying to get rid of me?"

He ran a hand through his hair, looking over his shoulder. The rest of the crew was descending the school steps—Willow and Luke on their skateboards, Lupo and Benji trotting alongside. It didn't take a rocket scientist to figure out what they were doing; we'd always gone out to work on our moves a few days a week after school. Mackinaw University, where my parents worked, was only a few blocks away, and it was full of accessibility ramps and handrails, benches and tall walls perfect for boarders and freerunners to practice on. Kyle was a competitive boarder, and I'd gotten into freerunning in junior high. Freerunning's a bit like gymnastics, but instead of practicing set moves in a gym, you find your own obstacles wherever you want and freestyle your way across them. There's something about treating the world like a playground to be explored that always appealed to me.

But now Kyle obviously didn't want me to come, and I tried not to take it personally. Getting sick had turned me from a jumper-of-random-objects type into a frail-patient type in a matter of weeks. But I was in remission now, and I hated that nothing had changed. I still slept all the time. I watched TV. I did my schoolwork at the kitchen table, and then I went back to bed again. The old Casey was gone, and I'd started to worry she wasn't ever coming back.

It was that fear more than anything else that made me push away from Kyle and greet the rest of the gang with a grin. "Hey, guys!" I said. "Mind if I tag along?"

Kyle fixed a pleading look on me, but I ignored it, sucking down the rest of my drink while everyone else cheered like my showing up was a major accomplishment. Maybe it was. Maybe instead of waiting for my old life to come back, I had to go out and get it.

We wandered down the street. Everyone was talking and goofing off just like old times, except that I didn't know what three quarters of their jokes meant, and I could either fake laugh along with the crowd or follow in stony silence. All overprotectiveness aside, Kyle seemed to pick up on how I was feeling; he trailed the group alongside me with his hands shoved into his pockets. We didn't talk, but then again, we didn't need to.

They went straight for the main parking structure without bothering to consult us, which was fine, because I don't know where I would have chosen to go had they asked. Prediagnosis, my mind had been full of new challenges to try and buildings to scale. But now I didn't even know where to start. Going back to precision jumps from brick to brick was depressing, not to mention boring as hell. But a full-on wall climb? I rubbed the patch of tender skin at the base of my neck where my PICC tube had been and tried to convince myself that it was adrenaline, not fear, building in my belly. As soon as I took my first step, the nerves would fade like they always did, and it would be just me and the obstacle. The way it should be.

As we climbed the stairs to the third floor of the parking garage, which was usually deserted by this time of day, I told myself to chill but failed to listen. The worried looks Kyle kept flashing me didn't help. Luckily, Luke popped his board up, snatched it out of the air, and dropped back to walk with us. It gave me something to concentrate on other than the urge to smack my best friend upside the head.

"So . . ." Luke was looking at me like I'd gotten topped with wings and a halo when I wasn't paying attention. Another person who thought chronic illness made you nigh-angelic. I was always tempted to spit on those people just to see how they'd react.

"So, what?" I asked, trying not to huff. Despite the doctor-prescribed walks, stairs still tired me out.

"You're coming back to school senior year, right?"

"Yeah," I said. "We decided I'd homeschool for the rest of junior year. I have a lot of ground to make up if I want to graduate on time. And the idea of staying in that hellhole another year without you guys?" I shuddered. It was only half theatrics.

He winced right along with me. "No kidding. Well, do you think they'd still let you do Spectacle? I'm putting together a sketch, and I need your mad ninja skills."

Spectacle was the school's spring talent show. I'd been in major demand for skits ever since freshman year, when I'd pretended to beat the crap out of the JV offensive line in mock combat. The best part about that sketch had been the costumes. I'd been dressed like Princess Leia, and the football players had worn Stormtrooper uniforms.

"You still got the moves, right? I mean, after . . ." Luke waved his hands, like he'd decided to finish the sentence in sign language because he couldn't bear to say the c-word out loud. Because if he said the word "cancer," he might get it. Wuss.

"I don't know if they'd let me in or not," I said. "You'd have to ask."

"Will do," he replied.

We emerged from the stairwell into the open expanse of the parking garage. And despite the fact that I was barely managing not to gasp for breath, I walked straight for the safety wall, propelled by frustration. Every time I tried for a little normalcy, the leukemia thing hit me again. It felt like people weren't going to see me as anything but a poor little cancer girl for the rest of my life, and it made me want to hit something.

I boosted myself onto the ledge, looking out into the empty space between the parking garage and the adjoining Arts and Sciences building, ignoring Kyle's worried voice behind me. "Be careful!" he barked. "That's dangerous." He must have thought I was stupid. Of course it was dangerous; that was why I was doing it. If I didn't push myself a little, I might just fade away entirely.

My heart began to thump as my body realized what I was intending, and my hands developed the familiar tremor that comes with a big jolt of adrenaline. But this time the rush held a new edge of fear, a little voice that whispered how stupid this was, that I should be resting, that I wasn't strong enough. *Little cancer girls don't do stunts,* the voice reminded me. *They decorate posters and look pitiful. That's what you're good for now.*

Damn voice. The only way to prove it wrong was to make the jump, and I couldn't do it while I was distracted. So I pushed away the doubt as best I could, reaching up to run my fingers over the smooth silver of my lucky katana necklace. I could do this. I knew that edge like I knew the back of my hand. Three stories up, a flat expanse of well-manicured grass at the bottom broken by a stretch of sidewalk. The side of the Arts and Sciences building, almost close enough to touch. A single bar atop the safety wall separated me from the air. I stepped over it, ignoring the assorted hoots and yells behind me as different members of the crew urged me forward or back. They'd understand later how much I needed this. I'd prove myself to them. And to me.

I pictured the trick from beginning to end, every detail sharp in my mind—the swing of my arms, the momentum in my core, the press of my foot against the brick, the precise placement of each step. Only then did I push off the ledge.

"Casey!"

Kyle's panicked yell threw off my concentration, and I felt the swoop of air as he reached for my legs and missed. I would have been offended if I hadn't been suddenly terrified. Why had I thought this was a good idea? Now that I was airborne, the three-story drop seemed much higher than it ever had before. I'd always felt immortal when I'd been free-running. But now I knew without a doubt that I was mortal. I felt a sudden urge to grab for the safety of the railing, but I was already committed.

My brain might have been scrambled with fear, but my legs remembered what to do. I planted my foot against the Arts and Sciences building as I fell, pushed off at an angle, and hurtled toward the parking structure again. I bounced back and forth between the buildings like a Ping-Pong ball, keeping my momentum in check as I descended toward the ground. My body was in it just the way it needed to be; it knew all the moves and executed them flawlessly. But instead of that feeling of freedom and triumph I'd always gotten from freerunning, I wanted nothing more than the safety of the ground again. It wasn't thrilling to defy death anymore.

My shoes touched the grass. I landed just right—knees soft to absorb the shock, body canted forward to transfer my momentum into an effortless run. But my legs buckled under-neath me, spilling me to the concrete. My jeans ripped; the skin underneath tore open. I reflexively threw my hands out to protect my face, sacrificing the skin off both palms.

I rolled into the cool springiness of the grass and just lay there, trying to catch my breath. I didn't know what had gone wrong. Had my mind been too weak, or had my body? Either way, the only thing I'd proven was that I'd lost my edge.

Kyle yelled, "Are you okay, Case? Stay there! We'll call an ambulance."

Very few things could have gotten me to my feet, but that worked. "No!" I yelped, shoving myself up. The scrapes weren't bad; I'd had much worse. It was the failure that I couldn't deal with. "I'm fine," I added. "Just a little road rash."

"Are you sure?" Willow leaned over the side of the building like she might be able to evaluate the state of my knees from thirty feet up. "That was a bad spill."

"Totally sure." I plastered a grin on my face and raised my stinging hands overhead in a gesture of mock triumph, trying to make light of the situation. "Next time, I'll stick the landing."

Kyle burst out the stairwell door like I was on fire. "Did you hit your head?" he demanded, rushing over. "Are you dizzy? Do you have any weakness? You should be sitting down, dude."

"I'm fine. I must have turned my foot on a rock. We forgot to scout the landing zone." I tried to sound nonchalant as I offered the lame excuse, but my voice wobbled. He only looked more concerned. "Honest. If anything's damaged, it's my pride."

His long mouth pressed flat with disapproval. "You should go home," he said.

"I want to stay. Please, Kyle. If I go home now, I'll never come back, not after that."

"You're not jumping again." It came out as an order, not a request. I would have been angry if I hadn't agreed wholeheartedly.

"I won't. Not today, anyway."

It felt like a concession of defeat. The best way to recover from a spill is to get right back up there and try it again. But I wasn't up to it. I might never be up to it again, and if that was true, who was I? Stunts had been my whole existence before I'd gotten sick. That left me with nothing.

He let out a long sigh. "All right. I'll sit here with you."

I flashed him a grateful smile before looking up at the rest of the crew. They still hovered at the ledge, waiting for the verdict. Luke clutched his cell, ready to dial at a moment's notice.

"I think I'll watch for a while," I said, swallowing the lump of shame in my throat. "Are you going to leave me down here all alone, or is anyone else tricking today?"

I didn't have to ask twice. They practically jumped all over each other trying to show me their newest moves. I pretended they just wanted my advice, but I knew they were secretly relieved that I wasn't going to kill myself with a repeat performance. Even worse, I felt the same way.

After about a half hour of watching my friends defy gravity, I was done. Kyle walked me home. It felt like I was slinking off with my tail between my legs. No one invited me back, and that was a relief until I got angry at myself for being relieved. At least I didn't have to pretend everything was okay; Kyle was pretty withdrawn too. I knew I should ask him what he was thinking, but I didn't really want to go there. We made plans to meet later that night for the annual Halloween Bash, and he gave me a gentle noogie before leaving me on my front step, so I knew we were cool. And really, I was too exhausted—in every sense of the word—to confront things if we weren't.

My parents were both theater profs, and they had Friday office hours, so I was free to go up to my bedroom undisturbed. Post-diagnosis, they'd turned my room into a little palace. I had my own mini fridge, flat screen, gaming console, the works. After a quick bathroom detour for disinfectant and bandages, I flopped bonelessly onto my bed and flipped through the channels. Nothing was on except *Jersey Shore* reruns, so I turned the TV off. For some reason, it was hard to get all emotionally worked up over orange tans and random hookups after the day I'd had.

My eyelids felt like concrete. I closed them for just a minute and didn't wake up until my older sister, Rachel, jumped on the bed and started shouting.

"Casey, you lazypants. Wake up!"

"Dude!" I flopped over in my cocoon of blankets and rubbed my face. "There's no need to yell. I'm right here."

"Hey, I can't help it if I'm a force to be reckoned with." She hugged me so tight, my back cracked. "Please tell me you did that to your head on purpose."

"Yeah. My hair came back patchy. I looked like I had mange."

She tilted her head. "It makes you look tough."

The comment made me feel instantly better. Rachel always knew what to say. My sister was two years older, but we'd always been close. If it hadn't been for her and Kyle, I would have gone completely insane in the hospital. The rest of the crew had come to see me, but they'd been so uncomfortable that I'd wished they hadn't. I'd never been able to talk to them the way I could Kyle. Not that I was holding a grudge or anything; that was just the way it was. But now I knew that the clichéd crap about how true friends stick with you when things go to hell wasn't just clichéd crap.

Normally I didn't pay much attention to my looks, but I wasn't a robot. It felt good to know that I wasn't completely repulsive. My problems were less about the hair and more about the rest of the package. I had sunken, reddish scars dotting my body from my neck all the way down my torso. Biopsies and aspirations, PICC lines, the Broviac catheter—each one had left its mark. I did my best to keep covered, even in hot weather. Not because I was vain but because I was tired of looking like a circus freak. At least I could pass the hair off as a fashion statement. Which it mostly was.

Rachel took one look at me and sat down, tucking a lock of long blond hair behind her ear and putting on her most serious expression.

"You look upset. What's up?"

I shrugged evasively. "I thought you weren't supposed to be here for another half hour."

"I cut out of sociology early, since I couldn't take you out last time I was home because *someone* had the gall to get pneumonia. What's up with that? Cancer isn't good enough and you have to hog all the other illnesses too?"

"What can I say? I'm an overachiever."

"I'm in awe of your mad skills." She snorted. "Now quit changing the subject and tell me what's wrong."

"I just . . ." I didn't know what to say. My eyes roamed the collage-covered walls, plastered with photos and magazine clippings that only reminded me of how I'd lost my edge. Levi Meeuwenberg, my freerunning idol, leapt into the air over a picture of pre-cancer me, my arms flung up in triumph. I would have given anything to be that girl again. She was fearless, and I had too much to lose. But I couldn't say that to Rachel. I'd already put her through plenty. "I don't know," I finished lamely.

"Well, then stop looking at me like I spit in your corn-flakes." She shook a finger in mock disapproval. "We're going to that Halloween party, right? Out with the crappy and in with the happy!"

"That's horrible." I threw my stuffed ninja at her.

"But still wise beyond my years," she said, tossing the toy back onto the bed. "So, what do you say? Are we going or not?"

"All right." I shrugged. "I don't have anything better to do."

When we were ready, I felt like a strange alternate-reality version of myself, a kickass Casey 2.0 who hung out in futuristic biker bars and didn't take guff from anybody. My costume consisted of Rachel's old roller derby uniform—red jersey, black shorts, fishnets, pads, and black roller skates. She'd drawn intricate curlicues all over my head with a hot-pink marker, which looked totally sweet. Makeup shaded my thin face into razor-sharp edges, and wide black lines traced my eyes, curling up into feline tips. My lips were so purple, they looked bruised.

I skated out to the sidewalk and spun to face my sister, regal and corseted in a Marie Antoinette costume. The skirt was so wide, she had to turn sideways to get out the door, and the bodice turned her already voluptuous figure into something wars were fought over. I would have been jealous that she'd gotten all the curves—I was compact and boyish, while she was tall and hourglassish—but people automatically assumed she was an airhead just because of her looks. I wouldn't have been able to handle that.

"Is my wig on straight?" she asked, putting a hand to her tower of white hair.

"You look hot." I waggled my eyebrows at her, and she pretended not to notice.

She double-checked the lock on our front door, which was shrouded by about five packages of fake spiderwebs. We lived in a gated community, but it was still technically downtown. Some moron had broken into our house a few years earlier. Afterward, I'd been afraid to step out the door, until I'd started martial arts. Black belts in ninjutsu are rarely abducted by random crackheads, and I'd learned a lot in the dojo before I'd had to quit that too.

We passed the parking lot and headed out the front gates and down the street. The university campus was only a few blocks away; I could already hear the low murmur of the crowd. I really wished Rachel would transfer colleges so we could see each other more often, but I also understood why she'd had to get out of the house.

Cars flashed past, random college guys hanging out the windows and shouting inappropriate things at us. And then we passed by some apartment buildings, where different random college guys shouted still more inappropriate things from the balconies. I didn't pay much attention to any of them and concentrated on my feet instead.

Rachel had been a derby girl in high school, and I'd tagged along to her practices all the time. I'd been really good at it too; I would have tried out for one of the junior derby teams, but the leukemia hit just before I got old enough. Skating is like riding a bike; you don't forget it once you've learned, but I was still extra cautious that night. The cuts on my knees and hands hadn't stopped throbbing yet, a constant reminder that I couldn't just slip back into my old ways, no matter how much I wanted to. The last thing I needed was to break something and get sent back to the hospital.

We passed a row of orange sawhorses that blocked off the street, and I stopped to survey the crowd. Halloween was always a big deal at the U; the school held a street carnival during the early evening so the local kids could trick-or-treat up and down Fraternity Row. I'd gone every year since I was little. I used to love getting my face painted and making spiders out of pipe cleaners. As the night wore on, however, the kiddie games disappeared and the booze came out, and there was a band. It was a college, after all.

"Wow." I rolled out a little farther into the street to get a better view. "They've really outdone themselves this year."

Main Street was packed. The pavement overflowed with carnival booths full of games, caramel apples, and hot spiced cider. Most of the fraternities and sororities had concession tables in their front yards, and herds of kids in costume ran from porch to porch with plastic pumpkin buckets, demanding candy. A large platform ran along one side of the street, empty except for a couple of girls dressed like Daphne and Velma from *Scooby-Doo,* setting up the sound system for the band.

"Come on," Rachel said, grabbing my wrist and lunging eagerly into the crowd.

"Not that way!" I twisted to an awkward stop. "The professors always hang at the Sammie House until the faculty costume contest."

"God, no." She turned around. "That's the last thing we want, to party with our parents."

"Exactly."

"Ohmigod." She skirted an elementary kid dressed as SpongeBob SquarePants and a pair of zombies that may or may not have been his parents. "Can we go to the Pi Kapps'? Dylan might be there."

I tried not to roll my eyes. As fabulous as Rachel was, she had crappy taste in guys, and Dylan was the worst ex-boyfriend of them all. He was the kind of guy who stuffed tube socks down his pants. Quite literally—I walked in on him once.

"You aren't going to get back together with Stuff Daddy, are you?" I asked. "Because you told me to throw shuriken at you if you did."

"No pointy ninja toys necessary." She adjusted her bodice. "But there's no harm in showing him what he's missing, right?"

"All right." I couldn't keep the reluctance out of my voice, but I tried. "I just want to sit down. These skates are killing my toes. Once we get settled, I'll text Kyle and tell him where to meet us."

"It's a deal. Follow me."

The front yard at the Pi Kapp house was packed, but Rachel walked right up to a guy with huge poofy hair and a Star Trek costume that exposed the beginnings of a beer belly.

"Eric," she said, "my sister needs your seat before her toes fall off."

He stood up immediately from his lawn chair, his eyes glued to her chest. I half expected his eyeballs to pop out of his head and bounce into her cleavage. But finally he turned to me and said, "Casey! I see you're rocking the bald look."

It took every ounce of self-control I had not to sigh. If wigs didn't make my scalp feel like it was on fire, I might have been tempted to wear one just to avoid having this conversation with every person I saw.

But that wasn't his fault. I nodded and changed the subject. "Hey there, Captain Kirk. You still rooming with Mr. Sock?"

Eric was Dylan's roommate and was just as laid back as Dylan was uptight. I liked him. He'd witnessed the tube sock stuffage too; it had been the kind of traumatic experience that makes people lifelong friends.

He snorted so hard that beer slopped out of his red plastic cup and onto his shoes. "Afraid so. Sweet costume."

"Thanks."

He helped me into the chair, which I didn't really need. But I let him because he'd always done things like that. I knew it wasn't just because he thought I was broken. And even if I didn't want to admit it, maybe I needed to be taken care of a little. After this afternoon's fall, I felt like I'd been run over by a truck, and my palms hurt.

When Kyle burst into the yard in a zoot suit and a pair of giant Day-Glo glasses, I didn't get up. He threw his hands up and yelled, "Hello, party people!" No one even gave him a second look. He flopped onto the patchy grass next to my chair and said, "This party sucks."

"You've only been here for five seconds," I said, stretching my legs out. My thighs weren't used to the extra weight of the skates, and I could feel the muscles twitching. They were going to hurt tomorrow.

Eric offered me a can of Coke from the cooler on the porch, and I practically kissed him. I took a long swig and said, "Kyle, this is Eric. He is cool. Eric, this is Kyle. He is also cool."

They nodded at each other.

"Hey, are you the clock guy?" Eric asked, his face breaking into a wide grin that almost rivaled Kyle's.

"Yeah." Kyle puffed out his chest proudly. "That's me."

"You've got to tell that story," Eric said to me. "It's hilarious. You mind?"

"Mind?" I shook off the malaise and smiled for real. It felt like I hadn't done that in ages. Here was something I could still do without feeling like a total poser. "I'm so happy to be out of social limbo that I might just kiss you." At his stricken look, I laughed. "Kidding, dude."

He gave me a gentle shoulder punch before gathering up a bunch of his frat brothers. For once, the glances they shot at my head were admiring instead of full of pity. It was a difference I could get used to. Kyle and I told them about the time we snuck into the gym right before graduation and filled the rafters with fifty windup alarm clocks all set to go off at different times. That had been a great prank, except for the part where someone saw us and called the cops. We'd ended up hiding on the roof and getting locked up there for a couple hours in the rain until we figured out how to get down.

We swapped stupid stories as the shadows grew longer. Dusk fell, and the little kids passing by on the street got progressively more tired and whiny. I could hear the loudspeaker down the block as they announced the winners of the costume contest, but I couldn't make out the words. Hopefully our parents had won the faculty division, because otherwise they'd mope.

Someone inside the house called for a beer pong tournament. Within minutes, the yard had emptied out. Rachel knelt down beside me, the hoops of her skirt rising bell-like around her torso. Kyle took the other side.

"Are you okay?" he asked.

"Having a good time?" Rachel added. "You're not too tired, are you?"

"This is awesome," I said. "I want to stay here forever. I think I might move into this lawn chair permanently."

"You say that now, but wait until they start puking." Rachel grinned. "So I hear Dylan's working the kissing booth. I'm going to go ambush him. Do you mind? I'll only be a minute."

"I meant what I said about the shuriken, Rachel. One smooch and I'm throwing."

"It's a two-person booth. I'm not going to kiss him; I'm going to kiss the other guy," she said. "He'll have a fit."

"Yeah, well, he can stuff it," I said, and we both started giggling. Kyle looked back and forth between us like we were nuts, which wasn't too far from the truth.

"Very funny." Rachel struggled to her feet. "Damned costume."

I watched her stroll away, leaving a trail of gawking guys in her wake. It was ridiculous.

"You look tired." Kyle looked at me over the top of his glasses. "Are you sure you're okay?"

I swallowed the frustration that came with constantly being asked that question. I just wanted to have some normal fun. Why couldn't people let me do that?

"Yeah." I pushed myself up from the chair. "But I've got to go to the bathroom."

It was meant to be an excuse, something to change the subject. But the moment I said it, I realized it wasn't just an excuse—I really did have to go. Unfortunately, my only options were to brave the innards of the Pi Kapp house or squat in the Porta Potties at the end of the block. I looked up at the house. Three guys in cheerleading outfits were doing keg stands in front of the door.

Which pretty much made the decision for me.

"Porta johns?" asked Kyle, reading my mind as usual.

"Yeah. If Rachel gets here before I do, tell her I'll be right back."

I half expected him to insist on accompanying me, but he didn't. A minor triumph, but every bit of independence I got felt like something worth celebrating. As I skated off, I felt a little better already.

The driveway, choked with cars, curved behind the house, and I slalomed down it, just for fun. A narrow alley ran parallel to the street; it would be much less crowded back there. When I emerged onto the empty pavement, I couldn't help letting out a sigh of relief. So much nicer than the mob scene out front.

About halfway down the alleyway, I heard it. "Rollergirl." A voice like dark chocolate and silk pajamas; I wanted to roll around in it.

I squinted in the dim light, but I couldn't see anybody. Just cars jam-packed down one side of the alley. Dark, dilapidated student housing. Shadows pooling on the bricks. The only illumination came from the streetlights on the other side of the houses, and the buildings blocked most of it.

"Who's there?" I asked, frowning.

"Roooollergirl," the voice repeated in a playful singsong.

A man stepped out from behind a peeling house about fifty feet in front of me. He wore all white, a fabric of such brightness that it practically shone in the dark. His overcoat flapped in a breeze I couldn't feel. And his face was as beautiful as his voice, with chiseled features so perfect, they didn't look real.

I rolled closer without even realizing I was moving. And when he reached out his hand, I took it without a thought. His skin felt mannequin smooth and cool to the touch. Its chill seeped through the Band-Aids that crisscrossed my palms.

When I lifted my chin to look at him, it felt like the movement took forever, like time had somehow shuddered to a stop. I could feel each thump of my heart and the eternity between the beats. My eyes met his, and his lips ever so slowly curved up into a smile, exposing perfect white teeth.

"I've been waiting for you," he said softly, the words sending a shiver down my spine.

And then his eyes caught fire.

Liquid flame spilled out of the stranger's eyes, leaving black-ened trails down his cheeks and splattering on the ground. The sudden smell of burning flesh and rotten eggs nauseated me, but I was too transfixed to gag. I knew I should move, kick him in the balls, *something,* but all I could do was stare as he pulled me closer.

"Your futile training won't save you, rollergirl."

He licked my cheek with a sandpaper tongue. Up close, his face seemed unreal, like the perfect skin was stretched too tight over something inhuman, something that seethed from within in an attempt to break free.

His hands came up to grasp my shoulders, and he pulled me violently against his body. Lava-like tears fell onto the front of the red jersey, burning right through the fabric and scorching my chest. The pain freed me, clearing the fog from my mind just as his head dipped toward mine, cheeks writhing like they were about to burst.

It had been almost a year since I'd taken ninjutsu, but my muscles responded as if it had been yesterday. I swept my arms up in effortless arcs, breaking his grip, and then rapidly sank down into *hoko,* striking his chest with both hands like an attacking bear and smashing him to the ground.

Then I started to hyperventilate. Flaming tears will do that to a girl. I was scared, and that made me angry, which made me feel like picking a fight, which made me remember that I'd lost my edge, which made me more frightened. It was a vicious cycle, and it only got worse with every passing second.

He twisted, snakelike, to his feet and meticulously dusted himself off, his eyes dry and his face unmarked. Was there a flicker of red deep in his eyes, or was it just the light? I couldn't tell.

"Was that really necessary?" he asked, rubbing ineffectively at a smudge on his lapel. "You've ruined my jacket."

His matter-of-fact tone snapped me out of the fear. Confused, I looked down at the pavement but saw nothing out of the ordinary. Had I imagined the lava tears? I was no stranger to hallucinations, but I didn't feel sick. Besides, there were burn holes in my shirt, and the skin underneath sizzled. It was the kind of feeling that promised lots of pain to come, once my nerve endings decided to spring the ambush.

"No matter. I'll make you pay for it anyway," he said when I failed to respond. "Would you like to scream for help? I'll take your friends as well if you'd like. The Master would be most pleased."

"Master?" I knew I sounded like an idiot, but I was having a really hard time figuring out what was happening. If I hadn't known better, I would have thought I was drunk. But I hadn't had anything stronger than Coke because of my meds. Maybe the doses were off. Maybe I'd taken the hallucinogenic pain-killers instead of my anti-rejection meds. That would explain it. I felt a huge wave of relief.

"You'll meet him soon enough. He'll drive you buggy." The man's eyes widened with maniacal glee. "That's a joke."

Okay, I might have been hallucinating the lava, but this guy was still super creepy. I began rolling backward, evaluating my options for escape.

"I have no idea what you're talking about," I said, trying to buy time.

"Mmmm. Well, you can't blame me for trying. Shall we get on with it, then? Without a Relic, you're as good as dead. There's no need to draw it out; I can't deal with tediousness." He rubbed his eyes irritably. "I don't have the patience for it."

"Maybe you have me mistaken for someone else?" I took a deep breath, intending to yell for Kyle. I'd never get to pee by myself again, but maybe that wasn't such a bad thing. Maybe I just had to come to terms with the fact that this was my life now.

The man's hand flashed out before I got out a peep. All I saw was a white blur of motion as he grabbed me by the neck and threw me to the ground. The landing knocked the breath from my body, and I skidded over the pavement, pebbles and bits of broken glass imbedding into my flesh.

He was on me in an instant, straddling my chest. A haze of panic completely obliterated all the techniques I'd worked so hard to learn in the dojo. I bucked and squealed as he slid down my torso, leaning over to mash his mouth against mine. I could feel his lips writhe, and something unspeakably vile tried to worm its way past my clenched teeth.

My neck felt like it was on fire.

I groped wildly at my skin, hoping to wipe away the man's flaming tears. But there weren't any. Only the delicate silver chain of my lucky necklace.

When I touched it, my hand went instantly numb. It felt like I was holding a bolt of lightning; the shock of it blazed up my arm. It burned; I had to get it off me. I yanked it off my neck and threw it blindly into the air, hoping against hope that it would distract him enough so I could get away.

Suddenly he was gone.

There was no weight on my chest. No pressure against my lips. I cautiously opened one eye and saw no one.

I scrambled up onto my skates, ignoring the sting of my abraded skin. The nape of my neck prickled; I knew he was watching me. It was impossible to look in every direction at once, but I tried.

"Rollergirl . . ."

The voice came from nowhere, floating bodiless in the air and tickling my cheek in an obscene caress.

I panicked.

I flew down the alley toward the Pi Kapp house, skating at full speed even though there was nothing behind me but a hint of mocking laughter on the breeze. Wild screams built up inside me, but my throat was so tight that I could only manage a series of little panting squeals.

When I rounded the corner, I smacked into a frat boy. We tumbled along the cracked driveway and landed with me facedown in a pile of old mulch and the guy sprawled heavily across my back. He rolled down my injured legs, grinding bits of glass farther into my skin, and thumped onto the ground.

"Ow," I said, wheezing.

"What the hell do you think you're doing?" demanded the guy. "You could have hurt somebody."

His voice was instantly familiar. Out of all the frat boys to crash into, of course it would be him.

Rachel's ex-boyfriend Dylan stood up without giving me a second look, straightening his gold Elvis jumpsuit with furious, jerky movements.

"Hey!" he snapped. "I'm talking to you."

I gaped, trying to regain control of my voice. No luck. He wasn't even paying attention; he had opened his mouth to berate me further, when he finally looked at me.

"Oh my God! Casey?" he asked. "Is that you?"

I nodded, rolling over and struggling to my feet.

"You're hurt." He turned, yelling toward the house, "Somebody get a first aid kit!"

"Dylan?" I wheezed. "Find my sister? She's at the kissing booth."

His eyes went wide, but I was beyond caring. I could see a tall spike of white hair bobbing through the crowd that was gathering at the end of the driveway, gaping at me like I was a bald-headed leper. And when Rachel emerged from the throng with Kyle in tow, both of them breathless and red-faced from pushing their way through, I let myself cry.

"So can you tell us what happened, miss?" asked the ruddy-faced police officer.

The party still raged on outside, but I sat on a ratty sofa in the middle of the frat house common room with Rachel's arm slung over one shoulder and Kyle's over the other. Dylan might have been a sock-stuffing dorkwad, but he was also a fourth-year premed student who worked at the local urgent care center in his spare time. He finished tweezing the last of the glass out of my leg and started to wrap it in layers of filmy gauze.

"Thank you," I said, gritting my teeth against the burn. At this rate, the only part of my body that wasn't going to be scabbed over was my right eyelid. My only defense was to joke about it, because otherwise I might start crying again. "I appreciate the help, Dylan."

He looked surprised, like common courtesy wasn't something he encountered very often and he wasn't sure how to respond.

"Oh. Sure," he replied.

"Miss?" the officer prompted, tapping his pen on his clipboard to get my attention.

"There was a man in the alley. He . . . I had to go to the bathroom. He jumped on me. He burned me." My hand fluttered up to skim the scorched circles dotting the front of my jersey, and I forced it back to my side. "I think he wanted to kill me."

Kyle muttered a long series of swear words, his fingers tightening on my shoulder.

The cop nodded, looking me over clinically. "Flicked a lit cigarette at you, did he? Okay, go on. How did you get away?"

I debated correcting him. But really, there was no way to say "the guy was crying fire" without sounding like a complete nutjob, so I didn't.

"Casey has a black belt in ninjutsu," said Rachel, squeezing my shoulder gently. "You probably kicked the crap out of the bastard, didn't you?"

"Something like that," I mumbled. I felt ashamed more than anything. I was a black belt, for God's sake, and ninjutsu doesn't require a lot of muscle strength. By all rights, I should have kicked that guy's ass, but did I? Nope.

The cop's attitude shifted a little; he looked at me with something like respect. "Good for you, kid," he said. "So you think you could describe the guy for me?"

"Tall, thin, wearing all white. Pale skin. Dark curly hair."

"Could it have been a wig?" he asked. "Halloween costume?"

I shrugged. "Maybe."

"Approximate age?"

"Not too old. Late teens, early twenties, tops."

"Good, good. Anything else?"

He cried fire, I thought. But I shook my head.

"We'll have you come down to the station tomorrow to make an official statement, okay?" the cop said. "But for now, I'll drive you to the hospital. Unless you're happy with Elvis here?"

I looked over at Dylan. "I just need some Band-Aids, right?"

"You should go to the hospital," Kyle said. He threw his hands up when I shot him a glare. "Hey, I know I'm over-protective sometimes, but this is common sense. Remember when I burned myself on those fireworks and my hand got infected?"

I did. It had been too gross to forget. To this day, the word "pus" made me shudder.

"Could you do anything for them, Dylan?" I pleaded. "They're just little burns."

"I don't know if you'd be comfortable. . . ." Dylan shifted awkwardly. "I mean, you'd need to take off your shirt."

"Just give me something to cover up with."

"I'll grab you a blanket." He dashed out of the room.

"See, Casey? I told you," Rachel said. "He's not such a jerk after all, is he?"

I nodded. "Yeah. He's been very nice."

A police officer with a long blond braid entered the house and walked over to us. Long hair could be used as a handhold in a fight; even before the radiation, I'd always kept mine short. Although it didn't seem to have done much good. I'd just gotten my butt kicked, and I was bald.

"Find anything?" the first cop asked.

"Just this." The blonde opened her hand.

My lucky necklace sat coiled in her palm.

I remembered the day Rachel had given it to me. I'd developed stage-four graft-versus-host disease after my marrow transplant, and even my eternally optimistic doctor had had to admit my survival chances were pretty slim. It got so bad that my parents even called in a priest to perform the Anointing of the Sick, and Rachel brought the little silver katana pendant for him to bless. He'd balked at blessing a sword, even if it was miniaturized, but she could be awfully persuasive. I could remember listening through a narcotic haze as the priest prayed over me. All three of my IV trees kept beeping because the alarms on the damned things were so sensitive. It sounded like the priest was being censored, and even though the situation wasn't funny at all, I kept biting back hysterical laughter.

When Rachel gave me the katana, though, I almost cried. I still remembered how it spun and glittered in the glare of the hospital fluorescents. I think that necklace might have saved my life because it helped me remember I was a fighter.

"Recognize it?" the ponytailed cop asked.

I blinked myself back to the present. The guy in the alley. The necklace had saved me twice now.

"Yeah, that's Casey's." Rachel held out a hand for it.

"The chain's broken. You'll need to get a new one."

"I'll take care of it." My sister stuffed the necklace down her bodice because her costume didn't have pockets. She and Kyle exchanged a look that was all too familiar. I was about to be coddled again, and I wasn't entirely sure I didn't deserve it. "Are we done now? I'd like to get her home so she can rest. She's been sick."

The officers exchanged glances and nodded.

"Great," she continued. "I'm going to go light a fire under Dylan's ass. Kyle, can you run to our house and get my car? You sit here and rest, Casey. We'll get you fixed up and I'll take you home. You're safe now."

She put a cool hand on my forehead. *Safe.* I touched the burn holes on my shirt again and tried like crazy to believe it.

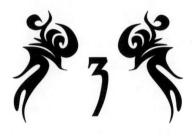

3

"How'd it go?" Rachel asked from her seat in the dingy police station waiting room the next morning. It smelled like old socks marinated in air freshener, and she had her sleeve pulled up over her nose to block out the reek.

I shrugged.

"You know, Casey?" She shook her head in mock exasperation. "Sometimes I wish you'd just shut up. You talk too much."

"Har har." I pushed the door open, the abrasions on my legs pulling and stinging with each stride. My muscles had tightened up; I felt like I'd been shoved into a dryer with a couple of bricks and left to rattle around for a few hours. "There's nothing to tell. Detective Johnson showed me a bunch of pictures, but none of them was the guy."

"So if it wasn't such a big deal, why are we running like the hounds of hell are about to pounce on us and devour our gizzards?"

"Dude, people don't have gizzards. That's chicken."

"Whatever."

Rachel pulled out her keys and pressed the button to unlock the doors to her Mini Cooper. We got in and immediately rolled down the windows. It was already warm even though it was still midmorning; the air felt soupy and on the verge of rain.

"Okay," I said. "I've got to tell you something. It's driving me nuts."

"All right." Rachel folded her hands and put on her best listening face, which normally made me want to laugh. Normally. "Spill."

So I told it all, starting with the disembodied voice and ending with the . . . well, the disembodied voice. And then I waited for her to call me a lunatic.

"You sound like Dad," Rachel said.

Our father believed in everything. His reality included things like men in black, alien abduction, spirit animals, demonic possession, voodoo dolls, Kyrilian photography, leprechauns, poltergeists, Ouija boards, reincarnation, pyrokinesis, subliminal messages that could be blocked by the generous application of tinfoil, and the theory that dolphins were really Atlanteans in disguise. The fact that some of these beliefs were incompatible never seemed to bother him. Frankly, he didn't even appear to have noticed.

"I know." I hung my head. "But I don't know what to think. At first, I figured maybe I'd gotten my meds mixed up. But I would have noticed that, right?"

"I'd think so."

"So . . ." I didn't want to say what I was thinking.

"It's the only logical explanation, Casey. He flicked a cigarette at you, just like that cop said, and you hallucinated it was tears. I mean, stranger things have happened. One time when I came to see you in the hospital, you were so doped up you thought I was Lady Gaga. And I wasn't even wearing my meat dress that day."

"Yeah, I guess."

"You sound less than convinced."

I threw up my arms. "Well, this sucks! I don't know what was real. Maybe the guy didn't look at all like I thought. Maybe he was an albino midget with only one arm. How do I know I'm even telling them to look for the right freaking person?"

Tears threatened to spill down my cheeks, but I wiped them away ferociously. I hated feeling scared, and things like this, inexplicable things, terrified me. Because there was another explanation I couldn't bring myself to say out loud. That stupid voice at the back of my head kept squealing, *Brain tumor! It's a brain tumor! It was only a matter of time!* I tried to tell myself the voice was full of crap, but if I hadn't dorked up my meds, it was the only other logical explanation. I was hallucinating for no reason. That couldn't be good.

"I hear what you're saying." She sighed. "But getting all worked up over it is only going to make you red in the face, and with the no-hair thing, you'll look like a tomato on a stick."

After a shocked moment, I started giggling. "I can't believe you said that."

"Me either." She flashed a grin, but it faded fast. "All joking aside, though, this pisses me off. It's like, we almost lose you once, and then some crack-smoking douche bag comes by and almost kills you in an alley? I'm seriously not okay with this."

I sighed. "I'm fine, Rachel. It was scary as hell, but I'm okay." What I needed was to go to a hospital, but I wasn't ready to face it yet. I could hide my head in the sand for just a little while.

"Did you tell Detective Whatshisname the whole story or the edited one? You need to tell him everything, even if it makes you feel stupid."

"I left out the parts that made me sound like a total lunatic. Can you blame me?"

"You need to tell him, Casey. If you don't, how can he get the job done?"

I looked at the squat building and envisioned walking back inside, through the sock-scented waiting room and into Detective Johnson's grotty little cubicle, and then admitting I'd been hallucinating last night. It was the last thing I wanted to do.

"I'll call him later," I said. "He seemed kind of busy."

"You better. No one messes with my little sister. We'll find the guy and hang his balls from my rearview mirror."

"Eeeeew."

Rachel finally put the car into drive and sped out of the parking lot like the hounds of hell were in fact following us, despite our lack of gizzards. Not that she was reckless; she just ran at a higher speed than the average human.

I braced myself against the armrest as we flew around a corner, and then I checked the dashboard clock. "Think you could drop me off at the dojo? It would do me some good to get out of the house under circumstances that don't involve any burning."

"Your wish is my command, dahling," she deadpanned.

My nerves stopped jittering as soon as I got out of the car, which was a major relief. I hadn't been to the dojo since I'd gotten out of the hospital. Every time I'd decided to go, I'd felt like puking and canceled at the last minute. But now? After what had happened yesterday, I felt like I had to come, despite the continued temptation to vomit. It was either that or be paralyzed with fear for the rest of my life.

The thwack of bodies hitting the mats was clearly audible outside the doors; sensei had probably propped them open in a vain attempt to make the thick air circulate through the building. I slipped inside, stepped out of my shoes, and bowed to the *kamidana* shrine on the wall.

About fifteen students milled around, shrugging on gi tops, stretching on the mats, and throwing each other around for fun. A couple of black belts came through the back door with armfuls of bamboo practice swords, and I saw Sensei's distinctive bristle-cut hairstyle among them. I sidestepped a white belt warming up on the floor and headed in that direction.

"Sensei?" I called out.

The acoustics in the dojo left something to be desired; everything echoed underneath the high ceilings. My voice got lost in the commotion, and he went back outside without seeing me.

One of the black belts intercepted me.

"Welcome to Black Sands Dojo! Can I help you?" she said, flashing a gap-toothed smile. Her hair was longer now and pulled back into a messy ponytail, but I would have recognized those teeth anywhere.

"Darcy, it's me. Casey."

The smile flickered and then pasted itself back on with fervor. Darcy fastened her eyes to my face, deliberately looking anywhere but at my bald head. I was beginning to regret shaving it. Even the leper 'fro would have been better than this.

"Casey! I didn't recognize you!" She gave me a one-armed hug that took me completely by surprise and nearly resulted in a face full of sword. We'd been training buddies for a couple of years, but we'd never hung out too much outside of the dojo because she went to Saint Joe's and I went to Mackinaw Central. But inside the dojo, we'd been pretty inseparable, which is what happens when you start training about the same time and you're both tiny junior high girls.

"It's so good to see you!" she said, her voice high and breathless. "Are you coming back to training?"

"I was thinking about it," I said. "Congrats on the black belt, by the way."

"Thanks! I had to work pretty hard, but you know how that is. You should come to the white belt class first thing on Saturdays. That would be a great way to get back into things! Today we're doing *gogyo* again." Darcy brushed a hair out of her face. "But next Saturday? I could give you a ride, if you want? I'm teaching the class, so I've got to be here early."

"I'll think about it."

"That's cool. Listen, I've got to get the rest of the gear for today, but I'll catch up with you after training, okay? Bye!"

She leaned over and gave me a quick smooch on the cheek like we were long-lost BFFs. We'd never had a huggy kind of friendship before; she'd always been the shy and reserved type. By the time I got over the shock, she was out the door.

Maybe that hadn't really been Darcy. It might have been an alien clone.

I took a seat at the back of the dojo, telling myself I wasn't wussing out; I was just respecting the rule about senior students not training without a gi. The students organized themselves into meticulous rows behind Sensei and bowed to the *kamidana* to officially begin the class. He began to lead them through the *gogyo,* a series of moves representing the five elements. I had always loved *gogyo;* it was amazing how each move felt different, like the elements were actually channeling through me. I liked the flash and arc of fire and the heaviness of my feet in earth, the buoyancy of air and the liquid way the moves rippled into one another in water.

Void was the most difficult element to master; everyone said so. But this time, something clicked as I watched Sensei punch, toss an imaginary *metsubishi,* and kick. I stood up without even realizing it and pictured the man from the alleyway, struck him with one hand, threw a *metsubishi* into his eyes to obscure his vision, shifted to kick. The moves blended together so it felt like I was striking from all directions at once. Being everywhere. Being void.

Once I started, I couldn't stop. The familiar cadence of moves carried me out of myself; all conscious thought ceased. I forgot all the angsty emo crap for a while and just moved. When the hand fell on my shoulder, it was like coming back to earth.

"Yes!" Sensei said. "That's exactly it."

I stopped midkick and bowed to him hastily. "I'm very sorry, sir. I know I'm out of uniform. I'll bring my gi next time."

"Oh, don't worry about it," he said. "You're not here."

I looked down at myself, trying to figure out what he was talking about.

"You're everywhere and nowhere, right?" He punched me lightly on the shoulder, the way he used to when he made a joke, regardless of how dumb it was. "You're void, right?"

Now I couldn't keep from smiling. "Something like that."

The flash of humor on his face was gone so fast, I almost thought I'd imagined it. "It is good to have you back, *Kunoichi*," he said, bowing deeply.

Tears sprang to my eyes, sudden and surprising. But I kept my voice steady and returned the bow. "It's good to be back, Sensei."

He straightened and winked, mercurial as always. "Now sit down, or I'll have to bust your butt for breaking my rules."

I plopped back onto the bench, and he returned to the other students, moving among them, making jokes, correcting with a light touch of the arm or a potato smack to the head. Then they moved into some basic sword strikes, and it was so hard to sit when my muscles itched to move, ached to quit surviving and start living again. Finally I'd found something that hadn't changed. If I could recapture ninjutsu, I could get everything else back too. Screw that theoretical brain tumor and the horse it rode in on. I was probably all freaked out over nothing. Heck, maybe I'd gotten roofied. Sad but true, that thought was reassuring. Here was a rational explanation that didn't involve my dying at the end, and it was totally feasible! That was why I'd hallucinated. No relapse. No metastases. No need to panic.

The wave of relief made me literally rock back in my seat;

it hit me that hard. I was going to be okay, and I was going to train again. I didn't have the stamina to pull off a ninety-minute class. Not yet, but I would.

After class was over, Darcy pounced before I could even stand up from my bench. She was practically squealing with excitement. I put my hands to my temples; I could feel the headache developing already.

"So are you allowed to go out?" she asked. "Because if you are, I could pick you up for the basics class on Saturday, and maybe we could go and get some coffee? Unless you don't drink coffee? I can't remember if you do or not. I love coffee. If I could drink it in my sleep, I totally would."

"Of course I'm allowed. I went to the Halloween Bash on campus last night," I said.

"Sweet! Did you dress up? I went as a ninja this year, which is so not creative, but it was all I had."

"I wore my sister's old roller derby uniform."

"Ohmigod!" Darcy waved her hands in excitement, agitation, or some combination thereof. "Do you like derby? You've got to come to these tryouts with me in a couple weeks! Say you will; no one else wants to come, and I don't want to go by myself."

I reached out and grabbed her hands before she stuck a finger in my eye. "What tryouts?"

"You know the Apocalypsies, right? One of the junior derby teams? They're looking for new skaters." She squealed. "I'm so psyched!"

"I wouldn't have pegged you as the derby type."

"Yeah, well, I've changed since you were here last." She tossed her hair. "So what do you say? I could really use a cheering section."

"Sure, I'll do it. But didn't the season start already? My sister skated with the Hotsies before she went to Smithton, and I'm pretty sure they'd already started by this time last year."

"Two of the Apocalypsies died in a car accident. Isn't that the most horrible thing ever? Anyway, if they don't fill their roster, they'll have to forfeit the rest of their bouts."

"That's terrible." I looked down at my legs. What I was about to say was stupid, but I had to do it. I had to ride the wave of my dojo triumph, if only to get my mind off the fact that I'd splatted on the pavement yesterday and then topped it off by getting beaten up. "I want to try out too."

"B-but . . . ," Darcy started sputtering. "But you can't do that. You didn't go to skills camp. It's a requirement."

"Why?" I put my hands on my hips. "You want me to come to the tryout; I'll come. But I'm skating. Skills camp is for people who don't know the basics, but I used to practice with the Hotsies all the time. They would have taken me if I'd been old enough. I could probably still do all that stuff—T-stops, plow stops, booty blocking. You name it."

"Well . . . okay. I mean, if it's okay with them, it's okay with me. Maybe we could each get a spot!" She almost visibly shook herself back into hyperactive peppiness. "I'll pick you up, and we'll go together. Isn't that perfect? I can't decide whether I'm excited or nervous! I've always wanted to be a rollergirl!"

A shiver ran down my back and out my toes. I wanted to try out, but the word "rollergirl" brought back that creepy feeling from yesterday. Even if it was totally irrational to be afraid now. It's not like the crackhead from last night was following me; that was ridiculous.

"Yeah," I said. "That's pretty sweet, all right."

"Wheee!" Darcy clapped her hands and danced around in a circle. "I'm so excited!"

I couldn't help it. I laughed.

After my dojo visit, I dorked around at home until Saturday-night dinner. Rachel got to the dining room right after me.

"When are you going back to the dorms?" I asked as I sat down. My chair was wrapped with orange and black gauze. At our house, Halloween decorations went up in early September and stayed until Christmas. Sometimes later.

"Tomorrow morning," she said. I couldn't keep the disappointment off my face, and she winced. "I know. But I've got an exam in Abnormal Psych this week, and I've got to make it to the study group or I'll fail."

"Maybe I'll come up sometime soon. I could take the train."

"That would be awesome."

Mom and Dad squeezed through the doorway, nearly up-ending the massive sheet cake they were supporting between them. It overflowed with green frosting; plastic ninjas competed for space with at least two boxes of candles. One of the ninjas had toppled headfirst into a candle flame, and his head was dripping.

"Happy recovery to you!" they sang. Rachel warbled along out of tune. "Happy recovery to you! Happy recovery, dear Casey! Happy recovery to you!"

They set the cake down on the table, nearly upsetting it into my lap. Then Dad said, "Blow out the candles, honey."

I didn't need to be told twice. Those poor ninjas.

Mom whipped out a knife and started cutting the cake into dinner-plate-sized slices. I got the first piece. It had a lot of ninjas on it, including the damaged one. A puddle of head goo encased his feet. Poor guy; I scooped him out reverentially and laid him to rest on my napkin.

"Uh, guys?" Rachel asked, taking her plate. "Isn't it customary to have dinner first? You know, vegetables, meats, that kind of thing?"

"Reverse dinner. Duh," I said.

My parents were big on themed meals. They did reverse dinners, where dessert was served first and appetizers last; alphabet meals, where every food item began with the same letter; and no-utensils nights, where they served things like chicken and noodles with no forks and lots of napkins. This kind of thing was one of the many reasons why I never invited anyone except Kyle over for dinner.

"Nope." Mom laughed. "Good guess, though."

"Just wait and see," added Dad, forking a piece of red velvet cake approximately the size of a baseball into his mouth.

"Whatever." Rachel rolled her eyes. "So how was the dojo thing, Sis?"

"I think it's great that you're getting out and about again, Casey," boomed our father. "And only one day after your traumatic experience. I'm proud of your bravery, kiddo."

I had to give my parents some credit; they were pretty chill. They had to be, with me as a daughter. I'd come home sprained, broken, or abraded more often than not. They'd clamped down pretty hard when I'd first gotten diagnosed, but I'd liked the fact that they'd been at the hospital every day. Mom would give me foot rubs, and Dad would debate with the doctors about experimental techniques he'd read about on the Internet. They were weird and embarrassing a lot of the time, but they'd known exactly what to do when I'd needed them. And, just as important, they'd known when to back off.

"There's not much to tell," I said, shrugging. "One of the girls invited me to try out for a roller derby team. Will one of you sign the release form? I called Dr. Rutherford's office, and he said it was okay. I'm allowed to go back to the dojo too."

Of course, when I'd spoken to my doctor, I'd failed to mention the hallucinations. And I might have downplayed the derby thing. In fact, I might have lied outright and told him I was going to be a mascot.

"How is Phil Rutherford these days?" Dad asked. "I keep leaving him messages about community theater tryouts, but he never shows. Pity, because the guy's got a natural stage presence."

"Not bad." I took a deep breath. "He said Little Casey's back on the floor. He thought I might want to know."

Little Casey had been my children's hospital fourth-floor neighbor for months. She'd had acute lymphoblastic leukemia; I'd had acute myelogenous leukemia. She'd been nine at diagnosis. I'd been just shy of sixteen. But the nurses had called us the Casey twins anyway. It was the only time I've ever been called big.

I hadn't spoken to her since I'd been discharged. I missed her, but she was a reminder of all the things I really would have preferred to leave behind.

"You should call her," Dad said. "Or go to visit. Take her some of this cake."

"I'll think about it," I replied noncommittally, earning myself a disapproving look from everyone else at the table. They didn't get it. And while Little Casey probably missed me as much as I missed her, I bet she understood the urge to leave and never look back. "So about that permission slip . . ."

"As long as Dr. Rutherford is okay with it," Mom said. "I don't want you to push too hard too fast. Especially after yesterday."

"Anybody can get mugged, Mom. That has nothing to do with my overall health. Dr. Rutherford said it would be good for me to be more active. Get my strength up." I kept my face straight. My parents had overactive BS detectors. It came with the theater-prof territory; they could spot a poor performance from a mile away. Either I was better at acting than I thought or they wanted to believe as much as I did that my health problems were over, because neither of them gave me a second look.

"Roller derby? Awesome! You'll be the star of the team. There will be blood on the pavement!" Dad gestured with his fork like it was a sword. Not like swords and roller derby had anything to do with each other; he just took any excuse to pretend to sword fight. "But it shall not be yours! Not this day, or any other!"

"You need medication," Rachel said.

Dad put the fork down. "I've been told that before."

"I think the tryouts are a great idea, honey." Mom sipped her wine. "You aren't happy just sitting around the house. Just promise me you'll be careful, yes?"

"Of course I will," I said dutifully.

"You'll need a fully defined character, though, won't you? Those derby girls always have great characters. I'll help if you like."

"Thanks, Mom."

I said it with a straight face, but no way was I going to take her up on it. I wasn't letting them turn my derby audition into one of their theater productions. They'd make me into Ophelia on skates. And I was not down with being O-wheelie-a. Not one bit.

"You'll need to explore her motivations," she continued dreamily. "Her aspirations. Her fears . . ."

I finished the cake, but she snapped out of her reverie

before I could move, swiping up the dishes and dashing back into the kitchen. Stereotypical Mom behavior, veering wildly between frenetic energy and complete crazeballs.

Moments later, she was back with parfait glasses full of some unidentifiable brown stuff.

"Oh God," Rachel said. "What is that?"

"Mousse!" Mom exclaimed. "Casey loves sweets, and it's her special celebration, so we have five courses of dessert tonight. Isn't that just the coolest idea?"

My parents looked at me with identical expressions of excitement and glee, and I smiled despite my roiling stomach. It still wasn't the same after all those months of chemo and hospital food. At the words "five courses of dessert," it felt like my stomach tried to jump out of my body and run for safety.

But I did love dessert. I shoveled a big bite of mousse into my mouth.

"This is really amazing," I said. "Did you make it?"

"Well, yes." Mom blushed. "I'm not much of a cook, but I know how much you love chocolate, so I got the recipe from Cherise. You remember her, don't you? She does the costumes for the theater. This is actually my third attempt; the first two were inedible."

"Completely inedible," Dad interjected, smiling fondly at her.

I couldn't keep from smiling too. "Thanks, Mom."

After the mousse course was over, she produced a big bowl brimming with apple crisp. It was heavenly. Or it would have been if I hadn't had a pound of dessert in me already. But I was still determined to eat it.

"I'm sorry." Rachel stood up. "I can't take this anymore."

"What?" Mom asked.

"You're going to make her sick. The dessert thing is a fun idea, but you don't stop to think things through. She's been eating like a bird ever since she got out of the hospital. How do you think her system is going to handle all this crap?"

"If Casey doesn't want the dessert, we'll make her a sandwich," Dad said mildly, but Rachel didn't back down. She grunted and shoved her plate away. "So what are you really upset about?" he continued. "I don't think this is about the cake."

"I'm just sick of it. You guys do this stuff all the time. Like the derby thing." She turned to me. Her face was all splotchy, the way it always got when she was upset. "I love you, Casey, but you haven't been out of the hospital for long, and you just got hurt yesterday. Don't think I haven't noticed you sneaking painkillers. Derby tryouts aren't a good idea for you right now, but our parents aren't going to say that because they're nuts. You know I love derby. I think it's totally awesome. But it's too dangerous for you, and the whole idea makes me sick to my stomach. We almost lost you once. I don't want to go through that again."

"Rachel," Dad said, glowering, "sit down right now. You're making Casey feel bad."

"I'm making her feel bad by telling her I care about her

well-being? I'm making a mistake by being concerned because she got mugged, and now she's having hallucinations—"

"Rachel!" I yelled. She wasn't supposed to tell our parents about that. It had been bad enough having to tell them about the attack in the first place.

"Hallucinations?" Mom blinked, looking at me.

"It's nothing, Mom." I forced a smile. "Rachel's *not thinking clearly right now* because she's upset."

"No, Casey. I'm thinking just fine. You're the one who's a little confused," Rachel said. "I don't mean to nag, but you really need to tell—"

"Shut up!" I snapped. Sometimes it felt like I'd suffocate under the weight of all the protection. I appreciated that they cared; really I did. But I'd survived. Plenty of kids from the cancer ward hadn't. And now it felt like everyone wanted me to just be satisfied with survival—they wouldn't allow me to *live.* My frustration over it all came out in a long, uncontrollable burst. "Can't you chill out and be happy that I've found something I want to do instead of sitting around on the couch by myself all the time? This is supposed to be my big celebration, don't you remember? It's like you don't give a crap what I want; you're too busy trying to smother out all the life I've got left!"

I threw my fork down; it skittered across the table and landed on the rug. Mom went pale and dashed into the kitchen, and after shooting a disapproving look in my direction, Dad followed.

Rachel and I stared at each other across the table. The silence got uncomfortable fast.

"That's not fair," she said quietly, standing up from the table and turning her back on me.

"Yeah, well, it wasn't very fair of you to decide what I ought to be doing without even asking me. I'm not stupid, Rachel."

"Could have fooled me."

She shoved the door open and stalked away down the hall. I knew I should run after her and apologize, but I was still pissed. She of all people should have known how much I hated being railroaded. So I got up, picked the fork up off the floor, and waited in lonely silence for my parents to bring in the next dessert.

4

I threw myself into skating practice for the next couple of weeks, partly because I needed the training but also because it gave me a handy excuse to avoid my family. After Rachel went back to school, my parents started speaking to me again, but it was that strained kind of talk full of things we weren't saying. Derby was the ideal distraction, and it made me feel more like my old self than I had in ages. Words were cheap; my family would understand once they saw me in action.

With that motivation in mind, I skated even harder, working out every day. Kyle wasn't fully on board with the derby thing either, but he didn't protest too much as long as I didn't go airborne, so we spent some much-needed time together at the skate park. At first, I couldn't skate for more than a few minutes without stopping, but it got better. I'd always been naturally athletic, and I had to concede that maybe I wasn't quite as out of shape as I'd thought. I was good with speed drills and plow stops—anything that required short bursts of energy—but my endurance was still pretty crappy. I tried not to let it get me down. I'd made a lot of progress, and I was determined that it would be enough. The derby team manager would have to see my potential; I'd only get better as I got stronger. And best yet, skating gave me that feeling of elation I hadn't recaptured in freerunning—probably because I was still too scared to try it again.

By the day of the tryouts, my toes were shredded from all the practice. My feet weren't used to the rough treatment anymore. It would take a while before I built up calluses again.

I'd just finished bandaging my feet when Darcy rang the bell. The moment I opened the door, she leapt into the car like we were twenty minutes late, but I knew we were early, so I followed at a more sedate pace. By the time I closed the car door, she was revving the engine and squirming in anticipation.

"Are you ready?" she chattered. "Yeah, you're ready. Okay, let's go! This is so exciting that I could totally throw up."

"I'm not so sure about the puking, but yeah, I'm psyched. I've been practicing ever since you told me about tryouts."

"So, what position do you think you'll get at first? I was telling my mom that I was worried I'd be a blocker, and she was all, 'What's a blocker?' Which seems pretty obvious, right? Like, a blocker is a person who blocks, duh. So then I was telling her that the jammers score all the points, and she's all, 'Then why don't they call them scorers?'" She snorted. "Moms."

"Well, she does have a point."

"And then she kept asking what kind of ball we use. I'm like, 'Mom, there is no ball,' but she still didn't get it. I tried to explain the rules, like, five times."

"It's not like they're complicated. Tell her the jammer scores points by passing players from the other team. The blockers try to help their jammer and block the other team's jammer. It's not rocket science."

"Dude, can you write that down for my mom? Because she just wasn't vibing me at all."

"Sure, I guess."

She paused thoughtfully. "I want to be a jammer so bad. I'll cry if I don't get to be one. I'm meant to score lots of points. I'm not a defensive kind of girl."

"Then you should give it a shot. It's worth a try, right?"

"Right. What about you? You'd make a really good jammer."

"I hadn't really thought about it. I just want to play."

"Well, you should think about it. Because they'll ask you what position you want, and then you won't know what to say, which would be really embarrassing, you know? But then you could tell them you just got out of the hospital and they'd understand. Not that I think you should use that as an excuse or anything, or that you *need* to. Gosh, I wasn't saying that at all. You're not offended, are you?"

Darcy's eyes rolled like she was a nervous horse, and the

car swerved as she waited breathlessly for a response. The tires scraped against the curb, a long, drawn-out squeal that made me wince.

"Hey, it's okay. I'm used to it," I said hastily, watching a fire hydrant grow inexorably closer to the passenger-side door. "Um . . ."

"Oh, good."

The car veered back onto the road, passing so close to the hydrant that I could have rolled down the window and touched it with my hand. Darcy just kept on going as if this kind of vehicular near-death experience were commonplace.

"So are you renting skates or did you buy some already?" I asked, white-knuckling the armrest. I was used to Rachel's speeding, but she wasn't overly dangerous. I'd defied death enough lately, thank you very much.

"Renting. I already picked out the skates I want, though. Most of them are so totally lacking in style, but I found a hot-pink pair that's cool. I love pink, just like the color you've got on your head. Is it a tattoo?"

"Not a tattoo," I mumbled, covering my hands with my face. Darcy's driving was scarier than a spinal tap.

The car skidded into the parking lot of the Skate Lake, one of the few indoor rinks that hadn't gone out of business yet. We had plenty of outdoor skate parks in town, but only one indoor track. It made most of its money from Mackinaw's derby leagues. Both the junior and senior teams held their practices there. Bouts were held at the university convention center; they almost always sold out, especially during the spring, when all the tourists rolled into town. Nothing says "family vacation" more than watching a bunch of girls on wheels beat the crap out of each other.

When we pulled into a spot next to a rusted-out El Camino, I heard the strangest noise. It sounded like a pterodactyl was about to dive-bomb the car. I stepped out, looking around in confusion. It didn't take long to locate the source of the noise: a derby girl was scuffling with what looked like a homeless vagrant girl against the wall of the building, and the vagrant kept letting out these animalistic screeches. As I watched, the vagrant grabbed the derby girl by the collar and started punching her in the face. Strangely, the derby girl just took the abuse. She didn't even raise her arms to defend herself.

That was totally uncool. I took a step forward and yelled "Hey!" before I even had a chance to evaluate whether this was a wise course of action. The two combatants froze and then turned twin glares on me like I'd interrupted something important. I put up my hands; if they wanted to thrash each other, it wasn't my business. But I couldn't help asking, "Are you sure everything's okay?"

No answer. Not the most welcoming of experiences, but I wasn't going to let it ruin my tryout. I turned to Darcy, who stood uncertainly by the trunk.

"Should I get our stuff out?" she asked, glancing nervously at the pair of crazies.

"Yeah, thanks," I said.

She handed over my bag and leaned back into the car to

collect a few things that had spilled out of her open knap-sack and scattered all over the trunk. I was waiting patiently when someone shoved me hard from behind, catching me completely off guard. I stumbled into a pothole so huge that our entire town house would probably have fit inside. Mud-swirled lukewarm water seeped into my shoes.

I whirled around, letting the momentum swing my back-pack off my shoulder. It flew right into the chest of the vagrant, whose expression of triumph faded when she got knocked back a step. She was younger than I'd realized, definitely not out of high school, and too clean to have been out on the street long. But the wild-eyed expression combined with the white crust of drool at the corners of her mouth suggested that she'd been into some illegal substances.

"What the heck is your problem?" I demanded, falling into a defensive posture.

She leaned toward me, her foul breath enveloping my head. Her pupils flickered red as if a flash had just gone off and I'd missed it. It reminded me of the guy in the alley, and not in a good way. My hand went instinctively to my lucky necklace, hanging on a new silver chain. Her eyes tracked the movement, and she immediately backed off, her hands in front of her face as if she expected me to stab her with a sterling sil-ver pendant. I might have if I'd thought it would do any good.

"It burns!" she squealed, cowering away from me. "It hurts!"

Then she turned tail and ran, the kind of flailing cha-otic flight that doesn't get you anywhere fast and manages to make you knock over everything in your path. She took out a snack bar sign and an empty garbage bin before disappearing around the corner.

"You okay?" Darcy asked.

I jumped; I'd forgotten she was standing behind me. "Yeah. You all right?" I shouted to the derby girl. She turned wordlessly and went into the building. "You're welcome!" I yelled after her.

"Weird." Darcy picked up her knapsack. "We should get inside."

"That's it?" I was more than a little shocked. It seemed to me that the situation warranted a bigger reaction, but Darcy was too obsessed with getting to the tryout before she turned into a pumpkin. And really, what was I going to say? I wasn't going to win points by observing that the crack addict's glowing eyes had reminded me a little of the guy who'd mugged me the other day.

"What?" she asked. She honestly seemed to have blocked out the weird almost-attack. Maybe I'd imagined it. "Oh my God. Look at your shoes!"

The once-white canvas was a murky brown, and pieces of unidentifiable muck clung to one toe. "Eeew." I stomped my feet, but the only result was a wet sucking sound from my insoles.

"Oh, yuck!" Darcy exclaimed, putting her hands to her mouth. "You want me to see if I have any extra socks? I might have some. I mean, not like I usually carry socks in my pockets, but—"

"It's okay," I said, resigned. "I'll live."

"Well, *yeah,* of course."

Darcy linked her arm with mine and tugged me toward the front doors, a trip that required multiple detours to avoid further exploratory pothole expeditions. When we finally made it into the rink, a blast of supercooled air slapped me in the face. It was so cold that my arms broke out in gooseflesh. I should have brought a hoodie.

A girl skated toward us, and I instinctively stepped back. I wasn't a coward. During my black belt test, I'd faced down two *shidoshi*—senior black belts—all alone. But just because I knew how to fight didn't mean I wanted to. This girl, on the other hand, projected a distinct aura of aggression, like the kind of person who picked fights because she thought bleeding was really fun. She wore a typically campy roller derby uniform: a yellow jersey imprinted with the number one, a pair of short purple shorts over black-and-white striped tights, and shiny silver skates. Her hair was done in two long braids and tinted an aggressive red, and heavy makeup ringed both eyes.

"You're late," she said, frowning.

I squinted at her. The attitude was totally different, but I could swear this was the derby girl I'd just saved from being throttled. "Um . . . yeah. Weren't you the one we just saw out—"

"I don't know what you're talking about," she interrupted. But from the tightness of her face, she did know and just didn't want to admit it. I was fine with not spilling her business all over the room, but to blame us for it was ridiculous. "Are you ready to get schooled?"

"Yes, ma'am!" Darcy said with a gap-toothed grin and a lot of nodding. "I'm so excited! I didn't want to be late, but I had to wait at Casey's house, and we lost a few minutes, and then there was that thing in the parking lot, although that wasn't really our fault, but—"

"Well, you're here now." The girl gave me a blatant once-over and then tried to stare me down. "Hi." She thrust her hand toward me as if it were a weapon and squeezed my fingers hard on the shake. "I'm RJ, but in Derbyland, I'm known as Ruthanasia. I'm the team captain."

"Yeah, Ruthanasia is totally cool—" Darcy said. She would have added more, but Ruthanasia interrupted her.

"Whatever." Ruthanasia pointed to the table clearly marked REGISTRATION. "Don't forget to sign in." Then she turned to me. "Moral support seating is over there."

"Actually, I'd like to try out."

She laughed right in my face. "Very funny, kid."

She did *not* just call me "kid." I folded my arms and tried to keep from scowling. I couldn't believe she'd write me off like that. Especially after I'd just gone to her rescue without even a thank-you. "I'm not joking. I can pass any skills test you throw at me. My sister was a Hotsie. I used to train with them all the time."

"How nice for your sister." Her eyes flicked up to my head. "But the answer's still no."

"So you're turning me down because I'm *bald*?" I demanded. This wasn't happening; she had to let me in. "That's not fair—"

"It wouldn't be so bad if she just tried out, right, Ruthanasia?" Darcy bleated nervously. "If she's no good, she won't get in. She'll sign the release form. Won't you, Casey?"

"Sure."

"Look, it has nothing to do with your head," Ruthanasia said haughtily. "Although I like the swirls. But you missed training camp. No camp, no spot on the team."

I took a deep breath. Obviously, I'd pissed her off; maybe she hadn't liked my seeing her so vulnerable in the parking lot, so she was trying to reestablish dominance. Antagonizing her further was only going to make matters worse, so I swallowed the angry retort I wanted to say and went for logic instead. But even though I did my best, it might have come out a little snippier than I'd intended. "The point of training is to teach me the skills. I respect that. But I've gone through skills camp before. With the Hotsies."

"Whatever," she said. "When we break you, don't come crying to me."

All my self-control went out the window. I could handle the witchy attitude, but calling me a baby? Writing me off as a wimp? Maybe I should have let her get pummeled after all. "Thanks. But you can drop the attitude. We can tell you're a badass from the way you're dressed."

"Really?" Ruthanasia glared at me. "Then maybe you shouldn't piss me off."

"I don't think it'll be a problem." I leaned against the registration table in a blatant display of casual disregard. "I'm a badass too. I just don't feel the need to shove it down people's throats two seconds after they walk through the door."

"We'll just go fill out that paperwork now," Darcy interjected, looking fearfully between the two of us. "Sorry to bother you."

"Whatever." Ruthanasia shot me an intense frown. I felt this urge to push things a little further just to see what would happen, but I shut my mouth instead. I needed to make this team, and taking the bait wasn't going to make it happen; I shouldn't have let her get to me in the first place. I knew I couldn't put all the blame for that argument on her, but recognizing that there was a chip on my shoulder didn't make it go away.

The rink was brightly lit, with a small snack bar off in one corner, newish tile, and about ten disco balls hung at what seemed like random spots around the ceiling. I found an empty bench near the locker room and tried to distract myself with all the paperwork. About ten minutes' and five pages' worth of monotony later, Darcy and I were lacing up our skates and strapping on pads. I tried to get all the water out of my socks, but it still felt like my feet were encased in moldy sponges. I'd just have to ignore it.

Darcy led the way across the worn carpet to the rink entrance. A few other girls were already out there, whizzing around in circles with long, graceful strides. There were only a couple of wall huggers; it looked like the competition would be pretty fierce. Good.

The smooth hardwood glided under my feet, and I instinctively sank slightly to maintain my balance and build up speed. My legs wobbled a bit and then locked in underneath me, and I rocketed past a gaggle of girls, who stared at my marker-scribbled head and whispered among themselves. I strapped on my helmet and pretended not to have noticed.

It felt good to spin around the track under the glare of the fluorescent overheads. The movement warmed up my frozen limbs and made the highly air-conditioned air almost comfortable as it whipped over my skin. Skating made me feel less paralyzed than I had in a long time. It made me not hate myself for almost dying. Or for living. I just felt like me, and that was really nice for a change. The only complaint I had was that my helmet kept slipping without any hair to help hold it in place. I took it off and began fiddling with the straps, making my way toward the benches.

Then I saw a guy standing at the railing. He had a surprisingly pale face under tousled surfer-boy hair. He was gorgeous, with the kind of angular features and broad shoulders that belonged in an ad for Abercrombie & Fitch, or maybe I just thought that because I was drooling over how his chest muscles filled out his Abercrombie tee. I knew I hadn't seen him before, because who could forget a face like his, but he couldn't have been too much older than me. I pegged him as a senior, or maybe a college freshman at the oldest. Frankly, I didn't care how old he was; he was made of hotness.

I rounded the track, drifting closer to get a better look. His white skin stretched over sleek cheekbones; his inhuman perfection reminded me of a mannequin.

Something wasn't right.

He noticed me looking at him, and his eyes widened. "You're bald."

I would have been offended if I hadn't been so busy trying to control the urge to shriek and run for it. It was the kind of voice that could defrock a nun. I'd felt something like this before, and it hadn't ended well. His voice and face weren't exactly the same as those of the man from the alleyway, but they were close enough to give me a serious case of the heebie-jeebies.

Any minute now, this guy was going to start crying lava, and I didn't want to be on the receiving end.

More than just about anything else, even the word "moist," I hated being scared. Fear had always hit me really hard. That was why I'd started taking ninjutsu. After our town house had gotten broken into, I'd been frozen with terror. Finally, after about a week of my not leaving my room, my dad had enrolled me in martial arts classes. That was in eighth grade. After that, I got into all kinds of extreme sports. I'd started freerunning, bungee jumping, and skydiving, and I wouldn't have stopped if my faulty bone marrow hadn't made me.

So the fact that I was running from this guy made me hate myself, but I couldn't help it.

The guy was standing next to the only rink exit, watching me. I pretended not to stare as I rolled up, but I couldn't help noticing the way his skin stretched to ripping point over the delicate bones of his face. He was still gorgeous up close, but it looked like someone had airbrushed his skin on.

I stepped onto the carpet, my hands nervously fluttering up to my newly repaired necklace. His eyes followed the movement, widening as he looked at the katana. I clenched the charm tight for reassurance. He started to say something, but then Ruthanasia interrupted him, leaning inappropriately close to whisper something in his ear.

While his attention was elsewhere, I fled. The best way to win a fight is to avoid it. I made my way across the matted carpeting as quickly as possible without falling over and didn't look back until I'd reached the ladies' room.

No one followed me. No one even seemed to notice I was gone.

But then the guy started twisting his head, scanning the room over Ruthanasia's shoulder while she continued to whisper sweet nothings at him.

Maybe he was looking for someone else—there was no reason to believe I'd captured his attention in a room full of wannabe derby girls in wild outfits—but my pulse thumped nonetheless. I pushed open the door and rolled into the bathroom before he could pin me with his eyes.

The longer I stood at the sinks, the angrier I got. I'd never run from a fight, so why was I so scared now? When had I turned into such a wuss? All because I thought this guy looked like a fire-crying crackhead? That was stupid, and it ticked me off. My fingers tingled with anger. My teeth ground together.

I'd felt like this once before, after the Anointing of the Sick, when Rachel had said goodbye to me. She'd always been the one who'd said I'd make it. And then it had gotten so bad that even she hadn't been able to deny it—I was going to die.

Just like that, it felt like everyone had written me off. I couldn't be angry at them, though; they'd kept on hoping long after the treatments had stopped working. That night, I stayed awake through a haze of morphine, wringing the sheets into tortured balls. I *wanted* the Angel of Death to come. I wanted to beat the crap out of him. I even came up with a fairly reasonable plan to thump him over the head with his own scythe, but he never showed. And then, over the next couple of weeks, I got better. Dr. Rutherford couldn't explain why. Everyone said it was a miracle, but I didn't buy it. I think maybe Death showed up, took one look at me, and decided he had better things to do.

Now I was scared again. It felt like everything frightened me these days, and that ticked me off. I was stronger than this, damn it. What was wrong with me, that I could face down death but not some random guy at a roller rink? It was either go back out there or resign myself to being a total loser for the rest of my life, and that was an easy choice. I thrust the door open just as Ruthanasia coasted up, wearing a pinched and disapproving expression.

"There you are," she snapped. "We're about to start, if you'd like to grace us with your presence."

I hit her with a glare and said, "Excuse me. Please." But it was less a request than an order.

She let me past, hostility practically sparking the air between us. I didn't particularly care what she thought.

The rest of the applicants were lining up in groups to do five-lap speed drills. I felt jittery and on edge; I wanted to blast through the girls in campy outfits and skate until my brain stopped snarling. But before I could move, Darcy pulled me into line in the second rank, edging out a chick in a purple pleather bustier.

"Are you okay?" she hissed.

"Yeah." I took a deep breath and let it out, determined to put all the stupid emotional crap behind me. It was time to quit looking back and start moving forward. No more guilt. No more wussing out. "I just had to go to the bathroom."

The guy was watching me again. I stared back, my jaw clenched so tight my teeth started to hurt. But he didn't react at all, just returned my gaze with an implacable expression until Ruthanasia sashayed over and gave him a clipboard. He rolled his eyes when her back was turned. Maybe he wasn't so bad after all. Maybe I could go back to lusting over him. That would be nice.

But I needed to focus if I wanted to make the team, because I knew I wasn't at my best yet, physically speaking. What I lacked in power and endurance, I'd have to make up for in technique and strategy. I watched as the first group of girls took their places on the track, jostling for the best positions on the inside.

"First wave," called a girl on the starting line, dreadlocks springing like a fountain from her ponytail. "Five-lap speed drills, starting now!"

She blew a whistle. The sound came out loud and sharp, and a few girls jumped, losing precious seconds. The pack moved around the first corner, quickly separating into three groups: agonizingly slow, fast, and really freaking fast. I watched the quickest skaters, the way the muscles in their thighs bunched as they squatted low around the curves, the thrust of their torsos as they drove ahead on the straightaways. I could do that. I could do better.

They whipped across the finish line one by one and rolled to the corner, where they stooped over with their hands on their knees, breathless and sweaty. The dreadlocked girl called for the second wave of skaters, and I rolled up to the line with Darcy at my elbow.

"Good luck!" she said, reaching over and squeezing my hand. I barely felt it; I was too focused on the expanse of lanes in front of us, the smooth grain of the floor, the flash of the lights overhead.

"On your mark, get set, go!" the dreadlocked girl said.

I surged forward, legs pistoning out in long, sure strokes, carrying me out into the empty air in front of the group. The first curve came, and I leaned into it, inertia tugging at my feet. The tips of my fingers grazed the floor. I felt like a million lava-teared freaks couldn't catch me if they tried.

When I whizzed past, the hot guy caught my eye for a fraction of a second, but this time I didn't feel afraid. I felt fearless and free and as fast as the wind.

At the beginning of lap four, I started to falter. By this time, I was way ahead; I'd even lapped a spindly girl skating with her elbows stuck way out to the sides for either balance or protection. Darcy was in second place, almost a quarter of a lap behind. But my speed started to decrease rapidly; my legs quivered as the burst of energy and adrenaline faded. I'd trained so hard, but apparently it hadn't been hard enough.

My skates felt like bricks, but I couldn't give up. I picked up one skate and then the other, over and over again until finally the end was in sight. The dreadlocked girl stood next to the finish line, a long red stripe that I focused on to the exclusion of everything else. I forced one final burst of speed. A flash of pink to the right drew my attention; I glanced over to see Darcy's sleeve . . . her shirt . . . her gritted teeth as she surged past me and over the finish line, in the lead by a second or two.

I coasted across the line behind her, rolled to the railing, and held on to it just in case my legs gave out. Second place wasn't bad, or so I tried to tell myself. But some of the girls in the first heat had been really fast, and there was still one group left to skate. If I didn't win the next event, I might not score high enough to make callbacks.

That wasn't an option.

"You okay?" Darcy skated over and put a hand on the small of my back.

I nodded, still too breathless to speak.

"I'm thinking it's totally time for some water. If I don't get a drink, I'll pass out!"

"God, yes," I croaked.

After we got our water, we sat down to catch our breath while the derby girls created an obstacle course out of dingy orange cones. We'd have to maneuver through a narrow, winding path around the rink. The other applicants pointed out the sharpest turns and whispered worriedly in their little cliques.

"Oh, dang!" Darcy said suddenly. "I've got to go potty."

"Go ahead, then." I pushed her gently in the direction of the ladies' room. "Watch out for the water on the floor. If they start, I'll hold you a spot."

"Thanks!"

After she left, I turned my attention back to the rink, leaning on the railing and evaluating the course. I felt someone walk up behind me, the prickling at the base of my spine that meant I wasn't alone.

"I think you set a bathroom record, Darcy," I said, turning around.

Only it wasn't her. The hot guy stood there with his hands stuffed in the pockets of his cargos and a confused look on his face. With that expression, he wasn't intimidating at all, and I felt a little foolish about the whole running-from-the-rink thing now that I was face to face with him. This guy was clearly not the tongue-molesting type. Or the crying-fire type either. And he probably thought I was a tool after the way I'd acted.

"Sorry. I thought you were somebody else," I said lamely.

He tilted his head. "How did you know I was here?"

"Oh. Martial arts. They teach a lot of awareness stuff. No big deal."

"No big deal? Unless you have eyes in the back of your head, I'd say that's pretty impressive." He paused, considering. "Actually, I think eyes in the back of your head would be impressive too."

I tried not to stare. His face was so perfect that it didn't even look real, as if he were computer generated. It was gorgeous and freaky-looking at the same time, and that made not staring pretty much impossible, so I looked away entirely.

"It's not that cool," I said, trying for nonchalance. "You should see some of the senior black belts. To get your fifth-degree black belt in ninjutsu, you have to kneel on the floor while somebody stands behind you with a sword. They try to whack you on the head with it, and if you move out of the way in time, you pass."

"You have to dodge it without seeing it?"

"Yep."

"Cool." He nodded, and I felt like I'd accomplished something. "And if you don't, you get bashed on the head?"

"Exactly. And the other black belts talk smack about you for the next year or so."

"I bet they do," he said, grinning. "So you're not a fifth-degree black belt yet?"

"Nah. I've got years of training before that happens. If it ever does."

"It will." He looked me over appraisingly. "I've done some

combat training, and you're a natural. I can tell by how you move."

"Thanks." I blushed.

"I'm Michael."

"Casey," I said, and then Darcy came back. This was probably a good thing, but I was vaguely disappointed.

"So when are we obstacle-coursing?" she said. "I'm totally ready now!" Then she noticed Michael standing there and immediately went mute.

"A few minutes, I think," he said. "I should probably get back." He nodded at me and then walked away without acknowledging Darcy's existence.

"Um . . . who—who is that hottie?" she stammered.

"No clue. But I'd like to oil him up and make him feed me grapes and fan me with palm fronds."

She let out a surprised laugh, and the tension went out of her shoulders along with it. Then the dreadlocked girl called all of us back onto the rink.

"All right," she said with a smile everyone in the room returned even if they weren't the smiling type. "I think I forgot to introduce myself before, and I see a new face in the group. I'm Barbageddon. I'm in charge of the Fresh Meat, and I'm begging you to not get yourselves injured and make me look bad in front of our new team manager."

She jerked a thumb toward Michael, who froze under the weight of all the female stares, and then gave a tentative wave.

"Anyway," she continued, "I want to give you a quick run-through of the course. We'll be splitting you up into pairs this time, so you shouldn't need to worry about bowling each other over. The pads and helmet should protect your most important bits, but the floor still hurts, and we don't want to break you just yet. That'll come later."

She grinned and walked us down the length of the course, pointing out the sharp corners and narrow stretches that were most likely to take weaker skaters out. There were a lot of them.

"Now we'll be pairing you up randomly. Just do your best to cross the finish line on eight wheels, okay?" Everyone nodded, and she beamed at us in universal approval. "Good girls. Bear with me while we split you up."

Barbageddon grabbed the clipboard from Michael and rattled off pairs of names. Darcy and I got called first, so we rolled into a corner to stretch out again and keep our muscles from getting too cold. I wasn't shaking anymore, but my limbs felt heavy with fatigue. A couple of weeks' worth of training could get you only so far after about a year of inactivity and illness. I only hoped my strength would hold out. At least we got to rest between events; if they'd been all in a row there was no way I could have finished.

"Darcy? Casey?" Barbageddon said, skating over. "Do you have any questions before we start?"

"Yeah," Darcy replied. "Is that really . . . That guy . . . Is he . . ."

"She doesn't deal well with hot guys," I interjected. "They seem to addle her brain."

"You think?" Barbageddon wrinkled her nose.

Darcy nodded and managed to squeak out, "Is he for real?"

"Mmmmm," Barbageddon said noncommittally. "Any questions related to the course?"

"No. Thanks," I said.

"All right, then. Let's get moving." She motioned us up to the starting line. "Let's see what you've got, ladies. On your mark, get set, go!"

We launched ourselves off the line in almost perfect unison, with Darcy quickly pulling into the lead. I didn't let it bother me, even when she edged a little farther ahead going into the first S-turn. After the last few months of perfecting my napping technique, I was physically weaker and knew it; I'd already blown my reserves in the speed drill. But I remembered something Sensei always said: "If you're not cheating, you're not trying."

Of course, since he was a ninja, he always followed it up with "If you get caught, you're not trying hard enough."

So instead of slowing down to maneuver through the twisty obstacle like Darcy did, I increased my speed with long, sure strokes, rocketing toward the cones on a collision course. Moments before impact, I cranked my torso down, elbows curled to my sides, and launched my legs into the air in a perfect aerial spin, like a cartwheel with no hands and on roller skates. Once I was completely airborne, I had to wonder if this was a big mistake, because being a good skater and a good freerunner didn't necessarily mean you could do both at the same time without splatting, and I hadn't been back on skates for long. But by the time I was in the air, it was too late.

I sailed over the first curve and landed on my toe stops, and then sprang back up into the air again, passing over the obstacle entirely instead of skating through it. That maneuver would shave seconds off my time. Darcy's startled face appeared in my field of vision as I flew through the air just inches away. Then I touched down again, bringing my body into a crouch to preserve forward momentum.

Well, that had been surprisingly easy. I'd tried a few aerials over the past couple of days, but not two in a row. The best thing about them is that they relied more on momentum than on strength, so my technique could make up for the fact that my muscles were taxed to the limit.

Behind me, I could hear the scrape and hiss of Darcy's skates moving at an even more frantic pace to try to catch up, but I blocked out the sound as much as possible. I focused on the next few obstacles instead, jumping over a hairpin turn, tucking my knees to my chest, and landing in a neat crouch on the other side. I kept going, my chest heaving with exertion. I skipped over or otherwise avoided as many of the obstacles as I could. I heard a smattering of applause as I passed the other applicants, but I didn't dare risk a look. Darcy was close on my heels as we skated toward the final obstacle: the narrowest of the corridors, banked all the way up against the wall.

It was dotted with random cones to make it even more difficult to get through, which made jumping a poor proposition. If I came down on one, I could twist an ankle, or do something even worse. I pushed forward desperately, feeling Darcy at my heels, knowing that all I needed to do was get into that corridor first and there would be no way she could pass me unless I fell.

Just as I reached the obstacle, she shot past me wrapped in a tight crouch, low on her skates. Her elbow whacked the back of my legs, shoving me toward a cone. My skate caught on the edge of the orange plastic and whirled me around. I windmilled my arms in a vain effort to maintain my balance.

Darcy didn't even look back; she just kept on skating as I went spinning out of control. I had a moment to feel grateful that I was wearing a helmet, and then I hit the wall with my face.

My nose wouldn't stop gushing. On the outside I was all, "It's just a bloody nose. Chill. It's not like my face fell off." But inside, I kept thinking this was the end; I was bleeding more than a healthy person should; the leukemia was back, and this time there would be no miraculous recovery. More than anything, I hated constantly second-guessing my body. Sometimes it felt like every cough was a death sentence. I knew that was stupid, but I couldn't help it.

"Oh my God, I am so sorry," Darcy said for the sixteenth time, patting my arm in an apparent effort to reassure herself it was still operational. I just wanted everyone to stop fussing and let me get up off the floor.

"Really, I'm fine." I pushed her hands away and checked the towel clasped to my face. "See? I think it's slowing."

"Let her up already," Ruthanasia demanded in a tone that made it clear to everyone she was losing patience with the whole situation. "We still have a lot more to do tonight."

Her attitude ticked me off on the one hand, but on the other hand, I was thankful not to be coddled. The irony of this didn't escape me.

"I didn't realize you fell." Darcy pulled me to my feet. "Really, I didn't."

"I know. It's okay, honest. It was just an accident."

Darcy took one arm and Barbageddon the other. It was embarrassing enough to have face-planted into the wall, but once Darcy shouted to the whole freaking room that I was a cancer patient in remission, they started treating me like I might fall apart at any moment. Literally. Like a leper.

I tried to skate away, and they tried to lead me toward the benches. None of us was successful.

"Let go," I said, my voice muffled from my already-swollen nasal area. "I'm really fine."

Barbageddon wouldn't let go. "You should sit—"

"I'm finishing the course." I set down the towel and probed tentatively at my face. No blood. About freaking time.

She still wasn't giving up, and I knew she just wanted to help, but it was hard not to growl. Couldn't she understand that I had to do this to prove to everyone that I could? Especially myself.

"But you need to—"

"Leave her alone," Michael ordered from his seat by the exit. It was the first time he'd spoken in front of the group, and some of the girls visibly swooned as his baritone washed over them. It tugged at the back of my neck, sending prickles up my spine. I wanted to look at him and maybe drool a little. But now that I knew to expect it, the urge was easier to resist. Not easy, but easier.

"Are you sure?" Barbageddon asked, her grip loosening but not releasing entirely.

"She's fine," he replied firmly. "Let Casey finish the course at her own pace."

I flashed him a grateful smile and tried to pretend everyone wasn't staring at me as I cautiously slalomed through the cone-filled track and across the finish line at a slow coast, but of course they were. Ruthanasia watched with distaste, Barbageddon with concern, and Darcy with hangdog guilt. Michael watched me too, but his eyes gave no hint of his feelings.

At least they weren't flaming.

The rest of the applicants made it through the obstacle course without beating each other into pulp. My nose and upper lip had started to swell, so I got to apply an ice pack on a bench right near the rink. I had a stellar view of the back of Ruthanasia's head as well as Michael's butt. Now that I'd gotten a handle on the whole panic-for-no-reason thing, I felt free to admire it as it should have been admired. The butt, not the head.

My rear-related reverie was cut short when Darcy said,

"Would you like some nachos? I'll get you some; just wait right here."

"No, thank you," I said, but she was already gone. Normal people don't gorge on carbs in the middle of a tryout, but she'd always been a nervous eater. The day we'd tested for senior green belt, she'd polished off half a box of Twinkies in about five minutes flat. I didn't share the habit, but I couldn't think of a graceful way to tell her that. The worst part about it was that I didn't really like nachos. The chips were fine, but the cheese looked too much like nuclear waste for my comfort. And now I'd have to eat them just so Darcy would quit guilting out.

Thrillsville.

"You might as well go home," Ruthanasia said, rolling toward me. "Did you drive?"

"I don't have a car."

She sighed like my lack of transportation was a personal affront. "Of course you don't. Fine, then. I'll get one of the girls to take you home. Hey!" she called, waving her hand. "Ragnarocker!"

"Darcy can take me home." I put down the ice and rose halfway from my seat. "But I didn't think we were done."

"Oh, we're not. But I figured you wouldn't want to stay." Ruthanasia's syrupy purr reminded me of every bad action-movie villain rolled into one. "You're injured, and you're just getting over this massive illness, right? I'm sure your doctor wouldn't approve."

"Actually, I've been cleared to play," I replied. I'd said it so often, I was beginning to believe it myself, but she wasn't even listening.

Ragnarocker detached from the gaggle of derby girls clustered by the snack bar and sauntered over, popping her bubble gum. She was one of the few members of the team still in street clothes, but the width of her shoulders and the cocky tilt to her smile suggested she'd be pretty formidable on skates. Hitting her would be kind of like running into a wall. As of about a half hour ago, I was an expert on that topic.

"'Sup, boss-girl?" she said to Ruthanasia.

"Can you take Casey home?"

"Yup." Ragnarocker turned and held up her fist for me to bump. "Nice spill."

"I don't want to go home, thanks." I bumped knuckles with her, though, because she seemed like the kind of person I should be nice to.

Ruthanasia was a different story. She'd been rude from the moment we'd walked through the door. And yeah, maybe I'd come here with something to prove, and maybe that made me a little oversensitive, but that didn't make her behavior acceptable. Under different circumstances it probably wouldn't have been a big deal, but between the lava-guy flashback and the brick facial, I'd had enough. I wasn't about to deal with a complete wench on top of it.

"What's your problem, RJ?" I asked.

"Ruthanasia," she corrected, looking down her nose at me.

"Whatever. You've been a total wench since we got here. What exactly did I do to piss you off?"

Ragnarocker backed away, holding her hands up in a gesture that clearly said she wanted no part of this conversation. But Darcy picked that moment to return with a giant plate of nuclear-orange nachos, and she nearly dropped them when she overheard me. "Casey?" she asked uncertainly.

Now we were the center of attention. The last two girls made their painstaking way around the obstacle course, but no one was watching. Even Michael had dropped his clipboard and was staring at us.

"Well?" I demanded.

"Look, I'm sorry if I offended your delicate sensibilities," Ruthanasia hissed, "but I've got a responsibility to my team. We're not one of those sissy leagues. Girls get into scraps here and people get hurt. You're damaged goods, and that really sucks, but I'm not going to be the one to go to your house and tell your mommy and daddy that I broke you." She looked me up and down, shaking her head. "You don't belong here."

"You can't make me leave," I said flatly. It took every ounce of self-control I had not to punch her in the face.

Ruthanasia opened her mouth to say something, but then she looked around the room at our audience. She closed her mouth, moved closer.

"Maybe you're right," she said quietly. "But when you get beaten down, don't come crying to me. I told you so. Excuse me for trying to help."

And then she stalked off. How she managed to do this while wearing skates on carpeting was a mystery. I wanted her to fall so bad, but it didn't happen.

"Wow," Darcy said. "I mean, really, wow. What was that all about?"

I shook my head, snagging a cheese-free chip and biting it ferociously.

"You totally told her off! But of course they're going to let you on the team anyway, what with those jumps and stuff, right? How did you do that? I mean, it was totally made of awesomeness, but I'm surprised you didn't fall on your head."

"I've been practicing. No big deal."

"Well, next time, invite me along. You made me look bad." She actually had the nerve to look sulky.

"You could have practiced too," I snapped. "That's not my fault."

She winced and ducked her head. "Sorry," she mumbled, and I immediately felt like I'd claimed the Complete Wench crown for myself.

"No, *I'm* sorry. I'm pissed at Ruthanasia; I don't mean to take it out on you."

"It's okay, really. Especially after I shoved you into the wall." She moaned. "I'm so sorry."

"It's really no biggie." I thumbed the end of my nose and tried not to wince. I'd probably have a pair of black eyes tomorrow. But on the bright side, maybe people would think I'd been in a fight. Maybe they'd stop treating me like I might shatter if they breathed on me too hard. "See? It's not broken."

I sat down next to her and took another nacho. But only one, because I didn't want to throw up. She started mowing through the plate as if it were her last meal on earth. I would have worried, but after the Twinkie incident, I knew she had an iron stomach.

We did booty blocking next, and I seethed the whole time. It wasn't my strongest suit, since I didn't have much to block with. But I kept imagining that Ruthanasia was trying to get around me, so when I did manage to get a hit in, it was a good one. Then we did some plow stops and single and double knee slides. I was usually pretty good at those, but by this time I was so tired that I couldn't bounce back up to my toe stops like I wanted to. After this was over, I was going back to bed and wasn't going to come out for a week. Fatigue didn't stop me from wanting a place on the team, though. I kept reminding myself that it would get easier. It was just a matter of time.

Once we were done, Ruthanasia climbed on top of a table, minus her skates, and shouted, "Okay, everybody. We've tallied all the scores, and we'd like to call back the top five to compete for our two open spots: Tanya Li, Shelby Shusterman, Monique Larribee, Sarah Smith, and Darcy Klinger."

Darcy let out a little squeal of excitement, but it faded when she saw how pissed I was. Ruthanasia very pointedly didn't look at me, but the satisfied smirk on her face was enough.

I hadn't even made it to callbacks.

I'd handled a lot. When Dr. Rutherford had told us that I had cancer, my parents had cried, and I'd stayed strong for them. I'd dealt with the bone-deep pain of biopsies without complaint. I'd lost all my hair. I'd puked until my mouth had grown sores. All of those things had been bearable, but this? It felt like I'd been kicked while I was still down.

"Congratulations, Darcy," I said, holding my head high with effort. "I'm really happy for you."

Ruthanasia interrupted before Darcy could answer. "Sorry, Kent. But you can't say I didn't tell you so." I couldn't decide what bothered me more—the fact that she referred to me by my last name like I was her servant or the fact that she was looking at me like I'd rolled in poop.

"Actually . . ." Michael cleared his throat, walking up behind her. "I was just going to say that I'd like to call Casey back too."

She gaped at him. And honestly, so did I. He must have seen something he liked in my performance, because the alternative was completely unbearable. If he called me back just because he felt sorry for me, I'd die of embarrassment.

"Um, yay?" Darcy said tentatively.

"We can't do that," Ruthanasia declared, folding her arms. "We said we'd bring back the top five. She didn't make it."

"So what?" he responded in a flippant tone. "It's not going to hurt anything to see her again. If she doesn't make it, that's fine. But I think she's worth a second look."

Ruthanasia glared at him, but she couldn't keep it up for long. "Right," she said reluctantly. "Come back tomorrow night at seven, Casey."

Then she turned her back on us.

"Thanks, everyone, for coming," Barbageddon said, rolling up on her skates and blanketing us all with a smile. "We're sorry we can't use you all right now; we're only filling the spots that were vacated due to a really horrible car accident. But we'd love to see you all again at next year's tryouts, and the league will have plenty of space on the roster then. Keep practicing and it'll happen! Have a good night!"

I sat back down and slowly unlaced my skates, trying to figure out how I was going to remove them without taking off my toes at the same time. My socks had dried, and it felt like they were fused to my feet.

"Well," Darcy said. "We both made it to the next round. That's great, isn't it?"

"Yep," I replied shortly. I couldn't decide how to feel, other than tired.

"I shouldn't have gotten the large nachos. Eat some of these, please? Or I'm going to turn into a big fat pig."

I took another chip to be polite, searching out the least-toxic-looking one on the plate. No way was I eating any more of these things after this one. "Maybe I'll see if they have a takeout box."

"Good idea."

There was a line at the snack bar. I got into place behind the girl in the pleather corset, who was so busy complaining about not getting called back that the guy behind the counter couldn't get a word in edgewise. I waited with uncharacteristic patience at first, but after a while the delay started to get to me. Pleather Girl wouldn't stop whining, and the counter guy kept coming back with a series of never-ending questions about the contents of her iced coffee. It was enough to make a Buddhist monk climb a clock tower with an automatic weapon. I cleared my throat loudly, and then someone else did it too, right behind my ear.

"God, this is annoying," I said.

"I guess," Michael replied, his deep voice sending a wave of goose bumps over my arms. "Waiting's not that bad."

"Come on," I said. "You're as impatient as I am. Admit it. You can't stop clearing your throat."

"I was trying to get your attention."

I didn't know what to say to that. Pleather Girl finally claimed her coffee and rolled out of the way, eyeing Michael with aggressive speculation. It was almost disgusting.

"Get a grip," I said, shaking my head at her. "You're practically panting."

"What?" asked the girl, thrusting out her chin and planting a fist on her hip.

"Nothing," Michael interjected before I could answer. "Casey, would you order already?"

I looked around in confusion before I finally remembered why I'd gotten in line in the first place.

"I just need a to-go box," I said. "Please."

The guy set the box on the counter, but Michael snagged it. "Let me give you a hand."

"I'm not an invalid, thanks," I snapped.

"I'm not treating you like an invalid," he said mildly. "I'm treating you like a lady."

I couldn't help it; I snorted. "I'm even less of a lady than I am an invalid."

"Fair enough." He grinned, offering me the box. I didn't take it, though. I was too busy staring at him with my mouth hanging open. That grin had taken his face from plastic perfection to new levels of amazing. When I realized what I was doing, I snatched the box and tried to look like I hadn't just been gaping. My ears turned red; I felt them burning.

"Thanks," I said, taking a deep breath. He was just a guy; I needed to chill. "And thanks for calling me back."

"Welcome." His eyes flicked down to the chain at my neck. He opened his mouth and shut it three or four times before he finally said, "Be careful going home. It would suck if you got mugged right before callbacks. Lots of crazies out there."

I snorted again. "You have no idea how right you are."

"You'd be surprised. I have both brains and beauty."

"And modesty."

He grinned, edging closer. "You noticed, huh?" He seemed about to say more, but Ruthanasia called him from across the room, and he frowned at me instead. "I guess I'll see you tomorrow."

"Yeah." I backed away, trying not to feel disappointed. Not that I was obsessing, but this was my first real flirtation since getting out of the hospital, and I didn't want it to end. It felt so *normal*.

Then again, it didn't have to stop here. I'd see him at callbacks. I found myself smiling as I slung my skates over my shoulder, and I kept it up all the way home, despite the fact that my nose still hurt and my eyes were already ringed with black circles. Darcy jabbered incessantly in the car about how excited-slash-nervous she was and what she was going to wear tomorrow. I just kept nodding and smiling. I told myself I was grinning like an idiot because of the callbacks and not because of the cute guy.

It was kinda true.

6

The next day crawled. Dad examined my swollen and bruised face with resignation—he knew from experience that arguing caution was futile—and worked with me on my derivative homework. It was like the blind leading the blind; he knew even less about math than I did. But I rushed through the work in the hopes that it might make the day go just a little faster. Unfortunately, all that sitting made my sore muscles cramp up, so as soon as I'd finished the math pages, I got into the tub and had a nice hot soak. That and some painkillers left me feeling vaguely human again.

As I was applying my post-bath moisturizer, my phone buzzed with a text from Kyle. LOLLIPOP CHAINSAW. YOU. ME. TONITE. He shouted even in his texts. And while I normally would have jumped at the chance to spend the evening wearing out the buttons on his PlayStation and eating popcorn, it just wasn't going to happen tonight.

I replied, SORRY, DUDE. CAN'T. CALLBACKS!

GOOD LUCK. His reply wasn't as excited as I'd hoped, but maybe that was just disappointment because we couldn't hang. And if I made the team, the schedule problem was only going to get worse. I'd have to practice a lot to get my endurance up. I sighed and set the phone down. Maybe Kyle could be Michael's assistant manager or something. It was the best way I could think of to have derby without totally ditching Kyle.

I took a little extra time getting ready for callbacks. This had nothing to do with Michael and everything to do with making a good impression on the team. Really, it did. I needed to show them I was good derby girl material. Something told me I'd need all the supporters I could get to make up for the fact that Ruthanasia wanted me dead.

So I dug through Rachel's drawers and came up with a pair of gold lamé hot pants, the fishnets from my Halloween costume, and a T-shirt that said TALK DERBY TO ME. I'd stopped by the store, so I had my own pads and helmet instead of my sister's ratty old ones. Now I looked about as authentic as Fresh Meat could, and I hoped it would score me some points.

When Darcy and I walked into the Skate Lake and removed our jackets, Ragnarocker took one look at the shirt and guffawed loudly. One point for Casey.

I grinned and walked over to her. "Awesome, isn't it? My sister used to skate for the Hotsie Totsies. I raided her closet."

"Yeah?" Ragnarocker asked, chomping on about five sticks of gum. "Who's your sister?"

"Buffy Slayzer? She skated for only a year; she started at Smithton, and it's too far to commute."

Ragnarocker nodded, rubbing her jaw. "Yeah, I remember her. She knocked me clear off my feet once during the junior-senior league bout. She's tougher than she looks."

I grinned proudly. "That's her."

"Awesome." She looked over my shoulder and then quickly away. "I should put my skates on." Before I could say anything, she was gone.

I turned around expecting to see Ruthanasia, but Michael stood there instead. He was still wearing Abercrombie. I was beginning to wonder if they'd rented ad space on his chest. If so, it had been a wise move on their part. I couldn't take my eyes off it.

"Hey," he said quietly. "Can I talk to you?"

My smile died. I felt it go, but there wasn't anything I could do to stop it. He'd decided he didn't want a former cancer patient on his team after all. He wanted to let me down easy; I just knew it. So when he pulled me into the tiny locker room and gestured for me to sit down on the warped wooden bench, I didn't waste a moment before going on the offensive. I'd been scared of him before, and I was determined not to let fear get the best of me now.

"You can't just let me go without giving me a chance." I stepped defiantly away from the bench and glared at him. "That's not fair."

He blinked. "What?"

"You're going to cut me, right? After going to all that trouble to invite me to callbacks in the first place. And it sucks!"

He held up his hands. "You need to chill. I'm not going to cut you. Who said I was? Ruthanasia?"

"No, I . . ." Felt a little like an idiot, now that I stopped to think about it. Maybe the problem wasn't everyone else seeing me like a poor little cancer girl. Maybe the problem was my constant quest to prove that I wasn't. Maybe the problem was me.

For some strange reason, that thought made me feel a little better; I might be stupid, but at least that was fixable. I forced my fingers to unclench and actually looked at him. His hair was even wilder than it had been yesterday, like he'd been running his hands through it. As I watched, he fidgeted with the hem of his shirt.

Holy crap. Was he going to ask me out? And if so, what was I going to say? He was the team manager. Was it a good idea for me to go out with him? I watched as the tip of his tongue flicked out to moisten his lips, and I decided that it would be a very good idea indeed.

Then he said, "Listen, I wanted to talk to you about—"

"Yes!" I interjected.

"About that katana necklace," he finished. Then he tilted his head. "Yes, what?"

Now I felt stupid. And disappointed, which was ridiculous. I barely knew the guy. And most of what I knew was that he was gorgeous. Not exactly the stuff relationships are made of.

So I took that feeling of frustration and choked it to death.

"My lucky necklace?" I asked, taking a deep breath and trying to ignore the heat in my cheeks. "What about it?"

He reached out to touch the chain, and the contact was like an electric shock. It spread in a tingling circle at my throat and then shot up through the top of my skull. My vision went white; it felt like the world was spinning around me. The sensation didn't hurt, exactly, but it seemed like it might choose to explode into pain at any moment. I straightened almost convulsively, pulling away and going straight into *ichimonji*—one leg forward, one behind, to maximize my balance. My left hand guarded my face, while my right was extended and ready to block. The defensive stance made me feel instantly safer, ready for whatever happened next.

"How did you do that?" I demanded.

But he looked just as shocked as I felt.

"Are you okay?" he asked. His hands hovered an inch over my skin, like he wanted to help but was too afraid to risk a repeat performance.

"What did you do to me?" I asked, not relaxing my defensive posture.

Now I was pissed. I knew better than to ignore my instincts, and my first impulse had been to stay as far from Michael as possible. Yes, he was hot, but that meant nothing. The guy from the alleyway had been pretty hot too, and he'd flicked lit cigarettes at me. It just went to show that you couldn't trust appearances.

Michael started pelting me with questions: "Are you dizzy? Do you feel faint? Do you need to sit down?"

"Quit patronizing me!"

He flinched, and I lowered my arms, partly because he didn't seem dangerous now, but mostly because I felt even stupider than when I'd assumed he was asking me out. He opened his mouth, and I think he was about to apologize, when Ruthanasia charged into the locker room.

"What's going on here, kids? You're making a scene," she said. Her voice was perky and playful and full of utter crap. "You're not going to faint, are you, Casey?"

"She's fine," Michael said.

He shifted to stand shoulder to shoulder with me, or head to armpit, I guess. He was a lot taller than me. I appreciated the gesture of solidarity and *really* appreciated the fact that he made it a point not to touch me. I wasn't about to risk a repeat of the shock wave until I knew what the heck was going on.

"Good." Ruthanasia took his wrist and tugged gently. Her hand didn't spark or shimmer or anything vaguely weird, which sucked. She could have used a good shock. "We need to talk about the plan for tonight."

Michael pulled his arm away. "I'll be there in a minute."

"We can't start without you; you know that," Ruthanasia said, pouting.

"In a minute," he growled.

But she didn't leave. She folded her arms and waited with ill-concealed impatience, practically tapping her skate on the floor. This more than anything else made me answer Michael's next question in the affirmative.

"So, Casey? Would you like to go out with me tomorrow

night?" he asked. "It's freshman night at the University Quad. I was thinking of checking it out after practice."

"Sure," I said, trying not to crow. Not only was he hot *and* a college guy, but it was going to piss off Ruthanasia. I couldn't keep from smirking when her mouth fell open. "Do you have my number? Just in case?"

He nodded. "It's on your derby paperwork, right?"

"Yeah." I made a big show of pulling out my phone and checking the time. I didn't want Ruthanasia to think she'd scared me off. "I should go put my skates on. Talk to you later."

I didn't need to look back to know that her laser eyes were burning a hole between my shoulder blades.

Darcy managed to contain herself until I sat down, but only barely. I got my skates out of my bag, and less than a millisecond passed before she started squealing.

"Ohmigod! What just happened? Because I was going to store my stuff in the locker room, and I couldn't help over-hearing! Are you really going on a date with Michael?"

"I guess." I looked over my shoulder to see Ruthanasia and Michael bent over a clipboard and talking quietly. As I watched, she sidled closer. If this went on much longer, she'd be in his lap. I almost felt bad for her.

Darcy was still talking. "Gosh, you're quick. I mean, not that I think you're a slut or anything, but you just met him, and he's like the team manager and stuff. . . ." She trailed off in embarrassed uncertainty.

"Frankly, I only said yes because I knew it would piss Ruthanasia off."

"Oh." Darcy considered this for a long time, longer than necessary. It wasn't that complicated. "Well, it's still awesome. And we're gonna be rollergirls too."

"Yeah, I hope so."

I tried to keep my nerves in check as I glanced at my competition. They looked good. Limber and toned and not hobbling around like they'd been in a train wreck. Only two of the six of us were going to make the team; I'd have to be on top of my game to avoid being cut.

Ruthanasia rolled up and looked us over. Actually, that's not entirely true, because she made a point of completely ignoring my existence, which was fine with me. "All right, ladies. We're going to start with suicides and burpees and then move into some jamming and pack drills before the scrimmage."

Practice was brutal. About halfway through the two-minute suicide drill, full of nonstop full-speed skating from cone to cone punctuated by double knee slides, I looked up to see Ruthanasia staring me down from her spot on the sidelines as if she was waiting for me to fall. I wouldn't have put it past her to pick endurance drills just to prove that I didn't belong there, so I pushed aside the burning in my lungs and the aching of leg muscles still unused to all the work, and skated harder. I brought up the rear, but I finished. By the time we were done, I had a killer stitch in my side and streams of sweat running into my eyes. I'd have to remember a headband next time. You'd think I would have remembered what it's like to lack the sweat-mopping protection of hair, but I'd already forgotten.

Everyone looked wiped, but I was the only one who couldn't stand upright. Ruthanasia had this triumphant expression like she'd managed to score a point. I straightened, lacing my hands behind my head to ease the pain, and breathed slow and easy. This was my lack of conditioning at work. This was not weakness. This was not cancer, part deux. And I was going to shove my skate up her butt if she didn't stop looking at me like that.

Michael took the stopwatch from her, and she gave him a flirty look from beneath lowered lashes that he missed or ignored. I was hoping for the latter, but I'd take either. And then he said, "My turn. Burpees. I want the whole team, not just the applicants. We're going to do them until you drop. Last one standing wins."

Michael and Ruthanasia turned to look at me in unison, and I knew what this was. It was a challenge, and I wasn't about to back down. Ruthanasia took a spot next to me; Michael blew the whistle.

It was on.

We began running in place, lifting our knees high, the wheels of our skates clomping on the floor in an increasing rhythm. Michael blew the whistle, and down we went, dropping onto both knees and then getting back up to run. Another whistle, and we dropped again. And again. And again.

The first applicant dropped out, chest heaving. Two more followed, so quickly that I knew they'd been holding on just so they wouldn't have to be the first to go. The other derby girls began to quit, slowly and steadily—they didn't have anything to lose, so I think they quit as soon as it started to get tough. Darcy began coughing hard, gasping for air, and fell to her butt on the floor. I couldn't even manage to ask if she was okay; I needed every ounce of oxygen to fuel my muscles. Pain flared in places that I'd forgotten could hurt. My knees ached despite the pads, and my feet felt like lead. Barbageddon dropped out. It was just me and Ruthanasia.

Her teeth were bared as she crashed to the floor again, but I was right there with her. Maybe she was stronger than me. Maybe I'd lost ground physically speaking, and maybe I never would have been able to rival her even if I hadn't. She was pretty cut. But I had one thing she didn't—I knew pain. I knew it like the back of my hand; I knew it like my oldest friend. I knew its shape and scope. I knew how to endure it. In the Olympics of pain, I was a gold medalist.

So I held on. I breathed through the agony, the firing of neurons that were decidedly unhappy with my stubborn refusal to quit already. I kept going as the world narrowed to the patch of floor beneath me and the sound of the whistle and the need to endure just one more drop to the floor over and over again. I would not stop. I would not give in.

But while my spirit was willing, my body wasn't. Michael blew the whistle again, and I dropped to my knees. The smooth wood of the floor went wavy; my vision wouldn't focus. Everything felt far away, like I was looking at my own hands through a telescope. I pushed weakly against the floor once, then twice, and then I collapsed.

7

I woke up sprawled on my living room sofa with the thick braided edge of a cushion embedded in my cheek. The bright midmorning sun streamed through a familiar picture window; pots and pans clattered in the kitchen. My mother was quite possibly the loudest cook in the history of the known universe, but I was used to it. I flipped onto my belly, wriggling into the depths of the couch, searching for sleep again.

When my nose pressed against the pillow, pain lanced my face. I pushed myself up to see Michael sitting on the floor next to the sofa. It all rushed back: the callbacks, the suicide drills, the whole hot-guy-with-a-shocking-touch thing.

"Holy crap!" I flailed in surprise, sending half of the cushions to the floor. "What're you doing here?"

"I just came by to check on you. Your mom said I could

hang for a while and see if you might wake up. And here we are," he said. His voice practically made me purr, but I wasn't about to let that show on my face.

"Wait." I settled back into the remaining cushions, glancing at the windows. "What day is it?"

"It's Sunday. Almost ten a.m."

My stomach clenched. I'd been out for about fifteen hours. I'd slept that long before, especially after a dose of painkillers, but this was different. Over the past few months, I'd gotten used to flipping out over every cough or sniffle. I knew it was just paranoia, and I could force myself to put the panic out of my head if I worked hard enough. But this time I wasn't overreacting; frankly, it seemed like everyone else was *underreacting*. Why wasn't I in the hospital? I should have been hooked up to about a billion monitors right now; my mom should have been studying my blood counts and helping me put on my lucky hospital pajamas, not dorking around in the kitchen.

"Casey?" Michael looked concerned.

"Oh. Uh . . . it's okay. But I'm assuming I didn't make the team?" I said. "That's probably a good thing. You can go now."

"You . . . you think?" He sounded uncertain. "I wanted to talk about possibly making you an alternate. I think I might be able to petition the league—"

"You're not listening to me." I stood up slowly, taking careful stock of my body. No dizziness, which was a bonus. I ached all over, but I couldn't honestly say whether that was from derby or something else. "I can't be on the team. Healthy people don't randomly lose consciousness. I've got to get to the hospital so they can see if I've relapsed. Maybe we can talk later. If you want," I added hastily.

It seemed like I should be panicking, but I felt this strange sense of relief. At least now I knew. No more worrying, no more fearing the worst. Because the worst was happening, and it left me exhausted and empty, like a scooped-out melon.

"Before you do anything, there's something I need to tell you." He gently pushed on my shoulders until I sat back down. It didn't take long, because I wasn't fighting. I needed to save my strength. "I promise it won't take too long. But here. Drink this first."

Michael handed me a glass of water, and only then did I realize how parched I was. I gulped it down and barely restrained myself from trying to lick the last few drops from the inside of the glass. My tongue probably wasn't long enough for that anyway.

"I'll get you some more," he said, holding out a hand. I gave him the glass and watched him walk into the kitchen. His shoulders were broader than I remembered, but maybe that was because I'd been too busy staring at his butt.

I heard the low rumble of his voice from the kitchen and the laughing tones of my mother's response. I waited for Mom to charge in and fuss a little, which kind of seemed warranted, given the situation, but it didn't happen. The whole thing was beyond surreal. I rubbed my temples and tried to put it all together in a way that made sense, but I failed.

"Here," Michael said, emerging from the kitchen with a

glass of ice water that tinkled musically as he carried it to the couch.

I wanted to push it away and demand some freaking answers, but I was just so thirsty. So I downed the second glass without stopping for breath, and then gasped the words out.

"So, what do you have to tell me?"

"Ah." He shrugged, looking over my shoulder at the wince-worthy painting of dogs in clown makeup that hung over the sofa. It was still a little singed in one corner from the time I'd tried to burn it. "Well, I didn't exactly tell your mom what happened yesterday."

I blinked. "So let me get this straight. You and Darcy brought me home unconscious, and I slept for about fifteen hours, and she thought that was normal?"

"No," he said. "No one was here when we came in yesterday. I stayed here until your parents got home around midnight, and I came back this morning. Your mother doesn't know how long you were out. I told her you fell asleep while we were watching a movie."

"Why would you do that? Don't you get it? I'm *sick*. It's not something you fool around with."

"You don't have all the information, Casey," he said, staring at his clasped hands. "There are some things I need to tell you."

"Like what?"

"What happened to you yesterday has nothing to do with your health. It has to do with what happened when we touched. You know, the whole shock thing?"

"You're certifiably insane." And it figured. The first guy I'd been even remotely interested in since I'd been sick, and he turned out to be a total loon. "I was probably hallucinating. It's not real. Look, I'll prove it to you."

I grabbed his hand. Nothing happened. No mysterious, semi-electrical current or anything else, except for the warmth of his skin. We locked eyes. His were wide and blue.

When it hit me, it was like a fireball.

The hair on my arms suddenly tingled with static, standing on end. A whip crack of electricity whirled through my torso; my face went immediately numb, all the soreness draining away. When I spoke, my voice vibrated, making me sound almost robotic. My lips felt like they were actually buzzing.

"You tell me what's going on right now," I said.

"Let go," he said, and if his voice had been awesome before, now I felt it thrum through my body like I was listening to it on headphones with the bass turned way up.

"Casey, you need to let go," he repeated.

"Not until you tell me," I murmured. "Not until you promise."

Now it didn't even sound like my voice anymore. It was too far away; I blinked and found myself floating near the ceiling. It felt so natural that I didn't even freak out when I looked down to see my body standing next to Michael. My arms were shaking uncontrollably; my skin glowed. Like, literally glowed.

He looked up and actually saw me floating, disembodied, in the air. Which was really freaky.

"Get back here," he ordered.

He pulled my body close and mashed his lips to mine.

I felt a rush of vertigo so intense that I nearly threw up, but the warmth of his mouth quickly distracted me. I was back in my body now without quite understanding how it had happened, and the electricity was muted, like he was sucking it out of me. He kissed me insistently, and I pressed against him hard, grabbing fistfuls of his shirt.

His mouth tasted sweet, like he'd been rubbing his lips with oranges. As if the whole situation could possibly get any weirder than it already was. I couldn't help myself; my tongue darted out to taste it, and the kiss slowed and deepened until we weren't trying to devour each other anymore. His mouth opened against mine, and his hands slid up to my jaw and cradled my face.

It was amazing, until I realized he was only doing it to distract me. I pulled back and slapped him.

"Ow!" he exclaimed, putting his hand to his cheek and looking almost comically surprised. "What did you do that for?"

"You were . . . I was . . ." I couldn't come up with anything to say that didn't sound totally insane. So I latched on to the one thing that did. "You were trying to distract me."

"No, I was kissing you. Unless that whole lip-contact thing means something completely different on whatever planet you're from."

My limbs were shaking pretty uncontrollably by this time, so I sat down and folded my arms.

"You were only kissing me because that was the best way to make me . . ." Return to my body? No sane person would say anything like that. "Shut up," I finished lamely.

"That's not the only reason," he said, not meeting my eyes.

"Oh?" I flushed. "I mean, *oh*."

"I was also kissing you to . . ." He made some vague gestures in the air above his head that may have referred to my out-of-body experience or may have been him trying to avoid saying anything else embarrassing. "Get your attention."

"You've got it. I want to know what's going on. Right now."

He nodded, and of course Mom picked that moment to come in with a couple of strawberry smoothies and some sandwich-type thing. Any sandwich made by her was an adventure. Most of the combinations she came up with were so bad that they qualified as cruel and unusual punishment, but some were surprisingly good. When no one else was around to witness it, I sometimes ate my mother's infamous pickle and mayo sandwiches.

"I thought you'd be hungry since you missed breakfast, honey." Mom put the sandwich on the table and followed it up with the smoothies. "And I made your favorite smoothie. I thought you might like one too, Michael."

"Thanks, Mrs. Kent," he said.

She kissed me on the top of the head. "I've got to get going, sweetheart. We're doing character-building exercises today. I mean, as long as you're okay? You slept in pretty late."

She stopped, shifting uncertainly from foot to foot as if trying to decide where she was needed most.

"I'll be fine, Mom," I said, not really sure but knowing that if she was hovering, I'd never find out what the hell had just happened. "Your students will be pissed if you don't show up to class."

"Yes, yes, of course." But she didn't go. She stood there for another moment or two and then finally turned to Michael. "Are you going to be around for a while? My workshop is only a couple of hours. It would make me feel better to know she's not alone."

"Mom!" I protested. "I do not need a babysitter! Let alone one who's a couple of years older than me, tops."

"But I'm mature for my age," Michael piped in helpfully, grinning like this was all really amusing.

"Humor me," Mom said, all the dreamy airheadedness gone from her voice. Now she was in stern-parent mode. It didn't happen often, but there was no budging her when it did. "I'd feel more secure knowing you have company. Do you mind, Michael?"

"Not at all," he said. "I like Casey."

"Of course you do," Mom said happily. "She's the nicest girl in the world. I hope you'll stay for dinner too?"

"I'd love to," he told her, but he didn't take his eyes off me.

She didn't seem to notice that she was intruding on our staring contest. "Great. Well, cheerio!" Mom kissed the top of my head yet again and then bounced out.

Michael and I kept staring at each other until the door closed. When he wasn't moving, he looked almost like a statue, with his too-perfect face and equally awe-inspiring physique. Not that I wanted him to kiss me again. In fact, I was concentrating very hard on not wanting to make out with him until he gave me some answers. It was more difficult than I would have liked to admit.

I opened my mouth to demand he start talking, but he spoke first. "Well, I guess I'd better just take the plunge."

"What plunge? Will you please for the love of God start making sense?"

He started to sit down only to pop up again, looking more than a little agitated. "Casey, I haven't told anyone this before, so I hope it will come out right."

"All right . . . ," I said cautiously. "I'm listening."

"Yeah." He held his hands out to his sides. "I'm not exactly human."

I didn't have time to scoff before a pair of flaming wings burst from his back and lit the dog painting on fire.

I found it difficult to argue with the whole I'm-not-human thing when Michael's blazing wings were immolating my living room. Something about those flickering wing-shaped flames convinced me. It's hard to argue with burn holes.

"Oh, crap," Michael said, glancing over his shoulder at the black circle of ash slowly growing on our wall. "I always forget how big they are."

"Put those things away, or whatever it is you do with them." I tore my eyes away from his wings and smothered the smoldering wall with a sofa cushion. "I don't think our insurance policy covers magical fire wings."

This time, I could almost feel the electric crackle in the air as the wings popped out of existence. Under different circumstances, I probably would have asked him to do it again, but

I had other things to worry about. The cushion was burning now too.

"Damn it!" I snapped.

"What?" He was at my shoulder instantly, looking down at the pillow like it might decide to pop out some wings too.

"Um, in case you haven't noticed, that wall is burning. And the ugly painting. And my pillow. Could you . . ." I gestured with my hands in front of my mouth. "You know, put it out?"

He only looked confused. "With my mouth?"

"Well, can't you breathe on it or something?"

"Ah." He shook his head. "I'm not Superman. If you have a fire extinguisher, I can get it for you, but that's about all I can do in the putting-out-fires department."

"Well, you're no help," I grumbled, taking the pillow to the kitchen. He followed.

"Not my fault. We don't exactly have fires where I come from." I glared at him, and he added belatedly, "Sorry."

I flicked on the cold water and shoved the cushion underneath. The smell of wet, scorched polyester quickly filled the kitchen. Sadly, it smelled better than most of Mom's cooking. It also set off the smoke detectors. We had three of them, all in one room. I didn't get it either.

"Take the batteries out of those things before we go deaf, will you?" I asked.

"Gotcha." He climbed up onto one of the breakfast-bar stools. Within seconds, the piercing noise stopped. "There you go."

"You were talking about heaven, right?" My voice came

out very calm, as if I weren't having a conversation with an angel in the middle of my kitchen. I'd been in shock before, and I recognized the faraway feeling, as if everything were happening at a distance from which I could safely make wise-cracks about it.

He blinked. "Heaven?"

"I was asking if you came from heaven. You said they don't have fire there."

He burst into laughter, and I threw the wet, charred pillow at him. Not hard; it barely grazed his stomach before splattering on the ground, spraying sooty water all over. But it definitely got his attention.

"I'm sorry." He didn't look it. His mouth kept turning up at the corners. "But the idea of me as an angel is pretty hilarious. I mean, *look* at me."

"I am," I muttered.

I looked again for good measure. He had a great mouth, and just thinking about that made me think of the lip-lock from earlier, and *that* made me flush redder than your average stop sign. He raised an eyebrow at me, and I decided it would be a good idea to do something else. Like maybe keep my house from burning.

I pulled out the biggest pitcher in our house, which was porcelain and shaped like William Shakespeare's head. The sculptor hadn't done a very good job; poor Will looked really constipated.

"What are you doing?" Michael asked, squinting at Will. "And does he need a laxative?"

"Shut up," I said, but without any heat behind it. "I'm putting out your fire here. Either help me or get out of the way."

I hurried back into the living room and hurled the water at the painting. The water splattered and hissed. And dripped. I didn't even want to think about how I was going to clean all this up.

"I'm way too impatient for this," Michael said.

He snatched the pitcher away from me so fast that my fingers stung. A mere second later, the kitchen door started ratcheting back and forth, almost tearing itself off its hinges. I heard the water running, heard it turning off, and then the water splashed onto the wall before I even had time to breathe. He repeated the process three times, moving so fast that all I could see was a blur.

Maybe he was lacking in the putting-out-fires-with-his-breath thing, but he had the super speed thing down pat.

When the wall was completely soaked and the couch dotted with random droplets, he stopped. The guy wasn't even breathing heavily, which I found really aggravating, considering that I'd had a hard time making it up the stairs not so long ago. But nothing seemed to be burning anymore, so I guess I had that to be thankful for. It distracted me from the fact that I had a not-an-angel in my living room. Or maybe I'd just had a psychotic break.

"Better?" he asked.

"Oh, yeah," I said faintly. "Much better."

"Good. Can we talk now?"

"It's preferable to burning down my house."

"You're taking this awfully well." He cocked his head. "Or are you in shock?"

"I haven't decided whether to believe you or not." I took a deep breath and sat down on the floor, as far away from the soggy bits as possible. "And yeah, I'm in shock too."

"Fair enough." He took a long, deep breath. "I'm a Sentinel."

He probably would have explained what that meant if his phone hadn't gone off. Sensitive-guy guitar music filled the air, and it took me a moment to figure out it was his text alert. The deductive process was aided by his taking the phone out of his pocket and glancing at the screen.

"Oh, crap," he said, not even glancing up from the screen as his fingers beat out a rapid return message. "I'm supposed to be at practice right now. Ruthanasia's going to kill me."

"Derby practice?"

"Yeah."

A wave of regret passed through me. If I hadn't fainted, or whatever it was that I'd done, I would have been able to go with him. Now I had bigger things to worry about, what with the out-of-body experience and the not-an-angel with the flaming wings, but that didn't mean I couldn't spare a moment to mourn my hope. I wasn't going to be able to go back to the way things had been. In a way, the cancer had killed me after all.

My complaint came out with less heat and more resignation.

"Well, you can't just leave. I deserve some answers. You can't pop me out of my body, burn my house, and then run for the hills. That's really uncool."

His hands dropped to his sides as he shot an exasperated glance in my direction, like somehow the flaming wings had been my fault. I would have smacked him if I hadn't been so desperate to figure out what was going on. My health and sanity had been compromised, and if the flaming-wing guy knew something about either topic, I wasn't letting him get away from me until he spilled it.

"I have to go, Casey," he said in a pleading tone. "I'm sorry; I know it's really crappy to leave you hanging like this, but I'll come right back after practice. We'll talk."

"Skip it." I sounded—and felt—desperate. "Ruthanasia would probably love to be left in charge anyway, and this is important. You can't just up and leave."

He shifted from foot to foot, looking increasingly restless. I wanted to grab the guy and shake him. Honestly, if anyone had the right to be a little shifty-eyed, it was me. I was the one who had fainted. I was the one who'd had an out-of-body experience. My health hung in the balance. And he was all worried about a derby practice? If one of us was certifiable, I was beginning to suspect it wasn't me.

"I *have* to go," he said. "I made a commitment, and breaking commitments makes me . . ." He trailed off, shuddering.

"Great," I muttered. "I got stuck with the OCD angel."

"I'm not an angel!" He threw up his hands. "I told you that already!"

"Dude, you have flaming wings and your name is Michael. What am I supposed to think? It kind of screams 'angel' to me."

He hung his head. "I did the flaming wings because I thought it would look impressive. And for your information, all the Sentinels in my pod were named Michael. I'm number six hundred ninety-two. We're not exactly creative in the naming department."

"So you're not an angel," I said. Frankly, it made me feel a little better about myself. Because if he wasn't really an angel, I didn't have to feel squicky about thinking lustful things about him. And if I decided to smack him upside the head for being difficult, I wouldn't be damned for that either.

"No. Sorry," he said, and it didn't sound like he was lying. It did, however, sound like his head might pop off at any moment from the pressure. He was practically hopping from one foot to the other like he had to go to the bathroom. The whole situation was getting increasingly more ridiculous, and I had to bite back a snort of laughter. "Can I go now? The longer I wait, the more uncomfortable I get. And the more uncomfortable I get, the more of a dick I become. It's a vicious cycle."

"I believe it." I sighed. "Well, that's that. I'm tagging along."

He shook his head sadly. "I'm sorry, Casey. I thought I already told you; you didn't make the team. I tried, but no one would listen to me after you fainted."

"So I'll be your guest. Or your assistant. Or the girl who won't stop following you until you tell her what the heck is going on. Take your pick."

"I don't really have much choice, do I?" he grumbled.

"Good Sentinel." I patted him on the head, or tried to. He ducked out of the way, knocking my hand to one side. "Actually, hold on a sec. Let me change into some clean clothes and then we can go."

He rolled his eyes and dropped onto the sodden couch. "Aw, crap!" He leapt back up to his feet, brushing at the damp spot on his shorts. Even with everything that had happened, I couldn't help but laugh as I climbed the stairs.

Michael's motorcycle was parked in our extra spot. That was one thing I hated about living in a town house; it was hard to convince your parents to buy you a car when you only got two parking spaces. Rachel had offered to leave her Mini, but I'd felt guilty taking her transportation when I didn't have anywhere to go.

The only problem with the bike was that we couldn't talk en route to the Skate Lake. But it gave me a chance to come up with questions. After twenty, I made myself stop and enjoy the sensation of snuggling against the hard muscles of his back. He might have been a Sentinel—whatever that was—but he was a Sentinel in a hot teenage body, and that had to count for something. Especially since I hadn't had many close encounters with hot teenage bodies. Or hot bodies of any age, really. And it mostly kept me from obsessing over questions I had no idea how to answer. Mostly.

When he pulled to a stop next to the Skate Lake doors, I released my grip on his shirt with reluctance. My cheek had been so comfortable nestled up against the soft fabric. I could have driven around town for hours, losing myself in the wind that whipped around his body and in the roar of the motor. It felt very peaceful, that bike ride.

"So I wanted to ask—"

I didn't even get the whole sentence out before Ruthanasia burst through the doors. She wasn't in derby uniform today but still wore enough eye makeup to cover an entire showgirl chorus. I couldn't help it; I stuck my tongue out at her. Not the most mature of choices, but it was better than slugging her in the face, which was my only other idea.

"What are you doing here?" she demanded. "You know you're not on the team, right?"

Her expression of triumph felt like a slap in the face. I tried to tell myself she didn't know how important making the team had been to me, but she had to know her words hurt. She just didn't care. So I didn't hold back. I retaliated with the thing I knew would bother her most.

"I know," I said. "Michael and I are going on a date to-night, remember?"

She glared at me, her brows drawing down into an angry furrow. I couldn't resist lacing my arm around his and lean-ing against his shoulder with a moony look on my face. It might have been a little over the top, but she bought it. She looked about ready to blow. Michael glanced between the two of us with an expression of dawning horror, like he'd realized belatedly that something was happening and he might not want to be in the middle of it. Too late, dude.

"Kent, I swear to God," Ruthanasia began, stepping forward with clenched fists.

Michael disengaged himself from my clutches with more grace than I would have given him credit for and intercepted her before she could get any closer. "Everybody chill out, okay? It took a lot of work to set up these extra practices, and we need to use the time wisely. Unless you want the Tilt-a-Girls to kick our butts in our next bout?"

Ruthanasia's eyes snapped to him, looking for a fight, but she didn't find one. "Yeah," she said, shooting me a nasty glare, "you're probably right. *Some* of us actually have things to do around here."

I tried not to envy her as I followed them through the doors. I tried not to feel like a useless weakling who had nothing better to do than pick arguments all the time. I tried, but I failed.

Once inside, Michael and Ruthanasia went off to do their official derby thing. I didn't have anything to do, so I went to the counter and was ordering a soda when Darcy rushed up and nearly knocked me over with a tackle hug.

"Oh my God," she said, "I'm so glad to see you! I have all your stuff in my car. Are you okay? What happened?"

I blinked, trying to sort out all the words and figure out which ones I was supposed to answer. I settled for, "I'm okay. Congratulations. I take it you made the team?"

"Yeah." She grinned. "I still can't believe it."

"Do you have my skates?"

"Yeah. Are you skating today? Yay!" She clapped her hands, bouncing on her toes. "I'll go get your stuff!"

Off she dashed, so fast that she actually tripped over her own foot before righting herself and heading out the doors. I wouldn't have believed it possible, but she was even more manic now that she'd made the team.

I sat down on a bench and began taking off my Chucks, because I wasn't going to sit around feeling sorry for myself *again*. I was going to train my butt off so that when the next tryout came, I'd make the team. Sure, I was still afraid of what would happen if I failed. But I was even more frightened of what would happen to me if I stopped trying. I'd fought through chemo; it was just a matter of figuring out how to fight this. I had to.

"What are you doing?" Michael ambled over and sat down next to me.

"Well," I said, "these are shoes, and when you pull these long stringy things, they come loose so you can take them off. You probably don't know this stuff, since you're not human and all."

"Quiet!" he hissed, putting a finger to my lips. "Someone might hear."

"Yeah, and they'd think I was teasing you. You've got to lighten up."

He took a long breath and let it out slowly. "I know. I'm just neurotic as all hell right now. I've never outed myself before."

"Now it's my turn to hush you," I said. "Or people really *will* get the wrong idea."

That earned me a grin. "Maybe I should reword that. Anyway, you're the first person I've told ever since I got this body."

"Why?" I frowned. The door opened, and I was sure Darcy was about to dash in and cut the conversation short, but it was Ragnarocker. She flashed me an approving thumbs-up before grabbing her knapsack and heading back out. At least two people were happy to see me, because everyone else was looking awfully worried that I might try to crash the practice and faint all over everything. "Give me something to tide me over, because the curiosity is killing me."

He leaned closer, and the door opened again. In flew Darcy with my backpack slung over one shoulder. I was hoping she'd trip again to buy us a few seconds, but I wasn't going to hold my breath.

"I train demon hunters," he said quickly. "And you faced a demon and lived."

"The guy who cried fire?" I asked, and Michael nodded. I didn't have any problems thinking of that guy as a demon. In fact, it felt good to have a name to put to him. It meant I wasn't crazy, for starters.

"How did you know?" I hissed.

Just as Darcy returned, he shot a significant look at the silver katana still hanging around my neck. "That necklace of yours zaps demons," he murmured in my ear.

She walked up with an unusually subdued expression. "Here, Casey." Then she took a furtive glance at Michael and plopped down on the bench opposite us. "I'm glad you're feeling better. Are you on the team, then?" She looked hopeful.

"Nope." I shook my head sadly. "I'm going to find a corner and practice on my own. I promise to stay out of the way."

"You don't give up, do you?" Michael said.

I thought of all the times I'd been tempted to quit, all the times I'd pushed people away, all the times I'd second-guessed myself or joked to avoid the uncomfortable truth. Near-death experiences give you way too much self-awareness, and I didn't always like what I'd learned about myself. But I'd made stubbornness into an art form. Maybe I hadn't made the team, but that didn't mean I wasn't a derby girl. I wasn't dead *yet*.

"Nope," I said.

I unzipped the bag and pulled out my skates. The wait was annoying, but I'd get my answers. I still wasn't sure what to believe, but if demons were real, I'd need all the physical conditioning I could get. I had gotten over my fears of the robbery by preparing with ninjutsu. Now it was time to get over the demon thing. I had more reason than ever to rediscover my inner ass kicker. Because if someone was going to take that lava guy down, I had dibs.

The team worked on jammer and pack drills before the scrimmage, and I wanted to jump in so badly, even though I knew I couldn't. My legs shook after just a few hockey stops in my isolated corner. I'd earned those shakes fair and square after pushing so hard at tryouts, but I still wanted to beat my thighs with my fists and tell them to get with the program already. But it wouldn't do me any good to drive myself into unconsciousness again. I forced myself to work on quality, not quantity; at least my technique was good.

Ruthanasia scowled every time she happened to look in my direction, but I didn't care. The skeptical looks the rest of the team kept shooting me really bothered me, though. "Do people hate me for being here?" I asked during one water break, when Ragnarocker rolled past.

She frowned thoughtfully, wiping sweat from her forehead. "What makes you say that?"

"I'm getting a lot of glares from the masses."

"Ah." She shrugged. "Some of the girls think you're getting special treatment because of whatever you've got going with Michael."

I swallowed the irate retort that rose immediately to my lips. Everyone else's opinions weren't her fault. "And you? What do you think?"

She grinned. "I think someone with the balls to keep showing up like you do deserves some respect. Besides, I figure if I butter you up enough, you might eventually teach me those aerial tricks of yours."

I had to smile back. She was my kind of person; what you saw was exactly what you got. "Keep buttering. I'll teach you eventually."

"A girl can dream," she said. "But for now, this girl is going to get a drink." And she skated away.

In the scrimmage, Ruthanasia scored a double grand slam while I tried to focus on learning strategy and not on trying to make her spontaneously combust with the power of my mind. After it was over, I asked Michael if he wanted help with all the cones. Darcy and Ruthanasia both looked dismayed when he said yes. I felt bad about Darcy.

"I'll give you a call later, Darce," I said. "Maybe we can get together after school tomorrow."

"All right," she replied reluctantly. "See you later."

She trudged out the doors, looking more dejected than

she had reason to. Although, maybe she'd been disappointed by more than my failure to hang out with her; she'd been stuck blocking the whole time, and I knew how much she wanted to jam. I felt like a pretty crappy friend after I realized that. I'd been so wrapped up in my own drama that I hadn't thought about anyone but myself. I'd definitely have to make it up to her.

Everyone else trickled out slowly, like they had no idea I was waiting to get the scoop on demonkind and might explode from the pressure if the delay went on much longer. Finally the doors closed behind Ragnarocker, who called out "Don't do anything I wouldn't do" just as they swung shut.

"I'm not sure there's anything she wouldn't do." I grinned.

"I don't know firsthand, but I suspect you're right," Michael said, walking out to the perimeter of the rink and picking up a cone.

"So." I glanced around one last time to make sure we were alone. The only person left in the place was the guy behind the snack bar counter, and he was watching bowling on TV. I got bored just thinking about it. "How does one hunt demons, and what do you do with them when you catch them? Besides throwing demon-zapping necklaces at them, I mean."

He straightened up with another cone in hand and a somewhat dumbfounded expression on his face. "That's it? Aren't you going to question my sanity?"

"I've had some time to think about this, and I saw what I saw. I can't deny the physical evidence. That thing burned me. So I'm not saying I totally believe you, but it's the best explanation I've heard so far."

"Wow." He sat down right in the middle of the rink. "Okay."

"Talk." I dropped down next to him and started taking off my gear. It felt so good to get the pads off my knees, which sported some nice greenish bruises from all the burpees. It was hard to believe that it had been only a day ago; so much had changed since then.

"Well, a Sentinel's an avatar of balance. Normally we live in the Between—that's the space between the physical and nonphysical planes. Our job is to preserve the balance between the two. If the universe goes too far out of balance, everything goes kablooie. Seriously. All existence, total annihilation."

"That's bad."

"No kidding." He flashed a grin at me. "So we keep an eye on things. Like, if one of the Elder Gods emerges from deep space and tries to devour a planet, we intervene, because that would screw up the balance. That's my job. Occasionally one of the Sentinels gets a little too involved in the physical world. And that throws him out of whack."

I nodded, stretching out my aching legs. It was too late to avoid muscle pain; I was definitely feeling yesterday's burpees, but at least I could keep it from getting worse. "Go on."

"The rules help us to stay in balance while we're here. I'm still new—only apprentice level—so I'm assigned to an older Sentinel who helps me get used to things like having a body.

Which is so weird. Anyway, once a Sentinel gets off-kilter, he starts consuming energy like mad, trying to get back into balance. But that usually just makes it worse. He wants more and more, and he becomes a creature no longer dedicated to protecting the universe but to eating it. A creature of total hunger."

"A demon."

He nodded, his face pinched and sad-looking.

"Can you fix them?" I asked.

"Not once they've crossed the line. The only thing we can do is take them out. But that comes with its own set of problems." At my inquiring glance, he said, "I like to fight. I like to move. Having a body, it's . . . intoxicating, and I've got a lot of power at my fingertips. If I decided to indulge, there wouldn't be much that could stop me. And demons try to manipulate everyone around them. If they used my desires against me, there's a decent chance I could end up just like them. If I let them jerk my chain, my balance goes haywire, and *poof.*"

"Instant demon." I let out a long breath, toying with my skate. "That sucks."

"But someone like you, someone who can reach through to the nonphysical, you could do it." Excitement was clear on his face and in his voice. "I mean, if you wanted to. I could teach you. That's why I'm here, to find people like you who can reach across the Between."

"And train us to fight the forces of darkness?"

"Bingo."

"Well . . ." I spoke slowly, considering my words. "No offense meant, but I'm not entirely sure I believe all this. It's a lot to swallow. But I'm still listening."

"That's fair." He held out a hand. "Then I guess I should show you something."

"You're going to burn somebody else's house down, aren't you?" My hand went to the front of my shirt. I could feel the healing scabs underneath. The burns had gone deep, and it seemed like my body didn't heal as fast as it used to.

Old Casey would have signed up to fight demons in a heartbeat. Now I knew how fragile life really was. I knew how much I had to lose, and I'd come way too close to losing it already. Either I was wiser now or I was a total coward, but signing up to fight the lava crier didn't seem like something I should just jump into without thinking it over first.

"Relax. I won't burn anything. And it's safe to touch me. I'll make sure not to . . ." He waved his hands around vaguely. "Pop you out again."

"I'm not convinced," I replied, but I put my hand in his. The contact was tentative at first, but my hair didn't light on fire and I didn't get thrust out of my body like I had the last time we'd touched. So I folded my fingers over his and held on tight. He pulled me up to my feet.

"I should put some shoes on. Unless this mysterious sight is in the locker room?"

He snorted. "No."

We got back on the bike, and he drove past my street, away from the university. It wasn't a direction I normally went; in fact, I made a point not to go down Washington at all. After about two blocks, the neighborhood quickly disintegrated into Slumville. The last time I'd been down this way was almost two years ago, and I'd stepped on a used syringe and a homeless guy in a cardboard box. Neither were experiences I wanted to repeat. So when Michael pulled into a gas station and turned off the bike, I was less than thrilled. I followed him onto the sidewalk, but I wasn't happy about it.

"You look nervous," Michael said, watching my expression but somehow managing to not run into anything while he walked, despite the random bits of trash dotting the sidewalk.

"I don't come downtown," I said, barely resisting the urge to hunch over like a frightened little girl. That kind of behavior practically begged for a mugging. "My friend Kyle got robbed near here once. It was a long time ago, but I think the neighborhood has only gotten worse since then."

"Ah." He considered this. "Didn't you say you've got a black belt?"

"Yeah, but I'm not stupid. People get hurt in knife fights. I'd rather pass."

He stopped in the middle of the sidewalk to stare at me, slowly shaking his head. Bald girls, and especially bald girls with random marker designs on their heads, get used to being stared at pretty fast, but this was different. There was the whole nonhuman thing, for instance.

I stopped and put my hands on my waist, boldly looking back. If he was going to give me the once-over, then I was going to throw it right back into his face. Unfortunately, the plan, while ingenious, kind of backfired. We stared into each other's eyes. He took a step closer. When his breath wafted into my face, I barely kept from swooning.

"You're pretty astounding," he said softly. "Wouldn't you expect the magic guy with flaming wings to come to your rescue?"

"What do you think I am? A total loser? I'm not."

"All right," he said agreeably. "If you say so." He took a step closer. I had to break the moment before I did something really embarrassing. I still wasn't sure where we stood or what I thought of him. Was he even allowed to date, or would that just pull him off balance? Whatever that meant. I wasn't sure, but it was all too easy to get caught up in the fun of flirting with him. Flirting was safe compared to all the other things we'd been talking about.

"Besides," I said, clearing my throat, "you'd probably end up burning the whole block down, and then where would we be?"

"Standing in the middle of a burned-out street, I guess," he said, still watching me intently.

"Good point." I forced myself to turn away and start walking again. "So, what are we going to see, anyway?"

"Oh." He cleared his throat. "Well, that." Washington Street dead-ended at Jefferson about half a block down, and he pointed at the large brick factory that loomed at the junction. It was one of those buildings that sit way too close to the sidewalk for comfort. If you looked up at the graffiti-covered walls while standing next to it, you were almost guaranteed a nice case of vertigo for your trouble.

"Wow," I said. "It's a building."

"Observant. Very observant."

"You didn't really haul me all over town to stare at a building, did you?"

"It's not just any building, Casey."

"Oh?" I folded my arms. "Well, enlighten me. Is this a demon in disguise? I expected it to be less . . . bricky."

He rolled his eyes, a big dramatic roll that made it entirely obvious how exasperated he was.

"So you can't see it, then?" he asked.

"See what? What am I supposed to be seeing? It's a big, ugly building. There's nothing to see."

He leaned down, his face looming closer to mine. For a moment, I flashed back to the scene in the alley, to the fire-streaked face of the creepy guy in white—the demon—as he'd tried to violate me with his tongue. But Michael worked for the good guys. I couldn't see him burning anyone, except maybe by accident.

I looked up at him, wondering if he was going to kiss me again and if I was going to slap him this time. Maybe I wanted to be kissed. . . .

He opened his mouth and blew gently into my eyes. It didn't hurt or anything because he did it so softly, but it felt awfully weird. I closed my eyes and took a big gulp of that citrus-tinged air. It smelled so damned good. I had to look away before I made a fool of myself by planting my lips on his and trying to suck all the breath out of his body.

And when I opened my eyes, I was looking at the factory.

Or rather, I was looking at the black cloud that hung around it like a cloak, choking the air.

"What the hell is that?" I exclaimed. It came out so loud that a couple of tat-covered guys at the gas station turned to look at me. I forced myself to speak more quietly. "Do you see that?"

I rubbed my eyes, but it was still there.

"I see it," he said softly. He sounded sad, but I didn't think it was a good idea to look at him, not while the pull toward him was still so freaking strong. "Now do you understand?"

"Well, no. Actually, I don't understand at all. It's . . ." I squinted at the building. "It's not smoke. It's not . . ." I felt sheepish saying this next part, but I was committed to seeing this through, so I went for it. "It's not even physical, is it? That black stuff."

"Nope." He stared at the building intently. "That's good. Most people don't get that so fast."

"Great," I said. "I'll put it on my college applications— 'Has a knack for seeing immaterial shadows.' And I don't even practice."

"It's nothing you can practice. You're just more sensitive because of what you've been through."

"What's that?"

"Near-death experiences have the potential to open people up. Or break them entirely."

"You seem to know a lot about this," I said accusingly. "I thought you said you were still an apprentice."

"We . . ." He cleared his throat and tried to rub the flush

from his cheeks. "My brother made me watch an instructional video."

"About what? What people say after they look at imaginary clouds?"

"It's not imaginary," he said, frowning. "I thought you understood that."

"Well, duh. I was just joking."

"But—" He stopped, sighed, and ran a hand through his hair, twisting it into random corkscrews that made him look even more like a model than before, if such a thing was humanly possible. Or inhumanly possible, as the case might be. Either way, it was entirely too distracting. "I don't want to fight with you, Casey," he said.

"I don't want to fight with you either. I'm sorry; I'm just feeling a little overwhelmed here." I turned to look at the building again, despite the sick feeling it gave me in the pit of my stomach. It was strange; it felt almost like I could taste that cloud of yuck even though I was only looking at it. "Okay, so whatever that thing is, it's bad juju. I may just be a silly mortal, but even I can tell that."

"It's demon-tainted. That building." He jerked his thumb toward it, turning his face away like he didn't want to look anymore.

I nodded. It felt pretty surreal to be standing on the sidewalk and talking to a Sentinel about demon-tainted buildings all nonchalant-like, but the only other option was to pee on myself and run away screaming, and that wasn't much of an option.

"What kind of building is it? I mean, what do they do there?" I asked, looking for a sign. The outside was so generic that it could have been anything: a gun factory, a porn studio, or maybe one of those places where they grow all kinds of drugs under a lot of really bright fluorescent lights. Now that I knew about the demon taint, the building's lurking façade seemed even more sinister. A guy with a shopping cart walked past on the other side of the street, and I barely stopped myself from shouting a warning, like the building might pounce on him.

I looked up at Michael just in time to catch a pained look on his face. He didn't say anything.

"Well?" I prodded. "What is it? You've got to tell me now. I can take it."

He sighed.

"It's a bobblehead factory."

10

"You had me going for a minute there." I leaned against a storefront, giggling. The mysterious black-cloaked building didn't seem so menacing now that I knew it was a toy factory. "Demonic bobbleheads. Very funny."

"I wasn't kidding." Michael scowled. "And it isn't funny."

"Aw, come on. There's nothing threatening about an oversized noggin that goes like this all the time." I wobbled my head around, grinning crazily and waving my arms. "I'm eeeeevil!"

"You think this is all a big joke, huh?"

"Well, *yeah.*" I gestured toward the factory. "I mean, you tell me it's a demon factory, so I expect it to make something dangerous. Guns, maybe. Or drugs or hazardous chemicals that turn entire ecosystems into toxic sludge. Not bobbleheads. I mean, how wimpy are these demons? They're going to trinket all the humans into damnation?"

"Have you ever heard of soul jars?"

"No," I said, still smirking. "Obviously not. Are you really trying to tell me this is serious?"

"Yes!" He threw up his hands. "People make deals with demons. The souls that don't get consumed immediately are sent here, and they get imprisoned in soul jars shaped like bobbleheads, where they're held until a demon gets hungry, and in the meantime, the imprisoned souls leak a nice spiritual taint into the area to make more people susceptible to making a deal. And then they'll all get eaten! Isn't that funny? Ha ha ha." He barked fake laughter.

"Well, this is all pretty tough to swallow. Give me a break!"

"Sorry," he muttered, but he didn't sound it. "I'll slow down a little."

"Oh, so now you're going to treat me like I'm stupid?" I knew I was being a little oversensitive, but I felt so overwhelmed, and he expected me to just nod and smile no matter how preposterous the whole thing got? I couldn't do that. "If you're going to talk down to me, I'm out of here."

"Fine," he snapped. "Do you need me to take you home?"

It probably would have been nice, but I was too proud to admit it. "I don't need anything from you."

"Fine," he repeated.

Michael stomped off, leaving me alone in the middle of Washington Street. I didn't even watch him go; I whirled around and stalked in the other direction. Flaming wings or not, the guy pissed me off. Did he expect me to fall down at his feet and take every word as gospel after he lit my wall on fire and popped me out of my body? At this point, I had every right to be rolling around on the floor and clutching my head. I'd listened much longer than the average person would have. Maybe because I was so desperate to find some identity for myself other than Girl in Remission.

The more I thought about it, the more aggravated I got. I deserved to approach things with a little healthy skepticism. Especially since it didn't seem too far-fetched to think that maybe the mugger in the white suit and Michael were somehow related. One cried fire; the other sprouted it from his torso. Just one more reason why taking a step back was a good idea.

I made it about a half mile before a lanky guy in a do-rag and a huge pair of sagging pants stepped out in front of me. He held his arms out, blocking the sidewalk.

"Hey, baby," he said, grinning. "Where you goin'?"

Then he reached out to grab me. I didn't want to be grabbed.

I couldn't help it. All the frustration I'd been carrying around leapt to my throat. I snatched his hand, locked the wrist, pushed, and turned. His own momentum carried him face-first into the ground with a grunt of pain.

"Leave me alone!" I shouted, releasing his hand and stepping over him.

"You stupid bitch," he snarled. "You need to learn some manners."

He swiped at my ankle, but I stomped down hard on his fingers and ran. I could hear him shouting, and other voices answering, and they shouted out the horrible things they wanted to do to me. I had no idea where I was, and I must have pulled a muscle because my side felt like someone had jammed a hot butter knife between my ribs, but I kept going as fast as I could.

Kyle started singing from inside the pocket of my jeans.

"Ra ah ah-ah-aah! Ra ma ra-ma-ma! Gaga! Oooh la la!"

It wasn't really him, of course, just my cell. He'd made the mistake of serenading me with Lady Gaga one day while I was in the hospital, and I'd ended up setting it as my ringtone. I slowed in front of a McDonald's and went inside.

"Hey," I said, panting into the phone.

"Did I disturb something exciting?" Kyle yelled. "It sounds like you're busy."

"Just getting chased by random crackheads." I tried to sound casual, but my casual setting must have been broken. It sounded like I was ready to cry instead. "What's up?"

"Did someone hurt you?"

"Why? Are you going to have someone hold them down while you beat them up?"

"It's not my first choice, but yeah. If I have to."

It was ridiculous, really, because Kyle had gotten into only two fights in his life, and he'd won the second one only because I'd showed up and bailed him out. Don't even get me started on the first one. But still, when he said he'd stand up for me, I felt better.

"Thanks," I said. "But it's not necessary. What I need is a ride. Are you free?"

"Yeah, sure. I was just on my way to the park, but maybe you need to go home instead?"

I considered. What I really needed was some time away from Michael, so I could process everything that had just happened. Figure out what I thought about it.

"No," I said, "the park sounds like a plan. Come get me."

It only took him fifteen minutes to arrive at McDonald's, and once I convinced him I was okay, he bought me a shake. I think he could tell I wasn't quite ready to talk about it all yet. Frankly, I wasn't sure I could without him trying to have me committed.

"Thanks, Ky." I drained the last of the chocolate-flavored awesome as we pulled into a parking spot at the skate park. "You are the best guy in the universe."

"I've got skills, baby."

"Dude, I love you," I said as we got out of the car. "Someone should clone you. The world needs more people who aren't douche bags."

"I'm all for this plan. I vote that the clone does my American history paper, because it's due tomorrow, and I haven't started yet."

I sighed. "That sucks. You pulling an all-nighter?"

"Probably."

We started down the path, looking for a free spot to practice in. The half-pipe overflowed with junior-high kids on BMX bikes, so that was out. I saw the rest of our crew jumping one of the mini ramps with their boards; Willow went up, grabbed some air, and made a silly face before she landed.

My feet slowed despite myself. "Hey," I said, "did you know everyone else was going to be here?"

"They usually are," he replied. It came out sounding a little defensive. "Why?"

As usual, Kyle's shouting attracted attention. Lupo elbowed Willow, who canted a hand over her eyes to shield them from the sun as she looked our way. Talking to them seemed inevitable, so I pasted a smile on my face, even though I really wanted to have Kyle to myself. But instead of skating up to meet us, they turned their backs, grabbing their boards and rolling farther down the path like we might have something catching and they didn't want to get too close.

I should have felt relieved, but it hurt. "What was that all about?"

He shrugged, dropping his board and rolling a little way down the path. "If we can find a free spot, I can show you the half cab impossible. You still haven't seen it."

"You're changing the subject."

He stopped but didn't turn around. "All right. How about I answer your question and you tell me what happened to you this afternoon?"

It wasn't something I looked forward to, but I knew I was going to have to tell him sooner or later. "Deal."

"Okay." He paused, rolling the board back and forth, testing the wheels. They looked new, the bright plastic smooth and unpitted. "They're pissed, Casey. And I can kind of understand how they feel."

"Pissed about what?"

"We understood when you were too sick to hang with us, but now you're not. And we only saw you that one time before you dumped us for the derby thing. You don't even text anymore, and you don't pick up when I call you. It's like you've written us off completely."

"I thought you didn't want me freerunning or boarding. The second I get near anything remotely dangerous, you get tense. So I started doing derby, which you don't like either." I threw up my hands. "I can't win no matter what I do."

"So I'm smothering you to death." He sighed. "Heaven forbid I actually care. Or have an opinion."

"Have all the opinions you want, but quit shoving them into my face."

"You know," he said in a sharp tone I wasn't used to hearing from him, "eventually, you're going to realize that the problem isn't me or Rachel or anything else. The problem is *you*. You're the one who can't get past your diagnosis. You're the one on this big quest to prove yourself. You're the one picking fights with anyone who will fight back, because it's the only way you can distract yourself from the fact that you're scared out of your mind. So maybe instead of blaming all your problems on everybody else, you could start realizing what you have. Like, for example, a friend who drops everything to come get you when you're in trouble, only you can't even be bothered to thank him."

The longer he yelled, the smaller I felt. "Thank you," I whispered.

He couldn't hear me over his own voice. "I'm going to work on the half cab impossible now, which you were supposed to see about a week ago, only you forgot that too. You can stay or leave. I don't care."

Then he stomped off. And boy did I feel like an ass as I watched him go. The word "sorry" didn't even begin to cover it. Because as much as I wanted to jump down his throat and defend myself, I knew he was right.

The benches overlooking the ramps were covered in graffiti, old bubble gum, and other unidentifiable gross things I didn't want on my shorts. So I sat on the edge of the ramp, my feet dangling off the side, while Kyle finished warming up. For someone so tall and gangly, he was a really graceful boarder. It was like everything jelled for him once he was on wheels. He was a good freerunner, but those skills were nothing compared to his boarding.

Kyle needed to cool off, and I needed time to think about what a mess I'd made of things and how on earth I was ever going to make it right. Because at this point, there wasn't anyone in my life who I hadn't neglected or pissed off or both. I'd dumped all my friends and shoved my family away. And now that I stopped to think about it, I couldn't believe how I'd bitten Michael's head off. Maybe he was nuts and maybe not, but it didn't change the fact that he'd trusted me, and I'd leapt down his throat. I had some serious work to do if I was going to fix it all. And I could start by watching Kyle skate like I'd promised to.

He paused at the edge of the ramp, his eyes flicking in my direction. Neither of us spoke, but he knew I was watching. My mind threatened to wander—there was so much I needed to think about—but I forced myself to focus as he took off from the top of the ramp, building up speed in ever-widening loops. Then he launched himself into the air, spun, and flipped the board over his foot like it was a freaking baton and he was a sequin-covered chick in a parade. For a heart-stopping second, I thought he was going to fall, but the board continued to spin, and he landed on it smoothly and rolled down the ramp with an expression of triumph.

"Wooo!" I launched to my feet, holding my arms up over my head. "That was awesome! Do it again!"

His face split into a reluctant grin, transforming him back into the friend I'd lost. "You sure?" he asked. "Don't you need to skate?"

"This is more important," I said emphatically. "I'll skate later."

"Cool." It didn't feel like everything was over, but maybe we were on the right track. At least he could look at me again. Then he added tentatively, "You know, if you wanted, I might be able to watch you skate in a while. Give you some pointers."

"That would be awesome."

We stayed there most of the afternoon. Every time his feet left the board, my heart stopped, and I waited for him to splatter on the pavement. And every time, he landed without a hitch. The irony of our switched positions didn't escape me. It was my turn to feel overprotective, not to mention sheepish because I'd always gotten so upset when he did the same thing to me.

We didn't talk much on the ride home; in this case I think our actions spoke more than words ever could have. Besides, I was preoccupied with the whole existence of demons and soul jars shaped like bobbleheads, and he was blasting music so loud that we couldn't have carried on a conversation anyway. But I made sure to give him a hug before he left. Neither of us could stay mad at the other for very long. And trust me, we'd both tried at one time or another.

The house was empty. Mom was catching up on things at the office, and Dad was directing a production of *Romeo and Juliet,* only all the actors were dressed like people from the Civil War, and Juliet's family had slaves and Romeo's didn't. I'd seen a couple of the rehearsals, and I had to admit that it actually worked.

Enough was enough. I was done hiding. And I was determined to prove it, to myself just as much as everybody else. So I went back to the one place I'd sworn I'd never go again.

11

The smell of the hospital hit me when I was two steps out of the elevator—bleach, air freshener, and metal. Air so sharp, it felt like it might cut your nose. That smell was associated with long days that ran into each other until they were one big blur of waiting for my cell counts to go up or a certain test result to go down. For ages, the quality of my day was predicated on a series of numbers on a piece of paper. One whiff of the fourth floor of Mackinaw University Children's Hospital, and my stomach started to churn.

This was not a place I wanted to be. What did I think I was proving? I leaned against the wall next to the circus mural with the dog that looked like it had hip dysplasia. I'd always hated the mural. Little Casey and I had once tried to draw a mustache on the dog, but the nurses caught us first.

"Big Casey!" Phoebe, one of the day shift nurses, spotted me against the wall. Her shiny face broke out into a wide grin, and her name tag pressed into my cheek as she folded me into a hug. "We haven't seen you in forever, girl. What's up?"

"Honestly?" I shuffled my feet. "I don't really know what I'm doing here. Maybe I should just go."

She tilted her head, her mouth twisting into one of those smiles that isn't really a smile. The corners of her mouth turned up, but her eyes were sad. "It's okay, baby girl. Sometimes our kids come back one last time to close the door on things. I'll give you a chance to look around. Just make sure to stop by the nurses' station before you go, okay?"

"Sure."

She hustled past me into room 402, which in my day had been occupied by a steady stream of short-termers. I'd never really gotten to know any of them.

I continued on to 409. My old room was now occupied by a baby in a bassinet dwarfed by a jungle of monitors. A man slept on the foldout, drool puddling under his cheek. It would have been wrong to disturb them by going into the room, so I moved on without feeling like I'd chickened out. I didn't want to go into that room ever again.

Little Casey's name was back up on the nameplate, door, and wall surrounding 411. It had become a thing—she had signs and posters and caricatures all printed with her name. Inside her room, the walls were covered with them. At least, they had been.

The fact that she was back after all this time did not bode

well. The question was not whether she'd be in bad shape, but how bad it would be. And if not for my blind luck, this would have been my fate too. It wasn't fair. If I could have changed places with her, I would have.

I wanted to leave. But I pushed open the door.

Little Casey stood beside the bed in her street clothes, shoving sketches and posters into a large cardboard box. She was taller than I remembered, and there was color in her cheeks. She turned to face the door with a smile.

"Oh my God! Big Casey!" she exclaimed, running and throwing herself into my arms. "Did you come to see me off?"

"Um . . . not exactly?" I rested my cheek against the smooth dome of her head. "Are you leaving?"

"Yep," she said proudly. "I'm back in remission. The docs gave me this super-secret experimental treatment that turned my pee pink. Isn't that the coolest thing?"

"Yeah! The recovery part, anyway. I'm not so sure about the pee." I grinned.

"Anyway, I'm outta here, and I'm never coming back." She pulled a decorative license plate that said CASEY #1 off the wall and tossed it into the box. "Want to give me a hand?"

"Sure." I took down a poster and started to roll it. "So, what are you going to do first?"

We'd played this game a lot—coming up with the most atrocious things to do on our first day out of the hospital. I'd say I was planning to build a glider out of papier-mâché and fly to Kansas; she'd say she was going to kidnap a sea turtle from the zoo and hide it in her bathtub, and we'd keep going and going until our creativity—or our energy—was exhausted. But when I'd first gotten home, all I'd done was sleep.

"I think we're going to stop at McDonald's," she said.

"Do they have sea turtles there?" I joked, but she didn't crack a smile. "What's up?"

"My mom's not doing so good," she said. "She hasn't come to see me in, like, a month. Dad says she won't even get out of bed. You'd think she'd be happy that I'm better, right?"

Her lip quivered, and I couldn't keep from hugging her. "Maybe she's sick. Like mono or something. That makes people really tired."

"Isn't mono from kissing?" She wrinkled her nose.

"Yeah."

"Eeeeew."

I chuckled. "Either way, I'm sure once she sees you at home, she'll perk right up."

"Yeah, prolly."

"So whatever happened to Malachi?" I asked, and we started running down the list—who'd gone home, and who'd died, who'd gone on a Make-A-Wish trip and whose parents had shaved their heads in solidarity. It didn't take us long to get the rest of the stuff off the walls; I'd just perched on the end of the bed when I noticed something on the nightstand.

I froze. "What's that?"

"It's Edward Cullen, duh."

She picked up the little figure and held it out for my inspection. The head jiggled back and forth as she thrust it at me.

I didn't want to take the bobblehead. Maybe it was from that factory. Maybe it was evil. Maybe Little Casey's recovery didn't have anything to do with that pink-pee drug. Maybe her mom didn't have mono. People would sell their soul for a lot of things. My parents would have done it for me in an instant.

Now I felt really horrible for laughing at Michael. Because either it was my imagination or this thing was evil. I couldn't see the black cloak around it, but I swore I could feel it.

"What's wrong?" Little Casey grinned. "Are you scared of vampires now?"

"Nah." I laughed it off weakly. "Just remembered there's somewhere I need to go, is all. I'm late."

"Awww." She hugged me. "Well, I'll Facebook you some-time, okay?"

"Of course you will," I said, but we both knew we'd talk once or twice at the most before we fell out of touch again. We needed to look forward, not back. Although, when I got to the door, I couldn't help myself. I looked back at that bobblehead.

After I left the hospital, I had dinner with my parents. It seemed like the least I could do after pretty much ignoring them all this time. I had every intention of calling Darcy and trying to hunt down Michael, but I actually fell asleep on my plate, and Dad had to carry me up to my bed. The last time I'd done that, I was seven. But I had to admit, this time I'd probably earned the exhaustion.

The next day crawled. I messaged Kyle with a bunch of derby videos and texted Darcy, with no response from either of them, since they were both at school. I didn't have Michael's number, which felt like a major oversight on my part. So I worked my way through a chapter on the Reformation and took the exam online before going back to bed. My body craved sleep; I'd been pushing it awfully hard, and it wasn't happy. At least I didn't hurt quite so bad anymore. I was beginning to think I might be over the hump.

I set my alarm to wake me up just in time for derby practice, because it was the only way I could think of to get in touch with Michael. Dad made me have some pizza before he agreed to drop me off. This time, I missed all the potholes on my way in, and no one tried to beat me up. I fully expected to meet Ruthanasia at the door and get thrown out on the street, since I technically wasn't supposed to be here, but for once things turned out in my favor. Barbageddon saw me first. One minute I was scanning the rink for Michael, and the next I was smothered in dreadlocks as she gave me a hug.

"Casey!" she exclaimed. "I'm so glad to see you! How are you?"

"Fine," I said, but that sounded really abrupt, so I added, "Thanks. Do you know where Michael is?"

"Not here yet, as far as I know." She slung an arm over my shoulder. With most people, the gesture would have felt fake, but Barbageddon was friendly to everybody and probably didn't have a poser bone in her body. "Hey, I know you're not on the team, but before we start, would you show me those tricks you did at tryouts? I've jumped fallen skaters before, but it wasn't half as fancy as those."

If I didn't find a way to distract myself until Michael showed up, the pressure would drive me mad, so I said, "Sure. We can start with the front tuck. That one's easy, and it should be legit to use in bouts. Some of the others aren't."

I sat down, pulled off my shoes, and put on my gear. Pretty soon, I had about half the team leaping over each other. The jump itself wasn't tough once you figured out how to handle the skates, but when you started adding defenders and turns, it got difficult quickly. Ragnarocker sent me flying twice, and the second time, I skidded right into the nubby carpet-covered wall with my head.

There was a shocked silence.

I leapt to my feet, whipped off my helmet, and exclaimed, "That was so cool! Let's do it again—"

But a voice interrupted from behind me. "Not now."

I whirled around. "Mike! I need to talk to you."

"Mike?" The corners of his mouth started to twitch, although he did a pretty good job of keeping them under control. "Really?"

I edged closer and said in a quiet voice, "It could have been worse. I almost called you Mikey."

He laughed out loud, and I swear I felt lighter.

"Let's talk after practice," he said, and I nodded. I needed the time to get my emotions under control. I felt like I might cry at any second. After an eternity of feeling guilty over things I'd done or said, it seemed like I might finally be free.

"It's nice of you to visit us, Kent, but those of us who are actually on the team really need to get to work. Can we start practice now?" Ruthanasia said, skating right past me like I'd suddenly developed a serious case of invisibility, and practically batting her lashes at Michael. "That bout with the Tilt-a-Girls is at the beginning of December, and I want to make sure we're ready."

"We will be," Michael said. "Now, before we start, I think we need a team vote. Casey's been coming to practice even though she didn't make the team, and it's pretty obvious she has valuable skills that could benefit us—"

Ruthanasia didn't even give him a chance to finish. "Even if that were true, we don't have any space on the roster. This conversation is totally useless."

"She could be an alternate," he persisted. "Her aerial skills alone would be worth the paperwork."

She just snorted, turning her back on all of us like she couldn't stand our faces any longer. I scanned the rest of the crowd, seeing expressions that were varyingly forbidding, approving, and something in between.

"Let's vote," Michael said. "Majority rules."

"Wait." I held up a hand. "Let me say something?" He nodded, and I continued. "I know I might seem high-maintenance. But I swear I'll play it smart. I just want to be a part of a team again. Heck, I'd dress up as your mascot if that's what it took."

Some of the girls giggled, and a few quit scowling at me quite so hard. I wasn't sure if it would be enough, but at least I'd tried.

"All right," Michael said. "Let's vote. Anyone who wants Casey Kent to be admitted to the team as an alternate in case of injury or absence, please raise your hand."

Darcy's shot right up into the air, followed only a moment later by Ragnarocker's and Barbageddon's. A few other hands went up, some more reluctantly than others. Ruthanasia, naturally, didn't budge.

Michael's lips moved as he counted up the votes. "Six . . . seven . . . eight. That's eight out of sixteen. Which means we need a tiebreaker."

"We already know how you're going to vote, Michael." Ruthanasia sounded beaten. As a knee-jerk reaction, I wanted to celebrate, but I squashed the feeling firmly. We could be an unbeatable team if we'd only work together. And right now I needed a victory.

He smiled at me. "That does it, then. Casey is our new alternate."

I grinned, and the girls broke out into uneven, scattered applause. But I didn't care. I'd win them over eventually, even Ruthanasia.

"Thank you so much," I gushed. "Let's start training before you all come to your senses."

Finally things were looking up.

I couldn't believe how tough practice was; the Hotsies had never worked me this hard. I was the newest, but there were two other Fresh Meat—Darcy and a chick named Monique, who looked more like a librarian than a derby girl. The Fresh Meat usually worked on basics separate from the rest of the team, but since it was already the middle of the season, we jumped right in with everybody else. First we did speed drills. This time, I easily outpaced Darcy, who didn't seem like herself. She'd barely said a word to anyone and was skating at about half the speed she'd skated at tryouts.

I edged up to her during our first water break. "You okay? I was hoping to ask you if we could hang out later, but you look like crap. I mean . . . Oh, heck. You know what I mean, right?"

She nodded, flopping onto a bench coated in peeling yellow paint.

"Are you sure you're okay? You don't look so hot."

"My throat hurts," she said, and it did sound a little scratchy. "I've got a cold or something."

Eventually Michael split us into groups. Some of the girls worked with Ragnarocker on booty blocking. It was a heckload of fun. If only I'd had more booty to block with. But I couldn't complain too much, because my no-curve boyish figure was good for acrobatic stunts. Even though I was having fun, it was still a relief when Michael pulled me, Ruthanasia, and Barbageddon aside to work on jammer stuff.

"You do know what a jammer is, don't you?" Ruthanasia said, and elbowed me.

"Yes, Casey knows," I said in a stupid voice. "Casey not idiot. Casey's sister skate for Hotsies. Casey wish you would give it a rest already."

"Hey." Barbageddon waggled a finger at us. "We're all on the same team now, right?"

"I guess," Ruthanasia said, and then she really surprised me by holding out a fist for me to bump. "I'm not going to make it a secret that I still don't think you belong here, and I don't like your attitude. But on the rink, I've got your back. All right?"

"Fair enough," I said, touching my knuckles to hers. "I don't like your attitude either, so I guess we're even."

A faint smile touched her lips. "Touché. Let's get to work."

The three of us made a good jamming team. We took turns trying to pass the defenders without going out of bounds. Ruthanasia was an aggressive skater; she barreled into people and sent them sprawling more times than I could count. Barbageddon was faster and had a knack for spotting the weak points in a defense. And I could squeeze through tiny spaces without losing my balance, even on one skate. We each had skills the other two could learn from, and a half hour passed without anyone making a single nasty comment.

Of course that had to end.

We'd just finished up and were guzzling water when Michael ambled over.

"Hey, Casey," he said. "Want a ride home? We could talk more about the . . . er . . . stuff from yesterday."

"Cool," I said.

Ruthanasia looked from him to me and back again, rolling her eyes. "We all know why you're on the team, but you don't have to flaunt it."

It felt like a punch to the stomach. It hurt even more because the thought had crossed my mind too. Had Michael championed me because of my derby skills, or did I really not belong here? Maybe he just wanted to keep a close eye on me.

From the look on her face, she knew she'd scored a point. I couldn't even come up with a witty retort.

"You're wrong," Michael said, but that just made it worse. I wanted to stand up for myself, but every time I did, I ended up picking fights and feeling crappy about it later. There had to be a sweet spot between being a doormat and a bully, but I hadn't found it.

"Whatever," she said.

Then she walked away, but she glanced at Michael first. It was the kind of look that begged him to notice. Like any second now, she'd be flinging off her clothes and throwing herself at him full-bodied. I wondered if all Sentinels had this effect on the ladies or if it was just him. It was going to be fun when she found out I'd kissed him. And that I wanted to do it again.

I'd just finished packing up my stuff when Darcy sat down on the bench beside me. I expected her to launch into a long-winded complaint about not getting to train with the jammers, or to twitter on about pink skates or random hairstyles or dojo gossip, *anything*. But she was uncharacteristically quiet.

"I really don't feel good," she moaned.

I put my hand to her forehead. Her skin was clammy; my hand felt damp after I touched her. I wiped it on my pants when I thought she wasn't looking, because it was kind of gross.

"Can you take me home?" She didn't even open her eyes. "I don't think I should drive if I've got the flu."

"Yeah, let me tell Michael. Do you mind if he follows? That way, he can give me a ride from your place."

"Sure," she said faintly.

It didn't take long to get Darcy settled at her house. Her mom took one look at her, thanked us for seeing her home, and put her to bed. Poor thing. I couldn't imagine skating with the flu. I hoped I didn't catch whatever she had.

As we walked down her street toward the parking lot where Michael had stashed his bike, I decided I really should hang out with her more. I'd never had many girlfriends before, because they weren't really interested in the same things I was. But maybe Darcy was different.

Michael and I made it halfway down the block before either of us said anything, and then we both spoke at exactly the same time.

"Listen, I need to—" I said.

"I'm really sorry—" he said.

Then we both stopped and laughed.

"You go first," I said.

He stuffed his hands into his pockets. "I owe you an apology. It's hard seeing that crap around the factory. It makes me feel sick, and I'm not used to having a physical body, let alone having to deal with it going all crazy all the time. How do you handle it?"

"I . . . What?"

"Bodies. Bodies confuse me. I've had this one for almost a year, and it still boggles my mind. One minute, I'm centered and focused and everything's going well. And the next, I'm getting just buffeted by all these different feelings, and my heart is pumping, and my hands shake, and I have these *urges*—"

"Oh my God," I said, covering my ears. "I am not about to have the sex talk with you. I couldn't handle it."

His eyes went wide. "No! Not that kind of urge. Like . . . I want to hit somebody. That kind of thing. I mean . . . I . . . You don't need to tell me about the other stuff. I've got a handle on that."

"How nice for you," I replied faintly.

By this time we could barely look each other in the eye, and I was entirely certain that I was just as red as he was. But how was I supposed to have known what kind of urges he'd meant? It's not like my mind was in the gutter, at least not most of the time.

"I've never had a temper before," he said. "It's hard to deal with. But I have no right to take it out on you. I'm sorry."

"Yeah, well, I'm sorry I jumped down your throat," I replied. "I've been doing that a lot lately, and I'm starting to feel like a real douche."

"Give yourself a break. You've only done it once."

"To you, maybe. But your head isn't the only one I've bitten off lately for no good reason. I'm just dealing with some stuff. I shouldn't have taken it out on you."

"Will you get mad if I agree?" He looked at me out of the corner of his eye, grinning tentatively.

I didn't answer, just punched him lightly on the shoulder. We walked for another couple minutes. "Will you tell me more about the bobbleheads now? And those jar things?" I asked. "Because I think . . . I saw one at the hospital. It scared the crap out of me."

He didn't answer right away, and I was starting to think he was going to turn me down, and then I was going to feel like a total fool. But then his hand crept into mine, and our fingers laced together.

"I'm sorry. I'll tell you whatever you want to know, but we can't talk about it in the middle of the street. Let's go somewhere a little more private."

"I know just the place," I told him.

We wandered down the winding backstreets leading away from the university; a warren of one-ways and dead ends lined with grubby houses for rent and apartment buildings with peeling paint. The sun began to set, reaching pink fingers across the sky, and the streetlights flickered on. I saw a front lawn full of laughing undergrads gathered around a huge pig on a spit, and about sixteen games of touch football. It was a nice walk, actually, and it gave me some time to chill out after the rampant embarrassment of the almost–sex talk. We didn't say a word until we turned into Clague Park.

My family used to play elaborate Lord of the Rings games here when my sister and I were younger. Dad always wanted to be Gandalf, and Rachel and I used to fight over being Arwen. She usually won; I got stuck being Legolas. Mom didn't care who she was as long as she got to use an accent. The playground equipment wasn't particularly impressive, just the basics, but the park itself was ringed by a thick circle of heavy trees that blocked out all hint of the city beyond, so it really felt like we were in Rivendell.

The playground was usually abandoned this late in the day. There weren't many families with young children in the neighborhood to begin with, and the college kids usually waited until around midnight to play on the merry-go-round. Of course, they were usually drunk, and they often puked all over everything. But if you could get over the faint scent of vomit that seemed to hang permanently in the air, it was a fun place to go.

We walked down the tree-crowded pathway leading to the playground. Under the canopy of green leaves, it felt like we weren't in the city at all but in some alien wilderness.

Michael steered me down the path with the barest touch of his fingers on the small of my back. I felt that current again, but this time it was muted to a pleasant buzz. So pleasant, in fact, that I didn't mind being steered for once. As we emerged from the arching branches into the open expanse of the playground, I said, "So are you ready to tell me what's going on?"

He didn't answer, and I looked up at him questioningly. He didn't even acknowledge my existence. He was too busy staring at the man in the white suit, the one who'd attacked me in the alley. He sat on top of the chipped monkey bars with a murder of crows clustered around him like little black-feathered worshippers. I knew it had to be my imagination, but it seemed like he sucked up every watt coming out of the park lights, leaving the rest of the playground in shadow.

The man in white flashed a sharklike smile at me.

"You're late," he said.

So there I was, stuck in a dark, remote park with one guy who supposedly wanted to train me to hunt demons and another who'd burned holes in my chest a couple weeks ago. I looked from Michael to Mr. Lava and back again with a sinking feeling in the pit of my stomach. How could I have been so stupid?

I should have suspected they were in it together.

It was so obvious now that I wanted to smack myself on the forehead. Guys like Michael didn't choose girls like me over girls like Ruthanasia. This was a trap, and I'd walked right into it.

I shifted away from them both, centering my weight in preparation for the inevitable attack. Michael glanced down at me, and I smiled at him quizzically, trying to look confused and pathetic, when what I really wanted to do was rip his nose off his face. The traitor.

The logical thing to do would have been to fend them off with my demon-zapping katana necklace, but I wasn't wearing it. The new chain was faulty and wouldn't stay clasped, and I hadn't had time to get another one. I'd just have to improvise. My hand slipped into my jacket pocket, and my fingers wrapped around my key chain. One jab with the edge to a pressure point would drop a charging bull. And hopefully a pair of demons too.

Air eased out from between my pursed lips. My muscles wanted to tense, but I forced my shoulders down. This was going to work. They wouldn't expect a fight. I could see the jump of Michael's pulse, the vulnerable spot where the neck met the shoulder. He would never know what hit him.

But before I could make a move, he said, "693." His voice was so cold that it could have frozen fire. It was not the kind of voice you'd use with your BFF.

I stopped. Now I wasn't just pretending to be confused.

"693? This is not the time for math," I hissed, clenching the key chain so hard that my fingers went bloodless.

"He's a Sentinel. We're not too good with the name thing, remember?" Michael said, not tearing his eyes from the man in white. "He's Michael #693."

"692." The man in white nodded at Michael. "I see you've picked up a parasite."

It was like I didn't even exist, for all the attention the

demon paid me. He leapt down from the monkey bars, the birds taking flight with caws of protest, and he rearranged his suit coat with fastidious care before ambling toward us. Michael shifted, edging in front of me and holding his arms out like I was in desperate need of protection.

On the one hand, it was nice to see that they weren't working together. On the other hand, I didn't enjoy feeling like the helpless sidekick.

"Okay, I am totally confused here," I said. "What's going on? Is he a good guy?"

There was a flicker of white in the dim light, too fast for my eyes to follow, and then 693 stood behind me, his hands on my shoulders. I could smell him, and it wasn't the sweet scent of oranges like Michael. He smelled like rotten eggs and burned coal. The stench was worse than I remembered from the alley; my eyes started watering from the stink.

He spun me around to face him.

"I am *not* a good guy, idiot mortal. I've turned demon." His eyes brimmed over with red, his cheeks sinking into cavernous pits while I watched. The lips pulled back from a leering mouth full of teeth that grew pointier before my eyes.

I froze. Running seemed wise, but how could I run from something that fast?

"Begone, demon!" Michael's voice was so deep, so loud, that it made my teeth hurt.

693's face melted back into its usual perfection as he laughed, light and mocking. "You're so cute when you're angry. But we both know you're useless on this plane. There's nothing you can do without jeopardizing your precious balance." He drew the last word out into a singsong.

"Stop trying to corrupt me. It won't work." Michael's voice was as hard as his expression.

"I'm not." 693 smirked. "The last thing I want is to be forced to spend more time with you. It was agonizing enough the first time around. Now, can we get on with this? I've tired of playing, and the outcome is inevitable. I'll devour your little pet, you'll rant and rave and ultimately do nothing productive. Then I'll move on and kill the rest of your humans, one after the other. The Master has decreed it."

I looked up at Michael. He just stood there, staring at 693's hands on my shoulders, his jaw clenched tight.

"He's kidding, right? You wouldn't just stand by while he killed me, would you?" I hissed at him.

His throat worked. "I won't let him hurt you," he said, but his voice was weird and growly, not swoon-worthy like usual. I was less than reassured. "Get behind me."

693 started to giggle, a high-pitched kind of noise that you'd expect to hear only in insane asylums.

"He can't do anything, cupcake," the demon said, squeezing my shoulder blades so hard they hurt. "He's bound by the rules."

"So are you," Michael said. I could see the muscles in his arms leap into relief as he shoved the demon away from me, wrenching my shoulder. "You're not supposed to touch them. You can't touch *her*."

The demon reached around him with giggling deliberation and poked me. "You mean like this?"

Michael smacked his hand away, seething. The demon seemed laughably infantile to me, but every taunt appeared to hit Michael like a punch. I swore I could feel heat rising off his body as his temper rose higher and higher. Eventually it was going to blow, and that seemed like a very bad thing to me.

"Hey," I said, putting my hand gently on his back. "He's not worth it. Let's get out of here."

Instead of soothing him, my words seemed to have the opposite effect. He shook me off like I was an annoyance. "No," he said. "I've had enough of this crap, and I'm not going to sit back and let him kill again."

"Wait, *what?*" I tugged on his sleeve with more urgency this time. "Kill who?"

"Ooooooh. Are you going to tell Mommy on me?" 693 cooed, dry-washing his hands. "Are you going to tell her that I've been bad? Because I have. I've devoured the souls of two of your skaters already, and it only whetted my appetite."

"Devoured?" I asked, proud that my voice wavered only a little.

"Didn't you know?" 693 licked his lips and shuddered with what looked uncomfortably like ecstasy. "The reason he held midseason tryouts is because I ate the souls of two of his skaters. Soullessness tends to be more than most humans can handle. They grew suicidal and crashed themselves into a tree. And he stood by and did *nothing.* So much for his stellar reputation."

"I'll tear you apart, and screw the consequences," Michael snarled. His head whipped around, and he pinned me under the gaze of his once blue eyes. Now they glowed a dull, faded red, like the embers of a fire left untended a little too long. "Get out of here, Casey."

For once, I didn't argue. I turned tail and ran. My frantic flight took me down one of the woodland trails, dimly lit by the light of the rising moon that filtered through the branches. Trees blocked my vision of Michael and 693, and the path was silent except for the usual rustling sounds of the forest and the crunch of my own footsteps. I paused, hands on my knees, chest heaving with exertion.

Dojo hide-and-seek had taught me a valuable lesson: when people search for a hiding spot, they rarely look up. My khaki-shorts-and-brown-tee combo would disappear against a tree, especially in the dim light, so I searched for and found a nice tall trunk that would defy most attempts to climb it. This wasn't the easiest of freerunning stunts, but if there was ever a time to get over myself, this was it. I could stand here angsting, or I could get to safety.

Marshaling my breath, I ran toward the tree, then planted my foot and shifted my torso the way I'd practiced a million times pre-cancer. My momentum carried me a few quick steps up the trunk, and a quick grab of a convenient branch got me to safety. I crouched comfortably in the crease of the fork, feeling an insane wave of accomplishment. I might have had a soul-eating demon on my hands, but at least I'd gotten my freerunning mojo back.

An earsplitting howl broke the silence of the forest. I had expected anger, but 693 sounded triumphant. Which was stupid, because I'd gotten away.

Unless I hadn't been the target after all. What if he'd picked that fight just to get to Michael? Those red eyes hadn't seemed like a good thing at all, and if Michael turned, I'd be hiding from two demons rather than one.

I shifted uncomfortably on my perch, squinting at the shadowy path with increased concern. How would I escape them both? And more to the point, why was I hiding when I could help Michael? He had said it from the start: I'd faced 693 before. Michael had been willing to stand up for me; maybe it was time for me to repay the favor.

There was no time to think about it. Either I was doing this or I wasn't. I pushed myself out into the air before I had a chance to question the wisdom of leaping onto an uneven dirt trail in poor light, windmilling my arms for balance. My heart leapt to my throat, because this landing would be even tougher than the descent off the parking structure, but Michael needed me. I landed with a crunch of dead leaves, transferring the force of my fall into a forward roll and rising into a graceful trot. Under different circumstances, I would have shouted in triumph. Instead, I ran.

When I reached the playground, I could barely believe what I was seeing. Michael and 693 rolled on the ground in what would have looked like a barroom brawl, except for the flickers of white and red energy that withered the grass underneath their bodies. I could hear the smack of fists against flesh and animalistic grunts of pain as they traded strikes, vying for dominance. 693 landed a strike on Michael's jaw and followed it up by wrapping his hands around Michael's neck. His gleeful expression told me everything I needed to know. If I planned to act, now was the time.

"Hey, demon!" I yelled, the strength of my voice surprising me. This was such a bad idea. The two of them turned identical red glowing eyes in my direction. "I've got a nice juicy soul over here."

The demon removed his hands from Michael's throat and started a slow stalk in my direction. His face rippled as he howled a challenge, the sound echoing off the trees and distorting into screams of what sounded like horrendous agony. The noise assaulted my head with an almost physical force. I fumbled the key chain out of my pocket and almost dropped it.

"Stop that!" I shouted.

The noise cut off as if someone had pulled a plug. I felt the same buzz in my spine that I'd felt when I'd thrown my necklace at him; it tingled up through my skin and made my hair stand on end. My hand went numb, as if I'd been sitting on it and now it was all pins and needles. Then the feeling was just gone, like someone had flipped a switch.

693 snarled like he'd been stung. Now he looked really angry instead of just playing at it.

For the first time, I began to wonder if that necklace fried demons because it was mine, not because the priest had murmured some mumbo jumbo over it. Maybe I really could touch the Between like Michael had said. It felt like I could turn this to my advantage if only I knew how to make it work at will, but my only potential source of information was lying motionless on the ground. I stared down at my hand. Was the key chain growing uncomfortably warm, or was I hallucinating? Everything kept whirling around in my head, the way my necklace had scared 693 off when we met in the alley, the mysterious rules that bound Michael but didn't seem to apply to 693, the fact that 693 had known to attack me in the first place. It didn't make *sense*. But maybe I didn't need to understand it. Maybe it was enough to believe in it. And in myself.

I was not going to let Michael down. And as I took my first determined step to confront the demon, the key chain began to burn with the same white fire that made up Michael's wings. It didn't exactly smolder; it vibrated, so hard and so fast that my teeth chattered.

It felt like an eternity had passed, but it must have been only a second or two, because when I looked up from the glowing key chain, 693 had just begun to reach for me. He pulled up short, wincing away from the light. I took another step forward, and he shrank before me. This was easier than I'd expected; I'd take him out quickly so I could tend to Michael. This whole demon-hunting thing was a piece of cake.

Then the demon's eyes met mine.

Black wings crept into my field of vision, cutting out all light. I heard his laugh, the one that felt like fingernails screeching down a chalkboard, only it was inside my head, and I couldn't make it stop. I felt him then, a pulsing, venomous presence inside me, unearthing every negative thought I'd ever had. The thoughts that said I didn't deserve to live when the kids in rooms next to me died. The ones that said I was a mistake. The ones that said I was a waste of a miracle.

Pain I could take, but this went beyond that. Every middle-of-the-night fear I'd ever had flashed through my mind in one agonizing second, and I fell to the ground with a shriek, dropping the key chain. My fingers clawed at my face; I would gladly have ripped it off just to make the agony stop. I deserved to die. I should have been dead.

Then I heard the demon's voice. "All you have to do is give up and all of this will end. I'll take it all away. It'll be like it never happened."

"No," I whispered, but it came out as more a question than a statement.

His voice was intimate and slickly smooth. It gave me goose bumps. "No more people staring at your head. No more wondering why. No more guessing how much time you have left. I'll take it all."

I found myself nodding, but that didn't feel right. I was the girl who picked fights with death. Yeah, maybe I felt a little guilty some days and angry on others. It was hard to be the miracle girl and walk out of the hospital, past the rooms of friends who you knew weren't going to make it. But I'd dealt with that. I could keep on dealing.

I pushed up from the ground as the word came screaming out of my throat. "No!" I yelled.

I reached out blindly for the key chain. And when my fingers touched it, the darkness dissolved. My vision cleared.

The demon loomed over me, his words blending into a stream of babble.

"I'll give you money. Power. Strength. The girl with the red hair, the one who hates you? She'll be on her knees at your feet. The team will accept you for real. Your friend and your sister? They'll give you the credit you deserve. I can give you Michael; I know you want him."

"No . . ." I shook my head. "I'm not dealing."

His voice came even more quickly. "Your body. I can heal it. I can make sure you never spend another night in the hospital, never worry if this is your last healthy day. I'll give you your hair back. I'll take your scars. You could wear a bikini in public without everyone looking at you like you're a circus freak. Wouldn't that be nice?"

I'd be lying if I said it wasn't tempting. It was. But this demon thought that having cancer had made me weak.

He was mistaken.

"I don't want what you're selling," I said, the words coming easier now. "Get your sorry demonic ass back to where you came from, and don't ever come back!"

There was no other choice. My fist jerked toward his neck, the key chain once again clenched between my stacked knuckles. The strike was nothing special, but it did the job. The fiery metal hit the demon and sank in as if he were made of Jell-O. The flames spread through him, and I felt them burn him into nothing, his voice fading away to silence. His body dissolved, the white clothes blowing away in a convenient gust of wind.

That was when Michael whooped so loudly, it scared the crap out of me.

"Yes!" he yelled, still lying on the ground. "That's what I'm talking about!"

My arms gave out, and I lay back on the ground, overcome by a heady wave of relief and delayed adrenaline. That could have gone wrong in so many ways. I could have died. I could have gone over to the dark side. Holy crap, what had I been thinking?

"What's wrong?" Michael scrambled to his feet, gravel crunching as he hurried to crouch by my side. "Casey, are you okay?"

"Look at me," I demanded in a shaking voice.

He did. His eyes were wide and blue. No more red flickers that made me feel like running off into the trees. "Are you hurt?" he demanded.

I shook my head. And then began to cry.

Once I started, I couldn't stop. The demon had stirred up so many feelings that I had kept struggling to bury, and I was so tired that I didn't know if I could bottle them up again. Michael sat down next to me in the middle of the path and slung his arm over my shoulders, pulling me to rest against him. I don't know how long we sat there, but eventually my sobs turned to hiccups and finally to hitching breaths.

Then my stomach growled.

"You need to eat," Michael said. "I'm taking you out, and we can talk then. Is there somewhere close?"

I wiped my face on my sleeve, snuffling. "Smuckers. Right

down the street. It's the best greasy spoon in town. But you don't have to pay for me," I added hastily. "I've got money."

"You agreed to go on a date with me. You're not going to go back on your word, are you?" He looked at me sternly, but from the way his lips twitched, I could tell he was kidding.

"I guess not." I took in a shaky breath and wiped my runny nose on my sleeve.

"Good," he said. "Because demon slayers eat for free around here."

"Oh, joy. And by the way? If my performance of a few minutes ago is any indication, I might need a little more info on this whole demon-fighting thing."

His mouth twitched. "First food. Then explanations. I don't want you fainting on me. I might have to give you mouth-to-mouth."

I couldn't help but flash back on that image of the two of us together, and I knew my face was bright red. So I ducked my head and said, "Okay. Help me up."

Instead of giving me a hand like I'd expected, he crouched down in front of me, presenting a very nice set of shoulders for inspection. His hair was wavy and kicked out in the back. I wanted to run my fingers through it.

"Get on," he said.

"What?"

"You're tired, so I'm giving you a piggyback ride to the bike. Get on."

I almost protested, but I really was exhausted, and there were worse things than being toted around on the back of a studly not-quite-mortal. He wrapped muscular arms around my upper thighs before standing easily. Then he started off at a light jog, which you'd think would have bounced me around like a ball but didn't. His stride was so fluid that I almost felt like I was floating.

"So do you know why this guy was after me?" I blurted out. "If I'm going to get attacked once every few days, I'd like to know why."

His shoulders tightened under my arms, and for a second, I got jostled around uncomfortably as his stride faltered, but then it smoothed out again.

"You're a threat to demonkind. Your brush with death changed you. A lot of people fold under that kind of pressure, but you just got more stubborn, as far as I can tell, and I mean that as a compliment."

"Thanks," I said dryly. "But I still don't get it. What does having cancer have to do with fighting demons?"

"It's not the cancer; it's how you reacted to it. Most people are stuck in the physical world; they're fixated on money and beauty and all kinds of physical things. Being sick forced you to confront the spiritual and come to terms with it. You've achieved sufficient balance that you are able to pull power from the Between like you just did with—what was that thing you hit him with, anyway?"

"My key chain?" I held it over his shoulder for inspection.

"Yeah. Anyway, weapons like these, charged with the Between, are the only way to kill a demon."

"And you can't fight them yourself because you'd become

a demon in the process. That's what was happening to you back there, isn't it?" It felt so strange to say it that way, all calmlike. But there were no words to describe how horrible the thought made me feel, and I knew if I tried, I'd break down again.

"Yeah." He sighed. "It was pretty close back there. If you hadn't interrupted when you did, I probably would have been a goner. And I can't stand to think about what I would have done then."

"What do you mean?"

He set me down next to his bike, answering quietly. "New demons tend to devour the things they love first. It would have been bad."

Did that mean he loved me? I wanted it to, but I worried about what that would mean. It was selfish to want him if those feelings were likely to doom us both. But that didn't make it any easier to stop feeling the way I did.

But I still couldn't help stepping forward and resting my cheek on his chest for just a second, thinking about how it would feel if we could just be together without all this demon crap getting in the way. His arms went around me in response. I knew if I kissed him, he'd kiss me back. We could shut out the world, just for a minute. I pulled back just far enough to look into his eyes, our lips only inches apart. Slowly, inexorably, we began to drift closer. But then, moments before our lips touched, I started to worry. Was I hurting him? Would the demons use me to make him fall like 693 had tried to?

He must have had the same misgivings, because he paused

too, our lips barely grazing. My heart hammered, and I could feel my hands tremble against his waist. I was torn between what I wanted and the responsible thing to do. One little kiss couldn't hurt, right?

If I really cared about him, I'd set those feelings aside and take care of business. I swallowed hard, trying to summon the willpower to pull away. His mouth quirked up in a wry grin that I felt more than saw.

"Crappy timing, huh?" he murmured.

"You can say that again."

"Crappy timing, huh?"

I let out a laugh that finally broke the tension between us, and we released each other. I knew it was a good idea but couldn't keep from regretting it. It would happen between us someday, but that wasn't soon enough.

He took a deep breath and let it out.

"Yeah," I said. "I totally agree."

This time he laughed. I rode the wave of it and then tried to come up with something constructive to say.

"So . . . about those demons . . ." I trailed off because I didn't know how to end the sentence.

"Yeah?" He arched a brow.

"What now? I learn how to hunt them myself?" I paused as a sinking thought occurred to me. "Were those other two derby girls demon hunters? Is that why 693 killed them?"

He shook his head, handing me a helmet. "You're the first fully manifested hunter I've seen. I thought they'd be so much easier to find. . . ."

"Well, the roller derby isn't the first place I'd look."

"I needed ways to meet people, and I thought athletes might make more likely hunters, since athletic training is a fairly strenuous process. I'm also playing in an Ultimate Frisbee league, and I coach high school soccer. And I take guitar lessons, but that's just because I want to."

"You have a very busy social calendar for someone who's only been alive for a year," I said faintly, climbing onto the bike behind him.

"Yeah, I take a class or two at the university each semester so I don't seem too suspicious. Plus, I live with a senior Sentinel who poses as my brother. He doesn't leave the apartment, but he's really good with technology, so he searches for and mentors hunters online."

"Oh," I said. Then I finally worked up the courage to ask the question that was really on my mind. "So why did 693 kill those girls?"

"He's trying to either recruit me or get me to give up and leave. I'm not sure the why matters; I'm more interested in how to stop him."

"Good point."

He fired up the bike, cutting off any further conversation for the moment. It was a good thing too, because all my witty banter had been designed to keep both of us from realizing that I was about two centimeters from complete hysteria. I needed the jokes to distract me or I'd be cowering in a corner. Good thing the ride wasn't long enough for me to really get thinking; we quickly pulled up in front of a fifties-style diner, one of those places where all the corners are curves and every surface is covered in spit-shined metal. I climbed off the bike and almost knocked heads with him.

"We should go inside," he said, taking me gently by the elbow and steering me toward the door.

"Yeah, that would be good."

It took us a few minutes to get seated; Smuckers might have looked like it was upholstered in disco balls, but they had the best fries in the city. The seating area was always packed. Finally we ended up in a saggy-springed booth in the corner underneath the brooding gaze of James Dean. It wasn't the greatest poster in the world; the camera angle made him look kind of like a bobblehead. But at least it wasn't dogs playing cards.

The bobblehead thought made me frown, my mind circling back to try to make sense of all the weirdness. Very unsuccessfully.

"What are you thinking about?" Michael asked, leaning toward me over the smooth expanse of pink Formica.

"Bobbleheads." I paused. "I found one in my friend's hospital room. She's miraculously back in remission, but her mom won't get out of bed. Could she have . . ." I couldn't say it.

But Michael could. "Sold her soul to save her daughter? I'm afraid it's possible, but there's no way to know for sure without getting a good look at the bobblehead. Demons are eternally hungry. If left unchecked, they'll consume entire solar systems. Soul jars are like little to-go boxes to them."

"I keep waiting for you to tell me this is all a joke and you've got a camera hidden in your hair or something."

"I wish. Black holes—you know how they suck everything in around them?" I nodded. "That's what happens when we miss a demon. They just keep eating until there's nothing left."

"So if there's a soul in the bobblehead, some demon's going to steal the bobblehead and eat it?"

He shrugged. "I don't know how it works, and I don't think I want to. They seem to be able to collect without having physical custody of the bobbleheads, though. I tried locking some of them up in our apartment, but one day, the souls were just gone."

"Oh." It came out as a whisper.

"Are you okay?"

"Well, I'm trying not to freak out." My eyes flicked back to the menu. "I'm also torn between the waffles and the chicken strips."

Of course, our waitress picked that very moment to scurry over and demand our orders in a voice so breathless that it was nearly unintelligible. Michael ordered a cheeseburger with a level of reverence normally reserved for the Pope, the Dalai Lama, and holy relics. Between his extra-polite demeanor, his overall hotness, and that voice of his, the waitress was practically purring by the time she left the table.

After she left, Michael just stared at me. I was pretty used to being stared at, but usually there was a good reason behind it. Pre-cancer, it usually had something to do with the fact that I was either hanging upside down from or jumping off something. Post-cancer, it usually had something to do with the fact that I was bald and marker-scribbled. But he wasn't staring at my scalp, and I wasn't performing any stunts. And it was hard not to stare back.

"So, what do you want me to do?" I asked. "Take my necklace and go out hunting?"

"Objects like your necklace are called Relics. I can teach you how to reach into the Between and make them at will," he said. "They're anathema to demons."

"Am I going crazy?" I asked. "Is this some elaborate practical joke? I've got to know, because I'm really starting to doubt my sanity. Like maybe I have a brain tumor, and this is all a hallucination. How do I know this is real?"

Of course, the waitress picked that moment to sashay over.

"Here's your coffee, honey," she said, batting her eyelashes at him so fast that I swore I could feel a breeze. "Cream?"

"We're fine, thanks," I said pointedly.

She flounced off with an extra wiggle in her step. Michael didn't even seem to notice, which was good, because I might have had to throw something at him if he had. He just smiled gently at me and laced both his hands behind his head. I attempted to ignore what this did to his pectorals, but trust me, a part of me noticed.

"There's no way to know for certain." He stretched. "I can show you the wings again if that will help, but some things you've just got to take on faith."

"Faith." I snorted. "I only believe in things I can beat up or jump off."

He smiled. "Yeah. That's why I like you more than I ought to."

13

My brain was struggling to parse everything I'd learned so far. It felt like someone had sprained my reality, which I guess wasn't too far from the truth. So I took refuge in small talk. I asked how long Michael had managed the team (one month), and what had made him interested in roller derby in the first place (he wasn't; he had applied to manage the men's rugby team but hadn't gotten that job), and what class he was taking this semester (Introduction to Philosophy, and his instructor always wore bolo ties).

When the waitress brought our food, I was beyond relieved. I sucked down my chicken in record time and drank enough Coke to flood Rhode Island. My appetite seemed to be coming back. I took it as a good sign. We exchanged numbers.

Then he drove me home.

"So," he said, rolling to a stop in front of our town house, "why don't you take a week or so to think about all of this? If you decide you want in, I can start teaching you what I know about demons and Relics and whatnot after derby practices."

"After practice?" I punched his shoulder playfully as I got off the bike. "Are you trying to kill me?"

He laughed low in his throat, standing up and capturing my hand. "I'm trying to save you, idiot. Make you tougher."

"Don't make me beat you up," I teased, leading him up the steps to our front door. I would have talked more smack if he hadn't leaned forward again. It was our third almost-kiss of the night, but somehow this one felt like it was a go. To heck with the ramifications. If we didn't kiss, it was only going to distract us from our duties, right? It would be better for us in the long run to get it over with. Our faces got closer and closer, and I felt strangely breathless, like I'd just been out running. It would have been very wise to look away, but I couldn't make myself do it.

My dad opened the screen door, nearly smacking Michael with the handle. We flew apart like we were on strings.

"Well, well," Dad said, looking Michael over and folding his arms. "I'll have you know I'm an expert swordsman."

"Dad!" I said, blushing. "He's just kidding, Michael."

"Mostly." My father shrugged. "But if you hurt my baby, all bets are off."

"That's fair, sir," Michael said.

"Sir?" I said, and snorted.

"My family's in the . . . ah . . . military. Remember?" Michael's cell rang, and he checked the number. "I should probably take this. It's my brother. He's acting as my guardian, because my parents are overseas."

"Okay. See you soon?" I said. I didn't know how long I'd make it without calling him. Not that I was turning into one of those obsessive stalker girls, but I'd probably have a new list of questions for him by about midnight.

"Yeah." He nodded. "Don't forget practice."

I expected the third degree when Dad closed the door, but he just kissed me on the forehead. "After teaching for fifteen years, I've learned to trust my instincts when it comes to people, and I like that one, Case. What's his story?"

"He's the manager of our derby team. I'm an alternate now."

"Congratulations!" He folded me into a hug. "I look forward to seeing you skate."

"I'll get you the schedule. But I'll only be in a bout if somebody's out."

"Yes, I understand the meaning of the word 'alternate.'" He softened the words with a smile and then ambled down the hallway, cleaning his glasses on his shirttail. "But no more staying up until all hours of the morning with him and sleeping all day, you get me? The deal was that you had to log your homeschool hours if you want to engage in activities. Dozing through them doesn't count."

"I know." I sagged against the wall, suddenly exhausted.

"And I'll keep up my end of the bargain. It's just nice to get out there again. I was starting to feel—"

"Lost?"

"Petrified. Like the wood."

"And this boy is the inspiration for your new zest for life?"

"Not exactly. Although, I do like him more than I should."

"How old is he?" And now we got to the third-degree bit. He replaced his glasses, looking at me with one of his rare keen gazes that miss nothing. The truth almost popped out of me, despite my urge to resist. My dad probably would have thought I was being a smart-ass if I'd told him Michael was only one.

"Nineteen, maybe? He's a freshman at the U."

"All right," he said. "I'm going to trust my instincts, but please be responsible?"

"Don't worry, Dad. I'm not going to do anything stupid."

"Of course you aren't," he said. "But I can't help myself. So I'll keep giving you my so-called wise advice, and you pretend to be floored by it on occasion, okay?"

"That's a deal."

He started down the basement steps, then paused to look back at me. "I'm downstairs watching a little *Inside the Actors Studio* if you're interested. Christopher Walken's on. Did you know he used to be a tap dancer?"

I shook my head. "Thanks, but I think I'm going to get in touch with Rachel. We haven't really spoken since . . . you know."

After all that had happened, I needed to let our argument go. Life was too short. And in my case, that could be a literal statement. When I thought about it that way, it seemed ridiculous to wait another second to call her.

"Good for you." Dad went down the stairs, humming tunelessly to himself.

Upstairs, I threw myself onto my bed and put my feet up on the wall. Normally I'd text, but this felt like the kind of thing that needed to be said out loud. The phone rang only once before Rachel picked up, and I didn't even say hello. I apologized right off the bat, because I wanted to get it over with.

"I'm sorry," I said, all in a rush. "I know you were looking out for me last time you were here, and you did have a good point, and I shouldn't have gotten my undies in a bunch over it. I just really wanted your support."

There was a long pause. "I'm sorry too. But I can't support the derby thing. I really want to, but . . . I can't. I'm glad to hear from you, though."

"Me too." I wanted to argue my case, but that didn't seem wise if I intended to avoid another fight. A change of subject was in order. "So, uh, how have you been?"

"Bored. Abnormal Psych is kicking my butt. I've got a ton of reading and no motivation whatsoever to get it done. What're you up to?"

I made my voice as light as possible, because she was worried enough without hearing about how I'd killed a demon at our favorite childhood park.

"Nothing, really. I'm only an alternate for the Apocalypsies, so you don't need to panic too much. I won't see much rink time, and maybe that's for the best. It'll give me a chance to get stronger. We'll be practicing extra this week to get up to speed for our next bout, but we don't have anything else planned. You?"

"Not much." She finally perked up. "How about I buy you a train ticket and you come and stay with me next weekend? You don't have practice, do you? I'll have to ask Sadie, but I'm sure she'll say yes."

"That would be awesome!" I said, so Rachel ineffectually covered the receiver with her hand and shouted at her roommate. Sadie was a tiny chain-smoking Brit who wanted to be a filmmaker and had as much luck with guys as Rachel. Between the two of them, they'd pretty much decimated every frat boy in a hundred-mile radius of Smithton.

"Bloody yes, she can come!" Sadie yelled in the background, and Rachel whooped.

I couldn't help but laugh.

The rest of the week was uneventful, with no attacks by freaky flaming guys, and I began to hope the demon-hunter training wouldn't be necessary. Maybe it was over. I was feeling pretty good when I left for my visit with Rachel. The train ride was only about forty-five minutes, which was long enough for me to write and delete nine texts to Michael. I hated myself for being so obsessed, but I couldn't help it. Finally I had to turn off my cell just so I wasn't tempted anymore.

I had a ton of stuff to learn about the whole demon-fighting gig, but first I needed to decide how I felt about it all. I kept hoping the defeat of 693 would be the end of the demon attacks, but he couldn't have been running that factory on his own, could he? I had to be prepared just in case. I needed to know whether I wanted to volunteer or hide under my pillow until it all blew over. Maybe if I stayed home for the rest of the year and homeschooled, dropped out of derby, and avoided the dojo, the demons would forget about me. I'd waited this long to put my life back together; I could wait a while longer.

It was tempting. I knew the bobblehead scheme was evil and needed to be stopped, but the whole experience with 693 had proved without a doubt that these guys were serious. I didn't want to think about what would have happened if I'd stayed hiding in the tree or if I'd taken that deal, but I knew it wouldn't have been good. My only options were to hide out or take the demons on. And wouldn't that be like putting a big demonic KICK ME sign on my back? The idea scared the crap out of me. I hadn't fought my way from the brink of death just to turn around and risk my life again.

None of the choices were good ones; I kept thinking in circles without making any progress whatsoever. Finally, in desperation, I distracted myself by mentally reviewing all the ninjutsu moves I could think of and making a list of tricks that Darcy and I could attempt on skates. Maybe we could come up with some legal derby moves to show our teammates once she was over that flu thing.

Before I knew it, I was sitting at the dining table in Rachel's so-called suite. Apparently, in college-dorm-speak, "suite" means "tiny room with rickety furniture linked to two equally minuscule bedrooms and a bathroom the size of a postage stamp." I had no idea how four people could cram all their stuff into such a small space. The only reason they had room for me was because their other two roommates had gone to visit their boyfriends for the weekend. That was just fine with me, because one was a hair-tosser, and the other laughed like a hyena.

But Sadie was pretty cool, so I was all for it when she plopped a grease-stained pizza box on the table and said, "Dinner's on me, girls, so long as you'll go with me to this party."

Both Rachel and I perked up. We really needed something to distract us from staring at each other and trying to figure out what to say. We fought so infrequently that neither of us knew how to handle it. Which would have been funny if it wasn't true.

Sadie shoved a flyer across the table, and Rachel and I bent over to read it: FOAM PARTY AT THE SPOTTED DOG!

"What the heck is a foam party?" I asked, flipping the box open and helping myself to a slice of pepperoni and mushroom.

"I'm not quite sure," Sadie said, "but I'm assuming it is a party with foam. Which seems like a brilliant idea to me."

"I've got to see this," said Rachel. "It's always been my greatest aspiration in life to party with foam."

"Hey, I'm game, as long as you can get me in the door," I said.

Sadie waved the flyer in my face. "I know the bouncer, love. We'll get you in."

"Woo!" Rachel shouted, throwing her arms up over her head and nearly upending the pizza in the process. "We're gonna get our foam on!"

About an hour later, we walked over to the Spotted Dog. It was your typical dingy college bar. Not that I've seen the inside of many college bars, because I'm only seventeen, but if you've seen one ratty old bar, you've seen them all. It was the kind of place where you squatted to pee and decided not to wash your hands, because it would actually be grosser to touch the sink.

So we walked straight through without touching anything, about seven hundred stamps on our hands proclaiming us to be under twenty-one, and went out to the patio. It was pretty big, with its own bar hung with strands of lights shaped like peppers and hula girls, and ringed by a big wooden privacy fence. Every available surface I could see was covered in plastic sheeting. I wasn't sure if there were tables or not, because the rest of the place was full of white, fluffy foam. It reminded me of a giant bathtub gone out of control.

I heard a low, steady hum from the far corner of the patio.

A stream of foam shot out into the air. A pair of guys stood there in Spotted Dog tees, spraying white clouds of dish soap out of a Shop-Vac. It was still early, but I could only imagine what it would be like once the place got rocking. The foam would be a big draw.

"I love this foam!" Sadie yelled, holding her cigarette over her head and wading into the stuff. She was so short that it came all the way up to her neck; she looked like this little bobbing head in a sea of white. Rachel and I couldn't stop laughing.

"Well, come on," Rachel said, grabbing my hand and plunging in.

The foam wasn't particularly wet, but it tickled something fierce when you moved through it. The bubbles popped against my skin, and if I put my ear right up to it, I heard the hiss of the foam as bubbles broke and reformed.

"This is the coolest thing ever," I said.

"Oh, pants," Sadie said, eyeing her foam covered cigarette.

I snorted. "It cracks me up that you think that's a swear word."

"It's a Brit thing. You wouldn't get it." She dropped the smoke into the foam and watched it disappear. "I've been meaning to quit anyway."

"Haven't you been saying that ever since I met you?" I asked.

She nodded. "But this time I have the power of foam!" Then she scooped up a big pile and dumped it onto my head.

It was mass chaos for a long time after that, because a

group of guys at the bar joined in the foam fight. I was having a lot of fun until someone spilled something wet on my foot, but I couldn't really see what it was because of the foam.

"I need to wring out my shoe," I told Rachel. "Be right back."

My favorite pair of orange Chucks smelled like beer. I dried them as best I could with a napkin and then couldn't resist turning on my cell to check my messages. Maybe Michael had called.

Unfortunately, my phone was not foam compatible. I didn't get any reception at all, not even roaming, and I started wandering around with it held up over my head, trying to find some corner where the stupid thing might work. I was changing service providers when I got home.

I'd just checked the screen again, when I heard a snuffling noise in the foam somewhere to my right. Was Rachel trying to sneak up on me? If it was her, I was going to get her so bad.

First, I'd have to flank her. I pushed away from the wall, staying beneath the foam and placing each foot carefully on the ground to avoid tripping. My hand in front of my face kept my eyes foam-free. The neon glow of the bar lights got dimmer and dimmer until I couldn't see it anymore.

Now I curved around toward the corner where I'd heard the noise, moving slowly and deliberately. I found a chair lying overturned in the foam and went around it. And then I saw another low shape off to my right. At first, I thought it was another chair, but then it moved. Someone crouching? I peered through the foam, trying to make out the shape. It trotted toward me.

A dog.

I huffed out an amused breath. I'd just stalked a dog. He'd probably snuck in under the fence. Somehow the poor thing had gotten stuck under the foam in this deserted corner, and it was probably scared stiff. I debated shouting for one of the employees, but it wasn't like I couldn't handle a dog, and I might scare it off and lose it in the foam. It would be much easier to let it outside myself.

"Here, boy," I said, pitching my voice low so I didn't startle it. "Come here; I'll help you get out."

It came closer. Its features were still distorted by all the foamy awesomeness, but it was big, with a black coat and long tail. A Lab, maybe? I wasn't exactly a dog expert.

I knelt down as it approached, and I put out my hand. I'm not sure what tipped me off that something wasn't right. Maybe I realized that the shape of its head wasn't quite natural. Or maybe I caught a glint of red in its eyes or a hint of the sulfuric scent that hung around it. Or maybe it was my instincts recognizing danger.

But the reason wasn't important. I was just glad I pulled my hand back before the demon dog bit it off.

I jerked back as it lunged. Its mouth opened on hinged jaws like a snake's, exposing curved fangs way too big for its head. They snapped shut on air inches away from my hand as I threw myself into a backward roll and came up in a defensive stance.

"What the hell?"

The thing had the build of a big dog, but instead of fur, it was covered in glistening black scales. The tail was tipped with a wicked-looking rattle, and the head looked like a strange hybrid of the canine and serpentine.

I was never going to escape these things. They'd never let me go; what had I been thinking? I'd taken out one of their demons. Of course they were going to hunt me down and make me pay. And now, my idiocy was going to get me killed, because I wasn't prepared.

Running wasn't an option, because I didn't want to let this thing loose on the other people here. My hand fluttered up to my bare neck. I really had to get that chain fixed. And my keys were back in Rachel's dorm room with my jacket. I'd have to try to make another Relic. I'd done it in the park with my key chain. How hard could it be?

All of this flashed through my mind as the snake dog crouched a few feet away, preparing to spring. I fumbled through the foam, knocking over a chair. Finally my hand closed on something slippery smooth, and I pulled it up to look at it. A beer bottle.

The dog leapt at me with a blurry flash of movement. I should have expected it to move faster than a normal dog, because 693 and Michael were both mega-fast, but it still shocked the hell out of me. I clamped my lips closed on a scream. I couldn't risk any noise; Rachel would come wading through the foam to help. And losing my sister to this thing wasn't an option.

The dog's heavy body knocked me to the floor, squeezing all the breath out of me. I desperately threw my arm up to protect my face as its slavering jaws closed just inches from my eyes. One fang opened a burning gash along the length of my forearm, and my hand went instantly numb.

The bottle was still clutched in my other hand, though. I broke it over the thing's head. Glass rained down on my eyes, and I barely managed to close them in time.

There was no fiery sizzle. No tingling in my fingers. No white light. I didn't know why it wasn't working, and I lacked the time to sit there and figure it out. I'd have to find another way to take this thing down.

The dog's triangular head shook back and forth; I'd clocked it pretty good. It didn't seem wise to give it time to collect itself, so I whacked it again. The jagged glass pierced the demon's reptilian skin, and then the gaping wound sprayed me with brackish blood that smelled like industrial sewage. It stunk so bad that I nearly puked all over myself.

It snapped at me again, and I just started hitting it, over and over. I dimly heard Rachel shouting my name, and all I could think was that I had to protect her. I had to kill it. So I kept on battering and didn't stop until the bottle broke into tiny little pieces and there wasn't enough left to hold on to.

When my head cleared, the demon dog's body sprawled limply on top of me.

"Casey?" Rachel sounded close by and very worried. "Where are you hiding? This isn't funny. You're scaring me."

The foam kept getting lower and lower, and the Shop-Vac guys weren't spraying any more of it my way. I crouched, waiting for something to happen, but the dog just lay there uncooperatively. If it was a demon, I knew a Relic was the only way to truly kill it, but hopefully, I'd bought enough time for us to get away. So I shoved it under the fence with my good hand. Maybe it would leave once it realized I was no longer there.

"Casey!" This time Rachel shouted.

I took a quick minute to rub at the stains on my shirt with a convenient handful of foam. I smelled beery and gross, but there was nothing I could do about that. Then I stood up, holding my injured arm against my side and flailing to clear the foam with the other.

"I'm over here!" I yelled back. "I just cut myself something fierce, though."

We waded toward each other, and I held my arm up for inspection. A pair of long furrows ran up the length of my forearm, and the skin around it was already puffy and red. It burned more than I thought it had a right to. Blood dripped steadily off my elbow and onto the floor.

"Sadie!" Rachel yelled, not taking her eyes off me. "Get a towel! We've got to take Casey to the ER for stitches."

"Aw, crap," said Sadie, emerging from the foam like a ghost and scaring the daylights out of me in the process.

"Sorry to ruin your foam party." I held my arm away from my body in a vain attempt not to bleed all over myself.

"Eh." She shrugged. "It's all right. It's not the end of the world."

I wished she hadn't said that. It felt way too much like she was tempting fate.

14

It took two hours of waiting, fifteen stitches, and about a half hour on the phone describing my injuries in detail to my mother before we finally got back to the dorms. I certainly wasn't going to tell everyone about the demon dog, so I settled for vagueness—I'd been trying to sneak up on my sister, only I'd tripped on something in the foam and cut myself. By the time I hung up Rachel's cell, which she'd kindly dialed for me since it was tough to do with one hand, I was utterly exhausted. I fell onto one of the empty beds and was instantly asleep.

When I woke up the next morning and turned my phone on to check the time, there were eleven missed calls and texts. All but two were from Michael.

Darcy texted to say thanks for getting her home when she was sick and to ask if I wanted to go to the movies sometime. I saved that one.

Then a text from Michael: WHERE R U?!?!?

The first voice mail was from Michael, his voice urgent: "Where did you go, Casey? I felt you leave, and you're not answering your phone, and I can't protect you if you leave the area without telling me. Call me right away."

A few hours later: "Just checking in. I'll be unavailable for the next hour or so, but if you get this, drop me a message? Maybe we should have started training immediately. Call me."

Then, right around the time I started fighting the demon dog, the messages started coming fast and furious.

"What's wrong? Call me right now, Casey."

"Call me, damn it."

He kept calling, leaving no messages.

Then there was an automated message from my cell company apologizing for the service interruptions last night—which explained the crappy reception—and offering to credit my account. This kind of thing happened all the time. Normally it was just annoying, but this time it had practically killed me. I was definitely changing my provider.

Then the last message, from early this morning. Michael's voice was strained with fear. "I know you're somewhere to the north. I'm coming, Casey. I'll find you."

I ended the call and frowned thoughtfully. It felt good to know Michael had my back. If I was hurt, he'd know. He'd find me. But a part of me wouldn't stop berating myself for being afraid. If I was tough, I shouldn't feel a wave of relief that he was coming to my rescue, right?

Enough of this. I could overanalyze things all day, or I could call and let him know everything was all right. It took two fumbling attempts to dial, but I finally managed. He picked up after half a ring.

"Casey?" he gasped.

"I'm okay," I said. "And I think I'm going to do the hunter thing, although it scares the crap out of me and I'm not sure I'll be any good at it. I'll try it. But if you have a dog, all bets are off."

He didn't say anything.

"Michael? Are you there?"

"Uh . . . yeah." He let out a shaky laugh. "I'm glad I don't have a dog."

"Good." I shuddered. "I'm not so keen on dogs right now."

"So, are you in a building named Murphy Hall, by any chance? Because I'm standing outside of it, and I'm pretty sure you're in there somewhere."

I nodded like he might be able to see me through the walls. "Room two twelve."

After I hung up, I rolled to my feet, cradling my injured arm. I needed to brush my teeth, but at least I didn't have to worry about bed head. Baldness has its advantages.

"Rachel," I called through her closed bedroom door. "I hope you don't mind, but we've got company."

"Mmmph," she said, and then I heard a loud thump. Either

she'd just fallen out of bed or she'd thrown something at the door. "Company what?"

"My . . . uh . . . boyfriend is here. At the dorm. Is it okay if he comes in?"

"You have a boyfriend?" Sadie shrieked, sweeping out of the room in a short filmy nightgown trimmed in feathers and printed with bright green skulls. She grabbed me by the shoulders and shook me. "Why didn't you tell us about this last night?"

"Sadie, unhand my sister," Rachel said. But then, as soon as Sadie vacated my shoulders, she took over and shook me too. "Why didn't you tell us this last night?"

"It's not that big a deal." I scratched at the edge of my bandages. The wounds were starting to itch already. I know that's supposed to be a good sign, but it was still annoying. "I mean, it would be nice if you guys put on pants, but otherwise there's no need to go all out."

Rachel looked down at her bare legs. "Pants. Yes. That's a good idea." Then she slammed the door in my face.

I'd just gotten a nice mouthful of toothpaste when he knocked.

"That must be our lover boy." Sadie breezed past the bathroom. She'd taken my pants suggestion literally; she was wearing a pair of what looked like black satin capris under the ridiculous nightie. The ridiculous part being that she actually looked *good*.

I choked out the word "Wait!" and managed to spray minty foam all over the mirror. By the time I'd rinsed my mouth out and cleaned the toothpaste off the wall, she'd already opened the door.

"Oh my God," she said, staring at Michael.

"Not exactly," he replied. "I'm Michael. You're not Casey's sister, are you?"

"Nah, I'm the comic relief. Name's Sadie."

"I'm the sister," Rachel interjected, toppling onto the thin cushions of the sofa. "And I'm happy to meet you, but I don't do mornings very well."

"I think they should be outlawed," he replied.

Rachel threw one arm over her eyes. "Casey, you should keep this one. Now, someone please make me coffee, and I will love you forever."

Sadie made the coffee, and then the uncomfortable staring began. Michael stared at the bandage on my arm like he had X-ray vision. Sadie, Rachel, and I stared at him like we were trying to figure out if he had X-ray vision.

"Well," Rachel said, draining the last of her mug. "I just remembered that Sadie and I desperately need to clean our bedroom for the next half hour or so. Don't we, Sadie?"

"Oh, definitely." She grinned. "Saturday mornings are always cleaning time. Nothing like getting up bright and early to tidy things up." She paused, and then whispered very loudly, "Do you think they're buying it?"

Michael and I both shook our heads, but it was too late. Rachel grabbed Sadie's arm and dragged her back into their bedroom, slamming the door behind them.

"I'm sorry," I said hastily, sitting down on the sofa. "Maybe

I shouldn't have told them you were my boyfriend, but it was the only way I could think of to justify your being here."

He sat down beside me and slung an arm over my shoulders. "There are worse things than being your boyfriend, Casey."

Did that mean we were officially dating? We'd never really had that conversation, and he had to stay balanced to keep from going demonic. I hadn't had many boyfriends, since I'd gotten sick just as I was reaching prime dating age, but I knew relationships were all about the push and pull. Loving someone gave them power over you, and that wouldn't be good for either of us. I was going to get my heart broken if I kept this up, but I didn't know how to make it stop. And if I was being honest, I really didn't want to.

This was why I was anti-romance. It turned people into idiots.

"Speaking of worse things," he continued. "Tell me what happened."

So I told him, keeping my voice down because I would have bet money that Sadie was listening at the door. Or Rachel. Probably both.

When I finished, he sighed. "I'm sorry, Casey. This is my fault. I intended to leave you alone because I thought you needed a little space to think things over. I figured I could keep an eye on you. I guess it would have been smart to tell you to stay in town, huh?"

I shook my head emphatically. "No, we're not going down that road!" His eyes widened, and I realized I was beginning to shout. I continued, careful to keep my voice down. "I'm responsible for me. You're not. And if we're going to be hunting demons together, or pretend dating, or whatever this is—"

"I'm not pretending," he murmured.

"Me either." Our eyes locked, but I pulled mine away before I got too swoony. "But I need to learn to stand on my own, you know? I can't be counting on you to swoop in and tell me what to do. It's not fair to either of us."

"So you want to hunt on your own? Without me?" He sounded wounded.

"I didn't say that, idiot. But it would be nice to understand what's going on so I can stop blundering around like I'm an idiot too."

"Done. Now, did you know you're very cute when you're irate?" he asked, leaning toward me and running a finger down my cheek.

I laughed. And then I got some more coffee and tried to think of anything but kissing him. It wasn't safe for either of us to get too attached, so I couldn't afford to encourage him, no matter how much I wanted to.

"I'm supposed to take Casey home with me," Michael said apologetically as we walked back to the dorm after runny omelets and black coffee at the cafeteria. Rachel and Sadie looked shocked, and his ears turned red. "I mean, back to her house," he clarified. "That's why your parents lent me the car."

"What?" Rachel asked.

"Um . . . the blue car? Your mom let me borrow it."

"Mrs. Kent loaned you her car? Dude, you are a god!" Sadie exclaimed, skipping down the sidewalk in front of us. "Next, you should ask if you two can have a sleepover."

"Sadie!" yelled Rachel, sticking her fingers into her ears. "You're talking about my little sister. I don't need to hear that. LA, LA, LA, LA!"

I tried not to laugh, but it came out as a snort instead. Nice.

It took a while to say our goodbyes because Rachel decided she had to wrap and rewrap the bandages on my arm three times, but I didn't mind. It was just nice to be back on speaking terms with her. About a half hour later, Michael and I finally managed to get into the car.

"Okay. So what next?" I said as we pulled away from the curb.

Michael glanced at me. "I was thinking about that sleepover." I punched him in the shoulder. "Ow. Or maybe we should just get you home and start your training. Unless you want to wait until you heal up?"

I shook my head. "If I wait, I'm only going to get hurt worse. I need to practice making Relics so I don't get demon dogged again."

"Agreed."

Back at my house, my mom fussed over my injury, making disapproving comments about people who don't clean up after themselves. She made me promise to keep the wound clean and bandaged, and then she excused herself to go grade papers.

"Are all mothers like that?" Michael asked, sitting on the couch and pulling me down next to him.

"What do you mean?"

"In the movies, they're always very emotional. But she seemed to take that well." I tilted my head to look at him. "Hey, you can learn a lot about people from movies," he added defensively.

"I guess. But I used to climb buildings for fun. Between that and the leukemia, she's learned to take things in stride."

I leaned over to look at him more closely. "You really have no clue what it's like, do you? Being human, I mean."

"No. But it's nothing you need to pity me for." But then his expression wavered. Sadness didn't sit right on his marble features. It looked off somehow, like his mouth wasn't supposed to bend that way.

"Michael, what happened with 693?"

"My thoughts are that obvious, huh?"

"Let's just say you shouldn't take up poker."

He shrugged. "There's not much to tell. He came into being just after me, and we did everything together. We trained in combat and learned the ways of demons and how to weave the power of the Between. Lots of aggressive testosterone stuff you probably wouldn't be interested in."

"Duh. Of course I would."

He chuckled weakly. "I was just a little older, a little faster, a little stronger. He grew to hate me for it. He pushed hard to be sent to earth before me, and even though I knew he had something to prove, I stepped aside so he'd be chosen. I thought it might make him feel better to finally be the first, but I think the jealousy only made him more susceptible to temptation. Ironic, right? I tried to help him. I didn't mean to send him to his doom."

"I'm sorry," I said, leaning my head on his shoulder.

"It's not your fault."

"It's not yours either." I rested my hands on my thighs. "So where should we go to practice?" I asked brightly. "I'm ready when you are."

He looked around at the overstuffed, brightly patterned furniture and the slightly scorched painting on the wall. My parents still hadn't noticed the new burned bits, or at least they hadn't said anything to me. Our living room wasn't particularly fancy, but it was comfortable. I was so glad my mother wasn't one of those people who bought furniture and then never let anyone use it.

"This looks good enough to me," he said.

"We're going to make Relics in my living room?"

"Where else would we make them?"

"I don't know." I shrugged. "Maybe I'm making this more complicated than it needs to be. But I know I'm missing something. I tried making one when that dog thing attacked me, and it totally failed. Do Relics all have to be metal? I wondered if maybe that was the problem."

"Relics can be anything. At some point, you won't even need an object to make one."

"Wow. I have no idea what you're saying." I glowered at him, only half serious, and he shrugged helplessly. "And thanks for the warning about the dogs, by the way. I didn't know they could be demons."

"Any living creature can be a demon. Sentinels don't always take human form."

"Yeah, I got that. So what did I do wrong?"

"It's all in the mind-set. Remember, all the power comes from balance between body and spirit. Feelings that pull you off-kilter like anger or fear will interfere with your ability to make Relics."

"There's no way I could look one of those dogs in the face and not be scared. I'm mortal, Michael. And I know it firsthand."

"Well, duh." I scowled at him, and he winked like he'd said something funny. "There's a difference between being scared and giving the fear power over you. Once you let your fear control you, it's impossible to be balanced, which makes it impossible to access the Between. Get it?"

"Uh . . . kind of. How do I know the difference?"

He shifted awkwardly, looking suddenly unsure. "Practice."

"Why am I worried that you have no idea what you're talking about?"

"Partly because I don't. I'm a creature of balance, so I haven't really experienced this firsthand. My job will be to put you into a bunch of different circumstances so you can figure out how to stay centered regardless of what the demons throw at you. You'll still be afraid, but you can use that fear as a tool instead of letting it force you into poor decisions."

I picked up one of the throw pillows and fiddled with it for a second while I thought about this. "So you're going to try to piss me off and make me scared."

"And then have you attempt to create Relics."

"That'll be great for our relationship," I said dryly, and then I felt like a bit of an idiot, because we were still in relationship limbo. Not quite together, but not quite apart either. "That was a joke."

"Was it?" he asked. The look he gave me made it so tempting to throw logic out the window.

"Yeah," I said, standing up before I did something stupid. "Should we get started?"

There was a long pause. I was all too conscious of his presence at my back. When he moved closer, I felt it without even looking. I wanted to turn around and kiss him. Part of the reason I wanted it so bad was because I knew I couldn't, but the knowledge didn't make it any easier to resist the impulse.

"That would probably be wise," he said.

"All right." I took a deep breath and let it out. "Let me meditate for a minute before we start. Because I'm not exactly centered right now."

"That's fair."

I sat on the floor, a meditation pillow propping me up so my legs didn't go instantly numb. Meditation was a big part of practice at the dojo, so I knew what to do even if it had never been one of my favorite things. I fell into a slow circle of breathing, in through the nose and out through the mouth. My eyes slowly closed. But still, it took a long time before my mind quieted.

"There's a chance they might try to get to you through your family," he said.

My eyes flew open. "What?"

"I told you I was going to jerk your chain. Now make a Relic."

"You expect me to create a Relic after that?"

He stood there silently, waiting. Part of me wanted to rant that this wasn't fair. He should have given me something easier to start with. But I'd seen how 693 had operated, and he'd been even younger than Michael. I didn't want to think about how much harder it would be to face an older, more experienced demon.

So I took a deep breath and pushed away the urge to smack him. How had it felt to make those first few Relics—the necklace and the key chain? If Michael was telling the truth, I'd made them into weapons; I'd channeled the Between into them without even knowing it. If I was going to do it again, I'd have to recapture how it felt. I remembered feeling desperate and afraid and confused, but then there was the part of me that had seen a challenge to be overcome. The part that wasn't afraid of death. It wouldn't go down without a fight. That part of me had taken my determination and honed it into a weapon. That was what I needed to access.

So I threw every ounce of my will into the throw pillow on the floor a few feet away. And for a second, I saw it flare with bluish, ghostly flames. A feeling of triumph rose in my throat; I let out a squeal of excitement. The flames went out, but I didn't care. I'd done it, and I could do it again.

"Good," Michael said, his voice stern and undeniably sexy. "Again."

I'd never been into shopping, but when Darcy invited me to the mall about a week later, I had to say yes. First of all, I still hadn't hung out with her except for at practice, and I felt like I should at least make an effort. And second, I would have agreed to stick bamboo sticks under my fingernails if it would have saved me from another afternoon spent trying to make Relics while Michael came up with new and interesting ways to screw with my head.

So she picked me up, and to the mall we went.

"Are you looking for something specific?" I asked as we walked toward the gleaming doors of the Wildwood Shopping Center.

"Actually," she said, "I just wanted to spend time with you. It seems like you're always with Michael these days. It's like I never get to see just you."

"I'm sorry." I nudged her with my elbow, trying for playfulness. "It's not because I don't want to see you. I'm just . . . you know. Thanksgiving family crap and homework and a new relationship and all that."

"Well, if you ask me, it's not such a good one if he's taking you away from all your friends."

"But he's not . . ." I trailed off. The reality was that I'd been doing my homeschool work every morning and Relic training every afternoon, followed more often than not by derby practice and more time with Michael. The only day I hadn't seen him was Thanksgiving, because I had to go to my grandma's and listen to her tell my parents for the umpteenth time that she wanted them to get real jobs. I'd talked to Kyle on the phone a few times and had gotten together with the crew once to play video games. After a few frosty moments, we'd shot at each other with virtual machine guns. That had seemed to help, although they still hadn't invited me free-running again. I wouldn't have had the time anyway.

I hadn't meant to blow them off, but I was doing just that. The saddest thing is that Michael and I weren't even really dating. Although, that saying about how you could cut the tension with a knife? I was starting to really understand what it meant. It was just a matter of time before something broke.

"I'm sorry," I said. "I don't want to be one of *those* girls. We'll hang out more; I promise."

"So you've got time?" She perked up immediately. "I mean, I've got to get a new charger for my cell, but can we stay for a while after that?"

"I'm not much of a shopper, but sure. Where do you want to go?"

"You'll see."

It took only a few minutes to buy a charger, and then she took off so quickly that I practically had to run to keep up. She had much longer legs than me. I was faster on skates now, but not so much on foot.

Finally I caught up to her in the middle of the Sears concourse. The area was pretty empty at the moment. In a month or so, the mall employees would decorate this space to look like Santa's workshop. But for now, it was just a big open space with lots of raised areas and random walls. It looked like a giant had dropped a big load of blocks on the floor, and instead of moving them, someone had decided to cover them with carpeting.

"Dude, what are we doing?" I asked, stopping at her side and panting a little.

Instead of answering, she flashed me an excited grin and sprinted at one of the mid-sized walls. It was maybe five feet tall. She ran straight up it, grabbed the top, and vaulted herself over.

Okay, now, this was cool. It didn't look like giant blocks to me anymore. It looked like one big freerunning course. We started leaping over blocks and tumbling down the other side. I ran up walls and did corkscrews and backflips and tic-tacs. I taught her some freerunning techniques on the biggest wall, a six-footer. Darcy did a few gymnastic passes across the floor, and then we started trying to outdo each other with the craziest flip combos we could come up with.

We gathered a small crowd of onlookers, and a few of them got out their phones and shot some video. The saleslady at the jewelry store next to us wasn't too happy about our impromptu show until one of our admirers went into her store and started trying stuff on. It bought us some time, but eventually the security guys showed up on their stupid Segways and told us we had to leave.

"That was the most fun ever," I said, wiping sweat from my forehead. "But I'm dying of thirst. Food court?"

"Definitely." She linked her arm with mine. It felt a little lame, but I didn't have the heart to pull away.

We got orange smoothies and sat down on the edge of one of the fountains in the middle of the food court, our legs dangling but not quite reaching the floor.

"So, what's up with you and Michael?" she asked.

I shrugged. "We're dating, I guess. He's pretty cool."

"Doesn't he seem . . . I dunno. Weird?"

I shrugged again. "All guys seem weird to me. I think it's in their DNA."

"Can't argue with that."

"What about you?" I looked her over. On the surface, she was still the same old Darcy. Gap-toothed, pigtailed, slightly dorky. "You've gone all quiet lately. You used to be . . ." I couldn't think of a way to say it that didn't sound like a put-down.

"A total spaz?" She smiled. "I think derby's settling me down. I feel very centered when I skate."

"And you're okay? Nothing you need to talk about?"

She cleared her throat and shook her head. "Nope. Nothing at all. Although, I wonder if that video of us is going to get YouTubed tonight."

"Oh my God, we totally have to check after practice."

We did. It was. And I have to say that we looked pretty darned awesome too.

I showed up at the convention center for our next bout assuming I'd be warming the bench. Of course I wanted to skate, but I kept reminding myself that it would come with time. With every practice, it felt like the team accepted me a little more. Regardless of whether I skated this time, I felt like I'd proved that I belonged, both to them and to myself.

I'd just sat down on a folding chair to watch the rest of the team begin their warm-ups, when Barbageddon hobbled up in an Aircast.

"What happened?" I leapt to my feet like a demon might pop out at any minute and try to take out her other foot too.

She shifted her crutches and patted me soothingly on the shoulder. "Calm down. It's just a bad sprain. My sister and I crashed our neighbor's trampoline. And I do mean *crashed.*"

"Oh." I sat back down, feeling foolish. "Well, that sucks."

"Are you kidding?" She flashed me a grin. "Once I stopped swearing, I realized this wasn't such a bad thing after all, because it gives me an opportunity to watch you skate."

I blinked. "Oh. I hadn't thought of that."

"What are you waiting for?" she asked. "Get your gear on, idiot!"

I stuck my tongue out at her first, but my heart wasn't really in it. It was too busy alternately racing with nervousness and leaping with excitement. I tried to play it cool as I joined the rest of the girls on the track, but Darcy squealed when I skated out to join them, and I couldn't resist echoing her. Besides, I was entitled to a little excitement after everything I'd been through.

After warm-ups, we reported back to the bench for our pre-bout strategy meeting. I tried not to take it too personally when Michael designated Ruthanasia as our first jammer. She smirked at me as she stretched the starred helmet panties over her head. I never understood why they called them "helmet panties," since they were really just stretchy fabric that you put on your helmet to designate what position you were playing at the time. I think someone just liked the word "panties."

"Okay, so Ruthanasia is jamming. . . . Ragnarocker, you take pivot," Michael said without even looking up from his clipboard. I opened my mouth to protest—after all the hard work I'd put in to get here, he wasn't going to let me skate? "We're going to keep Casey as our secret weapon for a little while. We'll tire 'em out, and then you'll skate their pants off. Okay, Case?"

"Call me Casaclysm," I said. I liked my new derby name. It cracked me up.

It felt good to be a secret weapon. But it still hurt to sit down on the row of folding chairs that served as our bench and watch as Ruthanasia, Ragnarocker, and a bunch of our other skaters took their places on the rink alongside the Tilt-a-Girls. My hands fiddled nervously with my official yellow and white Apocalypsies jersey. The longer I sat, the more nervous I got.

"Oh my God. I can't believe how many people are here," Darcy said, plopping down next to me.

I scanned the crowd. If I'd known I'd be skating, I would have invited my parents, but it was probably too late now. Not that I would have been able to locate them if they'd been there, because the place was nice and busy. About half of the five thousand seats were already full, and this was only the junior bout. People would keep trickling in for the main event. I saw signs and derby tees and lots of people with Day-Glo hair. The crowd hummed, a steady stream of sound that made it necessary to speak up if you wanted to be heard. I'd have to remember that out on the track.

"I think it's pretty average attendance." I tried to sound calm, but it was an uphill battle. My nerves would settle down as soon as I got out there, but I wasn't built for waiting.

"Yeah, but it's totally different when you're out here and all those people are staring at you."

"No kidding." I held out my fist to her. "Good luck, Dee Stroyer."

"You too, Casaclysm."

She bumped my knuckles with hers and gave me one of her gap-toothed grins. I was glad to see her in a good mood.

The whistle blew to start the jam, and the pack moved off their line, setting a fairly brutal pace. The second whistle— Ruthanasia and Hoosya Mama, the Tilt-a-Girl jammer, flew off their line, jockeying for position. Ruthanasia came in way too hot, hitting the pack like a bowling ball full of dynamite, and instantly earned a major penalty for illegal contact to the back. The ref signaled her out; she slid into the penalty box with a scowl. We watched as Hoosya Mama racked up an easy triple grand slam. I could have punched Ruthanasia right then for making such a stupid mistake. Her douche baggery was going to cost us the bout if she kept it up.

Frankly, I couldn't decide who to scowl at more. Ruthanasia for being her usual hotheaded self, or Michael for not seeing that I was the better choice to start, if only because I was a little better at keeping my temper under wraps these days. All the Relic training was starting to make me all Zen.

Darcy left with a squeal to skate in the second jam, and now I was one of the only players still warming the bench. I tried not to feel bad about that, with an emphasis on "tried." It got particularly hard when Ruthanasia got pinned behind the Tilt-a-Girl powerhouse blockers, Honey Beater and Skirt Cobain, and couldn't get anywhere. But Dee Stroyer, Ragnarocker, and Angel Pop kept Hoosya under wraps too, and the jam played out without much of anything happening.

Michael came up behind me. "It's time. Show them how it's done, Casaclysm."

I didn't wait to be told twice. I launched off the chair like one of those demon dogs was nipping at my heels. It was finally happening. When I hit the jammer line, I took a moment to look around at my pack. Ruthanasia at pivot, Dee Stroyer, Ragnarocker, and Dawn & Quartered blocking. Skirt Cobain was jamming for the Girls. I'd seen how she moved—quick and light on her skates despite her solid, muscular form. But I knew I was faster.

The ref sounded the first whistle for the pack to start moving, and my muscles tensed. I crouched low on my skates, balanced on my toe stops. He sounded the second whistle for the jammers. I flew off the line, my torso low, the hiss of skates hard and fast as Skirt and I fought for dominance. The pack was moving slowly, the blockers jostling for position too.

We reached the back of the pack; Dee Stroyer took my hand and whipped me forward, rocketing me past two of the Tilt-a-Girl blockers. I came up behind Ragnarocker, my fingertips light on her shoulder, using her as a shield while I looked for a hole in the defense. Stop Tart, another Girl blocker, came up alongside me, shifting her hips and trying to drive a wedge between Rock and me. We moved in automatic, well-practiced unison. Rock shifted right, hitting Stop Tart so hard that she fell over and skidded out of bounds. I shifted left, legs pistoning as I rocketed through the empty space that suddenly opened in front of me. I skated hard and fast, eyes and ears alert for additional defenders.

The announcer's voice boomed over the loudspeaker. "And

now, ladies and gentlemen, referee Edward Sullen points the fickle Finger of Power at rookie jammer Casaclysm, designating her as the lead jammer for the first time in her skating career!"

Sure enough, there he was, one hand pointing straight at me and the other up to the heavens like I'd been chosen by a divine power. Which I guess in a strange way wasn't so far from the truth. I couldn't resist a little hotdogging; I pumped my fist in the air, and the crowd cheered.

Enough of that. My skates hit the floor in an increasing rhythm. The pack lay ahead, just around the next curve, and I was dying to score some points. I crouched low, rocketing past the Tilt-a-Girl pivot before she even saw me.

"Jammer on right!" she shouted, her words distorted by the mouth-guard.

I dodged left, ducking under the outstretched arms of D&Q and Honey Beater as they struggled to own the space. Another blocker swerved in front of me, and I didn't even have time to see who it was. I spun, skimming past her by the barest of margins, and ended up out in front of the pack, rolling backward and not entirely sure how it had happened.

Before I could totally lose momentum, I spun back around and kept on skating, sparing an eye for the clock. Still almost a minute left in the jam, plenty of time to score another grand slam. Perhaps I was getting a little cocky, but maybe I deserved a little self-indulgence.

The next pass was even easier. It was like I felt the holes

before I even saw them. My body moved instinctively through the crush of the pack, and my blockers knew exactly where I needed them. They cleared the floor, and I charged through.

I would have scored another grand slam, or maybe even two, if Ruthanasia hadn't tripped me.

It was like one minute I was sailing out into the empty rink in front of the pack, and then there was a leg in front of me, a leg wearing tights printed with daggers and skulls, and then I was flying. There was just enough time for me to appreciate how much it was going to hurt when I landed, and then I was down. The pads absorbed most of the shock, but I still managed to ding my hip pretty bad. Another ref by the unfortunate name of Bustin Jieber sent Ruthanasia out again. I scrambled to my feet just as Skirt charged forward and scored. I called off the jam a moment too late, giving away two points.

As I made my way back to the bench, all I could think of was how I was going to kill Ruthanasia. Slowly. And with great pain.

17

Halftime came all too soon. I had only twenty-five minutes to corner Ruthanasia, so I didn't dork around. When she went into the ladies' room, I followed. By some miracle, the other three stalls were empty, so I leaned against the grungy tile wall and waited for her to open the stall door.

"What is your problem?" I snarled the minute she stepped out. "I thought we'd agreed to keep this out of the rink."

She took an involuntary step back, and I could see how much that ticked her off. So she got right up in my face, like aggression would make up for the weakness she'd just shown.

"I don't know what you're talking about, Kent. But I don't like your attitude."

"Well, my attitude might suck, but at least I don't intentionally trip my teammates."

Her face went blank. Only a jumping muscle in her cheek showed how angry she really was. As if she had anything to be pissed about. I wasn't the reason we were behind 47–40.

"You didn't just accuse me of tripping you on purpose, did you?" she asked, all cold and deliberate. "Because that's ridiculous. I might not like you, but I wouldn't throw the bout. That's stupid."

"That's what I thought about a millisecond after I vaulted over your leg. No way was that an accident."

"Why not?" She threw up her hands. "Christ, it's like you're determined to make me the bad guy. And from the get-go, I was just trying to make sure you didn't get killed. Sometimes I don't even know why I bother."

"No, you were trying to get rid of me because I threaten you. And that's not even bringing up the part where I saved your ass from getting throttled."

"What?"

"Why am I the only person who seems to remember this?" I sighed. "The parking lot at the Skate Lake? That random girl was beating the crap out of you until I intervened, and you didn't even thank me."

Her head drooped. "You don't know the whole story." For a split second, I thought we might have a bonding moment, and then she seemed to remember we were supposed to be fighting. Her head lifted, and she started in on me again. "Besides, I'm not the one who came through the bathroom door looking for a fight."

By this time, we were face to face, and it was only a question of who was going to throw the first punch. I didn't know how things had escalated so quickly, but I knew it had to stop if we were ever going to be truly teammates. I took a deliberate step back, inhaling a long, cleansing breath. Maybe the trip really had been unintentional. Ruthanasia seemed like the kind of person who really liked to win; no way would she jeopardize the team's standing because of her hatred of me. I'd jumped to conclusions once again.

"All right, all right." I held up my hands, urging calm. "Maybe you're right. I shouldn't have jumped down your throat."

"Damn straight you shouldn't have!" Her face was red with anger.

The door flew open and banged against the wall, saving us from further argument. Unfortunately, my relief was short-lived. A pair of guys ambled in, and I called out, "Wrong bathroom, dudes," before I got a good look at them. They looked like twins—with the same plasticky-looking, inhuman faces and expressions of gleeful menace. Demons, both of them. And from the looks of things, they'd stolen their hair from 1985. It was *feathered*.

"Oh, great," I muttered, automatically reaching up to unclasp my necklace, which I'd finally gotten fixed. "It's the attack of the demonic-hair band."

"You're in the wrong bathroom, losers," Ruthanasia scoffed, stepping away from me. I edged in her direction, because I wasn't going to abandon her to demons, no matter how much she ticked me off. Of course, she didn't understand that. She glared at me.

The demons stopped side by side in front of the door, blocking our only exit.

"The Lord of the Flies—" said one of them.

"Was most displeased when you banished his servitor," finished the other.

"Servitor?" I wrinkled my nose. "Do you mean 693 or the dog?"

"Silence!" they ordered.

Their mouths stretched like putty. The skin of their faces rippled, and I swore I saw hands underneath, pushing on the skin like they were trapped and wanted desperately to get out.

"Holy crap," Ruthanasia said, her eyes widening. "What the heck is wrong with them?"

"They're demons," I said. Under different circumstances, she probably would have argued, but it was hard to debate their inhumanity. "This'll protect you." I shoved my necklace into her hands just as they charged. She looked down at it with shocked eyes.

"Wait. Demons?" she asked.

There was no time to explain. "Make for the door!" I yelled, grabbing her hand and towing her after me. She didn't resist; I guess the one good thing about the freaky display they'd just put on was that it didn't leave much room for argument. We accelerated as quickly as possible in the short space we had. The demons waited for us, their clothes swelling and undulating as their bodies struggled to contain all the nastiness inside.

Just before we reached them, I called out again. "Double knee slide!"

We dropped in perfect unison, sliding on our knee pads underneath their outstretched arms. I struck fast as I slid, hitting pressure points on the inside of the thigh. Those strikes would have dropped a human, but the demon didn't even seem to notice.

I slammed into the door. I scrambled back onto my skates and put my back to the wall, Ruthanasia by my side. The demons leered, trying to frighten us into submission. Obviously they had no idea who they were dealing with.

"Get out of here." I jerked my thumb toward the door behind us. "Get Michael."

"Not until you tell me what's going on," she said.

This was the last thing I needed. I flicked a scowl at her, and one of the demons took advantage of my momentary distraction and sprang. I heard Ruthanasia shout as I went down, cracking my head on the tile. The demon pinned me to the floor before I could regain my bearings, his feathered hair tickling my nose. His eyes glowed red, and a forked tongue darted out to taste the air.

Out of the corner of my eye, I could see Ruthanasia and the other demon grappling on the floor only a few feet away. Its fangs were long and vampiric; it opened its mouth and displayed them to her, enjoying her muffled cry of fear.

I had to do something fast. All I needed was a second to focus my aching head, which was easier said than done when a demonic snake tongue was flapping in the air inches from my face. I'd made Relics so many times in my living room, but it was an awful lot harder in the middle of a fight for your life.

Those meditation exercises had seemed so stupid, so easy. But I would have gladly done a week's worth of them right then if it meant I could chill out enough to make another Relic.

The demon leaned slowly toward me, enjoying the horror written all over my face. I was losing the struggle against panic; this wasn't how it was supposed to go. Michael had been tough during training, but the fear and anger I felt completely eclipsed anything he'd put me through. It was more than I was prepared to handle.

But the only other choice I had was to concede defeat, and I wasn't ready to do that. My hand groped along the floor, searching for something I could use as a distraction. If I had a minute to regroup, we might actually survive.

My fingers encountered a wet puddle on the floor. Under any other circumstances, I would have recoiled in disgust, but I didn't have the time for that. I fought for focus. We were about to find out if I could make a Relic out of spilled toilet water. I got my hand nice and wet, sent up a little prayer to anybody that happened to be listening, and flicked shining white droplets right into the demon's face.

The demon recoiled, shrieking, and it was so unexpected that I just lay there and watched it for a second when I should have been getting the heck out of the way. I probably would have been in a lot of trouble if he'd still had a face.

The demon was dissolving. Apparently you *can* make Relics out of potty water.

His entire head quickly crumbled as I watched. When it was gone, the body started to topple, and I put up my hands to deflect it. It turned to ash when it hit them, spraying me in the face with powdered demon. I accidentally breathed in a big mouthful and began to cough and choke.

I rolled over onto my knees, hacking uncontrollably. My lungs burned; my eyes watered. And I could only wheeze as the remaining demon flipped Ruthanasia onto her back and pinned her there, opening its mouth wide to take a bite. Before I could even move a muscle, she shoved my necklace into the thing's mouth. It didn't even have time to shriek before it burst into incandescent flames.

She pushed away from it until she bumped into the wall. Then she wrapped her arms around her knees and began rocking back and forth.

"Ruthanasia." I took her by the shoulders. "Are you okay?"

"They . . . You . . ." She was shaking uncontrollably. It made me feel a little better about the fact that I was sick with delayed nerves.

"It's okay," I said. "Everything's okay."

We sat there for a few moments, clinging to each other. Strangely, it felt better having her there, especially considering that I'd been fully intending to pick a fight with her about ten minutes ago.

Finally she said, "So is this why you've been such a touchy wench all this time?"

"Um . . . yeah. The constant threat of demon attack will do that to you."

I pushed myself up on shaky legs and wiped the demon bits off my face with a wet paper towel. As I did, something crunched under my skates. My lucky katana necklace lay gleaming on the tile in the middle of a vaguely humanoid black splotch.

Ruthanasia picked up the necklace and put it in her pocket. I didn't stop her. At this point, she needed it more than I did. They might come back for her once that fly lord guy learned that she'd banished one of his demons too.

"I think we're okay now, aren't we?" I asked.

"Definitely okay." She took in a shaking breath. "Now hand me one of those towels so I can wipe this crap off my face. I'm not going back out there with demon slobber all over me."

After we cleaned up, I told Ruthanasia she should go find some ice. One of her eyes was purpling; the demon had popped her a good one in the nose. At least her heavy eye makeup made it difficult to notice.

"You don't want it to swell," I said. "It'll be hard to see, and we need you for the second half."

"Screw the second half!" she exclaimed. "I want to know what's going on!"

I couldn't blame her, but I wanted to talk to Michael first. I wasn't sure how much I should tell her. And besides, I was wondering why he hadn't shown up to help when the demons had attacked. He'd known something was wrong when I was fighting the demon dog. Was his Spidey sense broken, or did he just figure that my training wheels were off now?

"We'll talk," I promised, "but after the bout. Somewhere private. Right now, I think the best place for both of us is in the middle of a crowded room. It's safer."

She eyed me skeptically, but a quick glance at the scorch marks on the tile seemed to convince her.

"All right," she said. "But if you don't explain after the bout, I'm hunting you down and beating the answers out of you."

"Deal."

I opened the bathroom door and rolled out with her close behind. She had the look of somebody who accepts what they're seeing only because they expect to wake up any minute. I knew how she felt. Sometimes I still expected to wake up, and I'd had some time to get used to it all.

Michael wasn't in the locker room. Not on the bench or anywhere on the rink. And with each second that passed, I grew more and more nervous. He wouldn't just abandon me, not willingly.

I dashed past the concession stands and tried to ignore the panic growing in the pit of my stomach, but it was a struggle. Michael could take care of himself. So why was I so freaking worried? I made myself relax, the chaos in my mind slowly settling. Yes, I lost valuable seconds by doing that, but it was quicker than dashing around aimlessly like an idiot.

Now I knew where to go. I could feel the electric tingle of the Between that he carried inside him. And if I could feel him, he was alive.

I went up.

Michael was on top of the convention center. The roof was probably easy to reach for those of us with handy dandy pop-out wings, but I had one heck of a time finding an access door that would get me up there. Thank goodness it was unlocked, because by that time I was ready to scream.

I carefully climbed the metallic, gridlike ladder up to the rooftop, placing my skates with deliberation. Stealth would have been advisable, but there was no way I could make it happen without losing valuable skate-removal minutes. Besides, that ladder was so loud that I couldn't have snuck up on an eighty-year-old with a hearing aid. The roof was huge and mazelike, studded with random pipes and big concrete blocks with fans sticking out of the sides. But Michael wasn't hard to spot. In fact, it would have been impossible to miss the flickering white outline of my not-quite-boyfriend with a sword of fire in his hands and a halo of light emanating from his body. Black forms tipped in red flames fell to his sword; the weapon danced to music I couldn't hear. Sparks flew as he fought a small squadron of shadowy attackers. I tried to follow the battle, but it all happened at a speed that human eyes couldn't process.

So I bit my nails, waiting for the end. I was ready just in case he wasn't the victor. Or just in case what came out wasn't my Michael but a demon. I didn't know whether this kind of fight broke the rules or not. Fighting shadows wasn't exactly something I had experience with. And that worried me, because if he turned demon, it would be up to me. I began searching the rooftop for something I could make a Relic out of, but everything was bolted down.

Before I found a suitable weapon, the fight was over. Michael had won. When he walked toward me with little sparks of white light jumping off him like grease from a hot pan, I looked at him carefully.

"Is that you? Like, really you?"

He grinned. "Of course. Why wouldn't it be?"

I kept my distance, even though I wanted to run up and fling myself into his arms. Because really, that sparking thing was hot.

"I don't know." I eyed him warily. "It seems too easy. Ruthanasia and I just took out a pair of demons in the bathroom. The two of them put together weren't half as tough as 693. It doesn't make sense. I feel like maybe we're missing something. Like maybe these attacks were meant to distract us? And if so, from what?"

His smile faltered and then disappeared completely. "Yeah, maybe so. We should get inside, where it's safer. The second half starts in a few minutes anyway."

I followed, although I have to admit that the bout didn't seem quite as important as it had earlier. I couldn't believe I'd picked a fight with Ruthanasia over it and then let her watch my back during a demon attack. Apparently I didn't need brains to be a demon hunter. Or self-control either.

The Apocalypsies won the bout by two points. I scored five grand slams. Derby girls stopped by my spot in the locker room to give me a congratulatory pat on the arm as I put on my pants; fans intercepted me on the way out to the car to drop off my gear to ask for pictures and autographs. I should have been ecstatic.

Except I wasn't. I couldn't stop wondering what was going on. People didn't just walk off unmarked after facing down demons, especially when the demons had to have known what you were capable of after you'd taken out some of their soldiers. Why would they have ambushed me with so few fighters? The single demon dog made sense—that had probably been a spur-of-the-moment attempt to get to me before I was able to develop my abilities. But the demonic-hair brothers didn't compute at all. From what I'd gathered, demon lords had a lot of resources at their disposal, and they were smart. Why would the Lord of the Flies waste two demons when he could have sent five? No way could I have survived against five at once. The whole thing really bothered me.

So I smiled and nodded as I pushed my way through the crowd, but I didn't register half of what people were saying to me. I was more than a little surprised when I looked up to see that I was in the process of autographing Kyle's program.

"Dude, did you take a blow to the cranium or something?" he roared. "Because you are not all here."

"No," I said, shaking my head like that was going to magically clear it. "I'm sorry. I'm obsessing a little."

"You should!" He threw his arms around me and squeezed, hard and fast. I squeaked as he pushed all the air out of me. "You're going to be the best freaking jammer in the history of the world! Seriously, Case, I had no idea how tough this sport was. I thought it was fake, like wrestling. I already signed up to referee, and I'm hoping to get into managing a team. You'll have to help me come up with a name."

When I didn't immediately respond, he let go and searched my face. He knew something was up. If I didn't convince him otherwise, he'd follow me around in a misguided effort to protect me, which was the last thing I needed. I had to chill. And his newfound derby fandom was something to be thankful for. I'd get to see more of him, provided the demons didn't eat my soul first.

"We'll come up with something good," I said, forcing a smile. "Hey, check this out."

I twisted so he could see the bruise already surfacing on my hip. I'd taken that hit from Ruthanasia, or maybe I'd gotten it during the fight in the bathroom. I wasn't sure. The bruise was about the size of a dinner plate, and a dark crosshatch pattern ran over the top, like my fishnets had been implanted into my skin. In a way, I guess they had.

"Dude," he said admiringly. "That's awesome."

For once, I didn't worry about the size of the bruise or the potential ramifications for my health. I just soaked up the compliment. My face relaxed into a grin. No matter what happened next, I had this to be proud of.

Michael pushed his way through the crowd toward us. "Casey? We need to talk," he demanded, not even saying hello.

"Oh, hey." I snagged his sleeve and pulled him closer. "This is my best friend, Kyle. Kyle, this is Michael."

"Nice to meet you," Michael said automatically. Then he leaned down to whisper into my ear. "Listen, I've thought of something important—"

"So you want to go out for pizza, Casey?" Kyle asked. "I want to grill you about this derby thing. I'll need to get cracking on the rules."

I opened my mouth to respond, but Michael cut me off. "We've got to watch the second bout and go to the after-party," he said. "It's mandatory."

"Yes, thank you." I folded my arms, pulling away from him. "I can carry on my own conversation all by myself, you know."

The muscles in his jaw twitched. "Sorry."

I turned back to Kyle. "I do have to stay, but what are you up to tomorrow? I could come over and hang out."

Kyle perked right up. "That would be awesome. You might like this new game I got. *Gangland*? The minute I saw the flapper with a tommy gun, I knew she was meant for you."

"It's a deal," I said. "Call me when you get up."

"All right. I should run." He eyed Michael cautiously. "Nice to meet you, man."

"Likewise."

As soon as we made it back into the convention center, I frowned at Michael. "Dude, you've got to chill. I've got guy friends. If you can't deal with that, we've got a problem."

He looked around at the hordes of people waiting in line for hot dogs and pizza and shirts with derby girls outlined in sparkles on the front.

"Come with me," he said, taking my hand and pulling me toward the locker rooms.

In all the time I'd known him, I'd never processed how strong he really was. You'd think I would have realized, given all the times I'd swooned over his muscles, but I guess I'd been too busy appreciating them for their decorative value. Now I was pissed, and I didn't want to hold his hand, but there was no getting free. His fingers closed over mine like they were made of stone, and I didn't feel any give at all when I tugged.

"Let me go," I said. "Now."

He didn't respond, just pulled me past the sign designating the area for derby staff only.

"You are impinging on my free will here," I said, anger making my voice shake. "Let me go right now, damn it."

He released me so fast that I nearly fell over. Then he opened the door next to me and pushed me inside. We were in a small, unused dressing room; the only furniture was one of those vanities with the big lights all around it and an old couch with a popped cushion.

I didn't like being pushed, or herded, or ordered around. My hands shoved at his chest; its hardness bruised my knuckles, but I didn't stop. He'd never manhandled me before, and I was decidedly not cool with it.

"What is wrong with you?" I shrieked.

"Nothing." But the word came out all strangled, and my anger quickly dissolved into fear. If he really had turned while he'd been up on the roof, and he'd been acting normal while he waited to get me alone, I'd taken the bait.

"Michael, you're freaking me out right now," I said. "You're acting like a jealous ass."

He blinked then, and his pale eyes locked onto mine. I couldn't help searching for a flicker of red in their depths. I didn't see it, but I didn't know whether that meant I could relax.

"This is not about being jealous," he said. "Or about our relationship. This is about the fact that I think Ruthanasia might be demon-tainted, and every moment we waste gossiping is another moment she goes unchecked."

I literally felt my stomach drop. "What?" I demanded.

"Quiet." He pressed his body against mine, like he might be able to muffle the sound waves. "It's the only explanation for that attack. They keep me busy on the roof while she wins your trust by standing with you against two low-level demons. Then when your back is turned, she takes you out."

"Which is why she didn't totally flip out?"

"Exactly."

"But she doesn't look like a demon. I mean, it's usually pretty obvious that something's going on."

"That's true of young low-level demons. They often have no control over their hunger. But something like that factory would require an older, more established demonic presence. The demons in charge of the warehouse wouldn't be obvious, even to me."

"So what do we do?" I started to shake. I knew Ruthana-sia had been up to no good ever since day one, but I hadn't imagined this. Her plan had almost worked too; I'd just told her about the demons like it was nothing. What had I been thinking?

"I don't know." His brows drew together in a worried fur-row. "I need to report in. My brother might know what to do."

"Call him, then."

He shook his head. "I have to talk to him in person. We have pretty strict protocols about what we can say over the phone. It's safer that way."

"You're leaving me alone?" My heart leapt into my throat. He couldn't just leave me here alone with her. What if she tried something? Would my Relics work against a senior demon? I had the niggling feeling that I was missing some piece of information, something important, but it kept slipping out of my grasp. "So let me get this straight. First you manhandle me because I'm not acting fast enough, and then you expect me to sit around and wait? Are you nuts?"

"It's . . ." He blinked. "I didn't mean to manhandle you. But you weren't listening."

"From now on, if you tell me it's important, I'll listen." I fixed him with a stern look. "But if you drag me around like that ever again, that's it."

"I'm sorry." He folded me into his arms. "I may have gotten a little carried away. I've been waiting for this a long time."

"Don't be sorry. Just don't do it again."

He kissed the top of my head. "All right."

"I don't want you to go," I said, relaxing into his arms. "I'm frightened, and no amount of meditation is going to change that."

"Me too," he said. "I won't lose you, Casey."

And then his hands tilted my head up to his. His lips met mine. I knew I should resist, but pulling away wasn't going to change how we both felt. His body came up against me. I was pinned against the wall; my hands went into his hair. We fell onto the couch, and the damaged cushion spewed a cloud of fluff into the air. But at that point, I couldn't have cared less.

We kissed like the world was ending. Maybe it was.

Michael seemed just fine after the make-out session. I worried he might start crying fire once the lip-lock was over, but he just told me to be careful. After he left, I went out to the stands. Attendance at the second bout was mandatory, and if I stuck with the team, I'd be able to keep an eye on Ruthanasia. She was sitting two rows behind the rest of the team. I doubted she'd be able to do anything to me with everyone watching, but she still gave me a creepy-crawly feeling between my shoulder blades.

"There you are!" Darcy waved me over, pointing to an empty seat. "I saved you a spot."

I kept shooting glances at Ruthanasia as I edged past my teammates, and ended up stepping on Ragnarocker, who gave me a mock growl that made me laugh despite the huge ball of nerves in my stomach.

"It's a good thing you're such a kicking jammer," she said, grinning, "or I'd have to beat the crap out of you for stomping on me."

"You'd have to try," I shot back, and then it was her turn to laugh.

"So how's the bout going?" I asked, sitting down next to Darcy. She didn't even seem to have heard me. "Hey, D!" I poked her. "How's the bout?"

"Um . . ." She looked up at the scoreboard. "Well, the Hotsies are winning."

"I can see that," I replied. "How are the jammers?"

She looked blankly down at the floor, where they were setting up for a new jam.

"You know, I have no idea." Then she laughed. "I expected to be tired, but this is ridiculous. It's like I can't even think."

"There's an empty room with a sofa one door past our locker room, if you want to take a nap. I'll wake you up in a little while if you want."

She considered. "You know, I might do that. Otherwise, I'm going to fall unconscious at the after-party, and who knows what pranks you lunatics would play on me."

I held my hands up over my head in a mock halo, but she rolled her eyes. Evidently, she wasn't buying it.

"It's down the hallway to the right," I said, pointing. "No one will bother you there."

"Thanks," she said, stifling a yawn. "I'll see you in a little while."

After she left, I watched some of the bout. I liked the idea that we could scope out the competition. The best junior league team got to play a charity match against the senior league, and I was determined to skate in that bout. Although, if we lost Ruthanasia to the forces of darkness, I wasn't so sure about the team's chances of winning.

Then she sat down next to me, like my thinking about her had miraculously summoned her. I nearly jumped out of my skin.

"You okay?" she asked. She looked genuinely concerned, and I wondered if maybe she took acting lessons.

"Yeah," I said shortly. "Just jumpy."

I wanted to leap down her throat and ask her how she could work with the demons. I wondered what they'd promised her. Maybe it was Michael. She'd always seemed to have a crush on him, but there was no way I'd let her have him.

The Hotsies scored another grand slam.

"They're pretty good," she said.

I nodded.

"Last year, my sister Lauren and I got into Wicca," she said. The statement seemed to come out of nowhere, and I was pretty startled and confused. Why would a demon confide in me? Was she trying to make me empathize with her so I'd be more vulnerable? I told myself not to fall for it but to listen carefully. Maybe she'd tell me something useful. "I thought it was harmless, but then Lauren's boyfriend cheated on her over the summer, and she tried to call down this evil spirit to curse him and the other girl. It didn't seem to do anything, so no big deal, right? But after that she was different. She started doing drugs, stealing, all kinds of stuff.

"One night she attacked me with a kitchen knife, and it was like something else was looking out of her eyes. She left home, and I was kind of relieved, because what was I supposed to do, press charges against my own sister? She'd hunt me down every once in a while, demanding money. The day you saw us in the parking lot, she was really bad. I tried to get her to come home, maybe go into treatment, and you saw how that idea went over. Two days later, they found her body on the street. Overdose."

"Oh my God. I am so sorry." The words felt inadequate. Even though I knew this all had to be a put-on, my heart still went out to her. I couldn't help it.

She shrugged, a small, helpless movement. "Everybody blamed the drugs, but I just know that curse backfired. She let something out, and it got inside her and ate her up. When I saw those guys in the bathroom, that's the first thing I thought of. I knew they weren't right, just like her." She looked at me then for the first time since she'd started speaking. "I sound like a total nutcase, don't I?"

"No." The crowd erupted into cheers around us as someone on the floor did something interesting. I didn't even care. "I've seen some pretty weird stuff recently too."

"So what were those things?" Her voice stayed level, but I felt her shudder.

"Demons. People make deals with them. Can you believe that?"

"You'd have to be a total idiot to do that," she said, and her face was completely serious. "I wouldn't want to turn out like Lauren." She stuffed her hand into her pocket and pulled something out. "I almost forgot. Here's your necklace."

I didn't want to touch it. Maybe she'd put some kind of hex on it or something, because why else would the Relic have stopped working? Unless Michael had been wrong about her? I didn't know what to think. "You keep it. Just in case."

She nodded, her eyes back on the floor as the skaters went in circles.

"I'm sorry about Lauren," I blurted out, although I didn't know if I believed her. I was second-guessing everything and everybody now. But it seemed like the right thing to say, if you were talking to someone who wasn't a demon in disguise. And I had to keep up that façade, whether I liked it or not.

"Me too."

19

The after-party was at Bobbles, one of the many hole-in-the-wall sports bars around town that I'd never set foot in. The place wasn't very big, for starters. When you cram four teams' worth of derby girls into a small, narrow bar along with twenty assorted support staff and a couple hundred fans, it gets crowded pretty quick. Darcy drove me, since Michael still hadn't returned, and there was already a long line outside the door when we pulled into the parking lot.

At least the line moved fast, although I wasn't sure where they were putting all the people. I followed Darcy through the door, only to be stopped by a pair of fans in Hotsie hoodies who'd clearly been waiting to pounce on me. Darcy continued on, pointing toward the bathrooms.

"Oh, you're that new Apocalypsie jammer, aren't you?"

shrieked one of the girls at the top of her lungs, despite the fact that I was standing only about a foot and a half away.

"Yep. That's me." I craned my neck, looking around for Ruthanasia, but she was nowhere to be seen.

"Can we get a picture with you?" asked the second. She had orange hair that clashed with her hoodie.

"Sure." I posed for the pic and turned to leave, but the orange-haired girl grabbed my arm.

"We want to be derby girls so bad," she said, tugging me off into a corner. I could have resisted, but it seemed kind of rude. They were fans, after all. The fact that I had fans was pretty flattering when I stopped to think about it. "I want my name to be Orange Crush."

"And I'm going to be Anita Mann," added the other girl proudly.

"That's great," I said, putting my back to the wall and attempting to relax. "So how long have you been skating?"

"Oh, I haven't gotten my skates yet," said Anita. "But I'll do that soon."

"Me either. But I got some of the best tights ever from Too Fast. They've got daggers and roses printed on them, and . . ."

Orange Crush proceeded to give me a complete rundown of every kind of derby-appropriate clothing she'd ever purchased, and clearly she'd been at it for a while. I couldn't help but tune her out, although I kept nodding and making encouraging noises every time she paused for breath, which admittedly wasn't very often.

I scanned the crowd but couldn't see anyone I knew who

might come to my rescue. I assumed Darcy was still in the bathroom, and I couldn't see any of the other Apocalypsies from where I was standing.

"I like fishnets." Orange Crush kept prattling. "But it's so hard to find them in colors other than black, don't you agree?"

I nodded again, looking past her flushed and smiling face to the shelves behind her. That's when I finally realized why they'd called the place Bobbles—the walls were lined with glassed-in shelves full of bobbleheads. It was still hard for me to think of these silly little figures as instruments of torture. I wanted a closer look. The shelf nearest to our table held three random basketball players, a Carolina Bulldog, and Yoda.

My eyes were automatically drawn to the Yoda. He had a huge green head, ears longer than his legs, and a light saber that clashed with his complexion. It was strange, because his little bobbly head was rocking slowly back and forth, despite the fact that he was encased in glass.

Yoda blinked.

I jumped a little.

"Are you okay?" Anita asked me.

"Yeah," I replied. "Fine. Just got a chill."

That was enough for Orange Crush. She had to know that I wasn't listening, but she didn't seem to care. She kept talking.

That left me free to look at the Yoda a little more closely. Its beady little eyes darted from side to side. The movement was barely discernible, but I knew I wasn't imagining it.

I took a few calming breaths, the way I'd practiced so many times, and looked at it again. My eyes blurred as I tried to see past the physical and into the spiritual realm. I wasn't so surprised to see the cloud of black that hung around it. The whole place was choking with the stuff; I suddenly found it very difficult to breathe, even though I knew the pollution wasn't physical. And inside the Yoda's bouncing, cartoonish head, I could see the faint flicker of white light, bound in ropes of thick black fire.

That was somebody's soul. And it was watching me.

Once I realized that, I got mega-creeped-out. I needed to leave that building right away. I interrupted Orange Crush in the middle of an in-depth description of a do-it-yourself tattoo kit she'd gotten for her birthday.

"Hey," I interjected, "it's been great talking to you, but I'm late meeting up with my boyfriend. Maybe I'll see you later?"

"Oh!" She blinked. "Um . . . sure. See ya."

I smiled and ran for it. Once I was out in the comparatively quiet parking lot, I dialed Michael. It went straight to voice mail.

"Damn it!" I swore, nearly throwing the phone on the ground in frustration.

"What's wrong?"

Ruthanasia stood behind me with a bobblehead in her hand. I couldn't decide which one to stare down, so I settled for looking back and forth between them in complete paranoia. I didn't even realize I was backing up until my butt hit a car bumper.

"What's wrong with you?" she asked, looking around wildly. "More of those things?"

"No." I tried to get ahold of myself. "What's that?"

She shook the bobblehead. And now that I knew about the soul jars, I imagined I could hear it screaming wordlessly in panic or pain, trying desperately to get the attention of people who would never realize they were looking at an instrument of torture. The worst part? I wasn't entirely sure I was imagining it.

"Limited-edition derby bobblehead. They were giving them out at the bar. Didn't you get one?"

She thrust it toward me, and I backed up. "No!" Now she was looking at me very cautiously, and I realized I'd better tone it down. If she figured out that I suspected she was a demon, she'd have no reason to continue the charade of normalcy. And from the way Michael had reacted, defeating her wouldn't be as easy as defeating 693. If you'd call that easy.

"You're losing it," she said.

"Uh . . . yeah. Maybe a little." I forced a laugh, leaning against the car as casually as possible. "Can you blame me?"

"No." She shook her head. "Actually, I'm going nuts here. Will you please tell me what the heck is going on? I'll buy you pancakes. I think better while I'm eating."

The rest of the Apocalypsies came out the door then, buying me a little time to figure out how to handle this. They were laughing and shoving each other over some joke that was apparently both very funny and very offensive. And every one of them had a derby bobblehead in her hands.

"No fighting." Ragnarocker charged over and clapped beefy arms around each of our necks. "You two need to kiss and make up."

"No kissing," Ruthanasia said.

"Definitely not," I echoed. "But things are cool."

"Good." Ragnarocker smelled like the inside of a brewery; either someone had spilled a drink on her or she had a fake ID. Her bobblehead was about two inches from my face. And this close, there was no denying the fact that there was a soul in there. The plastic figure looked ready to cry any second now. If I didn't get away from it, I might join in.

I wiggled out from under her arm. "So . . . uh. Do you have a ride home, Rock?"

She nodded and jerked a thumb toward Hoosya Mama. "She's taking me. She owes me one after she elbowed my face."

"I did not!" Mama yelled, grinning.

"Liar, liar, pants on fire!"

They staggered off down the row of cars, arguing amicably the entire way. We watched them until the red taillights of Mama's car left the parking lot.

People spilled out of the bar, until the lot was more crowded than the bar had been earlier. A few people got into their cars, but most hung around outside the doors, chatting and smoking and being generally obnoxious. Apparently the party was over. The rest of the girls clustered around, organizing rides and making plans for an after-after-party.

I was surrounded by bobbleheads. Within seconds, breathing became a struggle. It felt like I was walking into a tiny, windowless room full of chain-smokers with particularly stinky cigars. The stench wasn't physical, but that didn't make it any less real. I started coughing and couldn't stop.

Barbageddon pounded me on the back. "You okay?" I nodded, rubbing my watery eyes. At least the coughing gave me an excuse for being teary. "This after-party is lame. Everyone's invited to my place," she said. "You want to come?"

"No thanks. I think if I party any harder, the world might explode from awesomeness." I grinned, trying to take the sting out of the rejection, and she laughed.

"Suit yourself," she said, hobbling off across the parking lot. "I'll see you at practice. Don't kill each other!"

I looked hesitantly at Ruthanasia. It wasn't safe to be alone with her, but how would I get any info on what was going on if I didn't take that risk? I didn't know what to do, and it was only a matter of time before someone noticed my shaking. I just wanted to go home and hide under the covers. But there was no way I could do that after what I'd seen. Which sucked.

Someone tapped me on the shoulder, and it took every ounce of willpower I had not to whirl around and take their head off. Didn't anyone realize I was about five seconds away from losing it completely? Of course, I didn't *want* them to realize it, but I was hoping for a little subconscious recognition here.

"I just wanted to know if you want a ride," Darcy said. "Unless you're going to the after-after-party?"

I looked between Darcy and Ruthanasia, and now I had an idea. This was the perfect way to stay safe and keep an eye on the demon girl at the same time. Pancakes. What could go wrong in the middle of an all-night diner? Especially if I had backup.

"Actually," I said to Darcy, "we were just talking about pan-cakes. You want some?"

"Gosh, yes," she gushed. "I'm so hungry."

Ruthanasia scowled at Darcy, and the fact that she clearly didn't want her along made me feel like I'd done the right thing. I relaxed just a little. "Are we waiting for your boyfriend too?" Ruthanasia snapped.

I wasn't about to admit that he wasn't here, because that might be an opportunity she couldn't pass up. "There's no way we'll find him in all this crazy. I'll text him so he can catch up in a little bit."

So I did. And then Ruthanasia led the way through the crowded parking lot toward her car. Navigation was much easier with her in the lead. People tended to step out of the way when they saw her coming, like she had some strange force field of kickassery. Or maybe they were just sensing the fact that she was a demon in disguise. I'd disliked her from the start; maybe I'd subconsciously realized it too.

She fished a set of keys out of her pocket and pointed toward a surprisingly generic four-door. "That's me over there. There's a twenty-four-hour Denny's not too far from here if that sounds good to you."

"Sounds heavenly," I said.

"Totally," added Darcy.

Ruthanasia leaned over to unlock the car, and I noticed for the first time how thin her face was. Maybe it was seeing her without her makeup for once, but I'd never realized how deep the shadows under her eyes went. I would have thought she had a pair of shiners instead of just one, but it looked deeper than that, the kind of weariness that went down to the bone. She looked fragile—no, that wasn't the word. She looked damaged.

Maybe I was judging her too harshly. Michael had admitted he was theorizing about the demon thing. He'd only been here for less than a year; he was still learning too. Maybe she deserved saving just as much as the bobbleheads did.

"Are you okay?" I asked.

She sat in the driver's seat, and I walked around to the passenger's side and settled down beside her. "Considering what happened tonight, yeah. Mostly," she said finally.

Darcy flung the back door open, making us both jump. "So listen," she said, and for the first time in ages, she sounded like old hyperactive Darcy again. At least something was going well. "You have got to tell me about those funky guys with the crazy faces. You know, the ones you beat the bleep out of in the bathroom?"

"They were demons," Ruthanasia said while I was still fumbling for an explanation plausible enough to make Darcy stop asking but dangerous enough to convince her she'd be better off leaving guys like that alone.

"Yeah," Darcy said. "I thought so."

I gaped. And gaped. Did everybody around me believe in demons? I was tempted to ask about aliens and tinfoil hats to see if they believed in those too.

"You did?" I asked.

"Michael told me there were lots of them in the area these days."

"He said that?" I felt like an idiot, but I couldn't believe what I was hearing.

"He's been teaching me for the past few months," she said. "I'm learning to be a hunter, Casey."

"You are? So am I!" I exclaimed. For a moment, I felt relieved because now I could share the burden, but the feeling didn't last long. "But he didn't tell me that! He's been training me too. Why didn't he tell me?"

"There isn't anything going on between me and Michael," Darcy said defensively. "I wouldn't do that to you."

Ruthanasia snorted, but she sounded less caustic than I would have expected. "Yeah, he doesn't have eyes for anybody but Casey."

For some reason, I found myself apologizing to the demon in disguise. "Sorry," I said.

She shrugged. "It is what it is."

"Anyway," Darcy continued, "he said you were having a really hard time dealing with things, so we agreed to keep my training a secret. I thought he should tell you, but . . . well, he seems to be struggling too. I think he's more emotionally involved with you than he's supposed to be, and it's dorking with his logic. He doesn't seem to deal with his feelings well."

"Oh," I said. My stomach plummeted to my toes. Michael didn't trust me. I wondered what else he wasn't telling me.

Suddenly pancakes didn't sound so good. I'd be lucky if I didn't throw up.

"Well?" Ruthanasia asked, looking between the two of us. "Are we going or not? I'm all for having this conversation, but

I'd rather do so in a well-lit public place. I'm feeling a little paranoid these days."

"Sounds good to me," Darcy said.

I nodded, because I didn't trust myself to speak.

"Good," said Ruthanasia. "Because I need coffee. Lots of coffee.

Darcy shuddered from the backseat. "Ugh. Coffee."

"I thought you said you'd drink it in your sleep." I looked over my shoulder at her. "I never thought I'd hear you turn it down."

"Demon hunting changes things."

She stared out the window, her face pale and drawn. I would have hugged her if the seat hadn't separated us.

"I know exactly what you mean," I said as Ruthanasia pulled out of the parking lot.

Under the bright fluorescent lights of Denny's, the whole situation felt distant and unreal. Like maybe I should step back for a second and reevaluate, because I was rushing into things without really stopping to think them through. I would have asked Michael, but after finding out that he'd hidden Darcy's training from me, I was starting to wonder what else he wasn't spilling.

I pushed the thought of him aside and sipped my coffee even though I knew it was still too hot. The liquid scalded the roof of my mouth, making my skin all wrinkly and tender.

I couldn't help probing it with my tongue even though that only made it feel worse.

"So," Darcy said, not even waiting until the tight-faced waitress was out of earshot, "when are we raiding the demon factory?"

"Hush!" I exclaimed, and it came out in such an unintentionally loud voice that I think it attracted more attention than Darcy had in the first place. Subtlety wasn't my strong suit.

"What factory?" Ruthanasia asked. "I'm lost here."

"Yeah," I added. "Apparently, you know more than the rest of us put together, Darcy. Why don't you fill us in?"

It came out a lot more accusatory than I'd intended. I was still feeling a little hurt that Michael had chosen not to tell me about Darcy's training. But it was the only way she could know all this. Normal people don't just go, "Oh, wow! Demons! Let's go kill them!"

"Michael showed me the factory," she said. "I really flipped out about it too. How'd you handle it when he told you? When he showed me those wings of his, I nearly died, I was so shocked." She jumped a little, like she was trying to show us how shocked she was, and the whole table clattered. "Whoops. Sorry."

"So he showed you the factory?" I asked.

"What factory?" Ruthanasia demanded in a voice that made Darcy jump for real this time. It also ticked off the waitress, who had picked that moment to deliver pancakes for Ruthanasia and me and a Moons Over My Hammy for Darcy. She shoved our plates in our general directions like she didn't want to come into accidental contact with us and contract something. Then she stalked off.

"Apparently she doesn't like factories," Darcy said, deadpan.

I couldn't keep from cracking up. It was good to have someone to back me up. Now I wasn't alone, and that was a good thing. Between mouthfuls of crispy bacon, Darcy and I told Ruthanasia all about the factory and the soul jars.

"I wonder if Lauren's stuck in there," she murmured, staring down at her untouched plate.

"There's no way of knowing," I said. She looked devastated by that, and I knew it was probably all an act, but it felt so real. My mind went straight to Little Casey's mom. If she'd really sold her soul to help her daughter, nothing could make that right. I was starting to empathize with Ruthanasia despite myself.

"But there's no way to know that she *isn't,* is there?" she demanded.

I shook my head.

"Then that does it. We've got to do something about that factory."

"I'm totally down with that," Darcy said.

I opened my mouth. Closed it. Opened it again.

"Have you fought them yet, Darcy?" I asked.

"Just a couple demon dogs. Piece of cake." She snapped her fingers and grinned proudly, like demon hunting was a terrific hobby and I should try it sometime. She seemed to have recovered from her bout of nerves in the car, while I was getting edgier by the minute.

"I don't think you realize how dangerous this is," I said. "I'm not talking physical danger. They just . . ." It was the first time I'd spoken about what 693 had done to me in the park, and it made my hands shake so hard that I slopped hot coffee all over myself. Darcy wordlessly handed me a napkin. "They get inside your head. I absolutely believe they could make you kill yourself."

"Well, that's exactly why we need to do something." Ruthanasia must have seen the look on my face, because she added, "I mean, it might not be exactly the same guys who took my sister from me, but at least I've finally got some way to get back at the bastards. So you can either help me or get the hell out of my way."

"I'm going." Darcy looked at me, her eyes bright.

"Maybe we should wait for Michael," I hedged.

"Why?" Darcy took a big bite of her sandwich and swallowed it down. "He knew we'd go for the factory the minute his back was turned. Why do you think he left? He wants us to do this."

There was no way I could let her go alone with a demon. And maybe there would be some way to save Ruthanasia in the process. Maybe she could get her soul back.

"All right," I said reluctantly. "Let's do it."

"Tonight," Ruthanasia said.

I nodded and shoved a big bite of pancake into my mouth. If we were going to be fighting demons, I needed to carb up.

20

It was almost midnight by the time we arrived at the factory. We parked the car at the gas station where Michael had parked his bike, praying that it wouldn't get stolen while we were battling the forces of darkness. My nerves jangled like wind chimes in a hurricane, partly from the neighborhood we were traipsing through and partly because of what we were about to attempt. This was going to be a real battle, and I wasn't looking forward to it. Not that any of us intended to fire a weapon. I was a hunter, not a gangbanger. We'd come armed with dojo weapons. Darcy had her staff. It didn't look like much, just a solid length of ash, but it was super sturdy. It would make a good Relic.

I hadn't felt comfortable arming Ruthanasia, because who knew who she was going to be attacking? And she'd already taken my necklace. Although, now I was wondering how she'd managed to do that without getting blasted. Did Relics expire? I couldn't remember Michael saying anything about that, but he'd obviously been selective about what he'd told me. It brought me back to the growing suspicion that he'd been flat-out wrong. Maybe she wasn't a demon after all. It was a frustrating situation, because I didn't know whether I should be watching my own back or watching hers.

An empty plastic bag blew across the deserted intersection about a hundred feet away, but otherwise I didn't see any movement at all. It should have made me feel more secure, but instead I felt nervous. Like a hundred unseen eyes were watching me but I was never quite fast enough to catch them in the act.

The dingy brick of the factory looked almost black in the light of the flickering streetlamps. A metal gate covered the glass entryway, throwing faint crosshatched shadows onto the floor inside. And if that wasn't bad enough, I could see the sticker from a security company on the door.

"Aw, drat," I said, trying not to sound as relieved as I felt. "Looks like there's no way in. Guess we'll have to do this another time."

"Don't give up so easily," Darcy said. "Let's look around first."

Ruthanasia pressed her face up against the door, trying to get a better look at the lock. "I'd say screw it and break the glass, but there's no way we're getting through that gate unless you happen to have a blowtorch in your pocket." She eyed me. "You don't, do you?" I was pretty sure she was kidding.

"It's locked up tight, guys," I said. "And we are not breaking and entering. Seriously, let's come back sometime when we have a plan." And when we weren't towing around a maybe-demon who might decide to stab us in the back at any moment.

"Let's go around the building," Darcy said, totally ignoring me. "Maybe the cleaning crew propped the back door open. It's worth a look, right?"

I wanted to argue but couldn't come up with any reason why we shouldn't at least try. So when she took off down the claustrophobically narrow alley alongside the building, I followed. The ground under my feet crunched, and the dim light made it impossible to see what we were stepping on. Something told me I didn't want to know anyway.

We emerged onto the loading dock, which was illuminated by a pair of floodlights with sickly yellow bulbs. But it was still all too easy to see the glint of the huge silver padlocks securing each of the bay doors. Darcy tried the employee entrance in the corner. I just wanted her to get it over with so we could go home and I could go to bed. I was clearly not meant to be a bobblehead avenger.

The door opened.

"See?" Darcy flashed her gap-toothed grin. "My mom got fired from a cleaning crew once for leaving the back door unlocked, and somebody came in and stole a bunch of stuff.

People come out to smoke or to throw trash into the Dumpster, and they don't lock it again until the end of the night."

"So there are cleaning people in there?" I frowned. "I thought the building would be empty. I don't want them to get caught in the middle of something."

"Well, let's start in the basement, then. Usually the cleaners spend the most time on the public areas and the bigwig offices, which are on the upper floors. At least, that's what we did this summer when I temped with my mom," Darcy said. "Besides, if these really are demons, don't you think they'd be . . . you know? *Down?*"

I concentrated hard, trying to sense something that would help. I'd felt demons before, so it seemed like I ought to be able to tell if they were around. But the air was full of that choking blackness, and I couldn't sense a darned thing. So I quit trying.

"It sounds like a good enough place to start," I said. "Let's go."

She opened the door wider. Something slithered out of it.

So far, all the demons I'd seen had been creepy for sure, but they'd been just human or canine enough to slide under the radar as long as you didn't look too closely. But this thing was totally alien. All I could see was a burst of tentacles, sucking mouths, and sagging flesh. I had the instant, immediate sense that I was in the presence of something *other,* something that didn't belong here and never would. My mind recoiled; I wanted to run away, but I forced myself to step forward instead.

Darcy crumpled to the ground, babbling incoherently, and the door would have swung shut if the thing hadn't grabbed it with a tentacle, ripped it off its hinges, and thrown it across the loading dock. The door hit one of the floodlight poles with a clang, and the light rocked back and forth in sickening arcs before it hissed and went out entirely.

Strangely, that was better. Now that I couldn't see the creature very well, it was much easier to advance on it. I felt numb; my hands tingled with adrenaline, and it seemed like everything was suddenly moving in slow motion as my body readied itself for those instantaneous decisions that could mean life or death. I remembered this feeling from my black belt test, the sinking knowledge that yes, I was going to get hurt, but I was going to do this anyway.

One of the tentacles wrapped itself around Darcy's leg and started pulling her through the doorway. Red streaked the ground underneath her, and she moaned as her body skidded facedown over the broken glass and small pebbles strewn in front of the doorstep.

The smell of blood hit me, and it only managed to piss me off. If it hadn't been for me, she wouldn't have come. I had to protect her.

Suckers dotted each of the tentacles; I could see Darcy's jeans steaming where they came into contact with the greenish flesh. No way was I going to touch that. Now I was doubly glad we'd brought the arsenal. I grabbed her staff from the floor of the loading dock and spun it into action, whacking the tentacles wrapped around her leg with a swift double strike. I expected to feel the usual heat and vibration that came with using a Relic.

But it didn't happen.

I couldn't understand. There was no reason it shouldn't have worked. Maybe I couldn't use another hunter's Relics? It sure would have been nice if Michael had told me that.

The useless weapon clattered to the ground as the demon continued to drag Darcy inside. I needed to keep my hands free to defend us, so I knelt on her back to hold her in place. She screamed as I mashed her into the assorted sharp things beneath her. But it was better than her getting dragged into the darkness.

Now that I knew she wasn't going anywhere, I fumbled at my side for my *kusari-fundo,* a length of chain with a heavy weight at either end, but it was all tangled up in my belt. I batted away a searching tentacle with one hand and struggled with the chain with the other. This was not going well. At all.

"What the hell is that thing?" Ruthanasia yelled.

She was frighteningly pale, and the ground in front of her was splattered with puke. But she was still there, holding my necklace in one fist and a flimsy pocketknife in the other. You'd think she would have gone all pointy-teethed and fiery-eyed by now if she really was a demon. This would be an ideal time to strike, and *bang!* Two hunters out of commission. We had to have been wrong about her. Strangely, even though I'd never liked her, I wanted to be wrong.

"Casey?" she shrieked. "What do I do?"

"Just stay there." I finally freed my weapon and began to swing it, gaining momentum. "I'll handle it."

"No. These things took my sister." Her eyes flashed in a very familiar way.

"Wait!" I yelled, but it was too late. She leapt toward the thing, and a mass of tentacles shot toward her. They whipped around her body, curling up to encircle her neck. One quick twist, and she'd be dead.

"No!" I leapt to her rescue. But once I let Darcy go, the demon jerked her through the doorway. I heard her faint wail of panic from somewhere in the darkness. She sounded impossibly far away.

I hovered indecisively in the doorway, torn between my friends. How was I supposed to decide which one to save? I knew that if I didn't choose fast, I'd lose both of them, but how could I choose? There was no right answer, nothing I could choose that would make it easy to live with myself later.

Ruthanasia struggled against the constricting tentacles, her hand worming free. I saw the glint of the cross in her hand.

"The necklace!" I yelled, even though she was only a few feet away. "Use the necklace!"

"Duh," she replied.

Then her wrist twisted, and she shoved the bright silver right into one of the gaping mouths. The tentacle whipped away from her like she was made of acid, and then the beast stiffened in what looked like pain. I felt more than heard it shriek with frustrated hunger. Then it exploded, raining greenish goop and gobs of flesh onto the loading dock. And on us too.

I ducked, covering my head with my arms to protect myself from the globs dripping off the building, and charged inside. It was even more disgusting in there; the creature had been stuffed into the small hallway beyond the door, and I found myself wading through knee-high muck. When my foot hit something hard, I recoiled in disgust because I was sure that I'd just kicked a demon bit, but then I thought I saw a hint of yellow down there in the slop.

Darcy. She'd been wearing her jersey. I plunged my hands into the quivering, jellylike stuff and pulled her out, willing her to gasp or scream or something. But she just hung limply in my arms, rivulets of putrid guts running down her face. Was she breathing? I couldn't tell. I dragged her out onto the relatively firm ground of the loading dock. Ruthanasia rushed to help as soon as she saw what I was doing.

I couldn't remember CPR; my mind was whirling so fast that I couldn't think straight. Lucky for me, Ruthanasia knew what to do. She tilted Darcy's head back with what looked to me like an expert hand, stuck a finger into her mouth, and pulled out a clump of demon slime. Then she tilted her gore-streaked face to listen at Darcy's mouth.

It felt like my heart stopped beating and my head would burst any second. If Darcy was dead, those demons would pay.

She started coughing. I nearly lost it right there, but then she tried to sit up, and I forgot about the stupid hysterics and knelt down to help my friend.

"Thanks," she gasped. "What happened?"

"You almost suffocated on demon goop," Ruthanasia said as if this were something that happened all the time. But when I looked, her hands were shaking.

I felt so grateful that I thought I might faint. But I stayed conscious through sheer willpower. "We should get out of here," I said to Ruthanasia. "Darcy needs help."

"I'm not wussing, Kent," she growled. "I took that thing out, remember? We can do this."

I closed my eyes, trying *not* to remember. "I know. And thanks. But it's insane to do this when one of us is already hurt. Let's get Michael or get a plan or a flamethrower or something."

"You have a flamethrower?" She eyed me skeptically.

"Well, no. But Darcy's injured. You can't deny that."

"No!" Darcy croaked. "Don't even try to send us home now. Because we're going into that warehouse with or without you."

Ruthanasia hauled her up, and they folded their arms and stared me down with identical expressions—stubbornly set jaws and narrowed eyes. Going into the warehouse wasn't the best idea, but I couldn't abandon them now. I was sure by this point that Ruthanasia wasn't demonic—the whole dissolving-her-demon-brethren thing seemed to have eliminated that option—but she had no idea what she was up against. Darcy did, but she could barely stand up straight. So I had no choice but to give in and try to make the best of it. It was time to stop yapping and start moving. Because if the demons hadn't known we were coming before, they had probably figured it out after we'd exploded one of their buddies on their back porch.

"All right. But you two promise to stay behind me and watch our backs. I don't want to get flanked by a bunch of demons and have no way out." I looked them over. "Deal?"

Darcy nodded reluctantly, and after a moment's thought, so did Ruthanasia.

That would have to be good enough. I went through the door. The sludge was noticeably shallower already, about ankle height now. Either this stuff was draining out somewhere or it was dissolving. I voted for the latter, because the thought of demon guts in the water supply was enough to make me swear to drink canned beverages for the rest of eternity.

Doors on either side of the hallway led to rooms full of maintenance equipment and empty pallets, but I checked them briefly just to be sure demons weren't waiting for us to pass by before they jumped out at us. Maybe I was being a little paranoid, but that's the kind of thing that keeps people alive in combat situations—being thorough. Darcy and Ruthanasia hung back as I explored, Darcy muffling the occasional cough into her slimy sleeve.

The rooms were clear. But I did find a crowbar on top of an unopened crate of toilet paper and tossed it to Darcy, since she'd lost her staff. She took it and swung experimentally.

"You should Relic that up," I said. "Or do you want me to do it?"

"I'm not that damaged," she said, looking irate. "I'll handle it."

I pointed down the hallway and said, "This way."

At the end of the hallway was a door clearly marked with a glowing red EXIT sign. After what had happened outside, closed doors made me nervous. I motioned Ruthanasia and Darcy back until they were hugging the walls again, and cautiously opened the door. We didn't get tentacled, spewed on, or otherwise demon-assaulted, so I slowly looked around the door. Nothing there. We all let out breaths that none of us would have admitted we'd been holding.

The stairway was about as generic as they come. It had cream-colored tile walls. Metal steps that made more noise than I would have liked. Bright fluorescent lights overhead. But I could have happily stayed there forever.

We looked at each other cautiously, and then, without saying a word, we turned right and took the first step down. My instincts told me that Darcy was right. That was where the demons were.

I held the *kusari-fundo* loosely in my hands, the chain clanking softly as we descended the steps. Ruthanasia had her pocket-knife, and Darcy watched the rear with the crowbar held high. No way were we going to be taken by surprise.

As we got closer to the bottom of the stairs, the smell of burned plastic filled the air. The scent was undercut with something rotten that turned my stomach. I refused to think about what it was and started breathing through my mouth. Dingy brown paint covered the entire door—even the little window—so there was no way to see inside. No sign on it either, although I hadn't really expected one. Finding a door marked DEMON SOUL-SUCKING MACHINERY INSIDE would have been too easy.

I jerked my thumb toward the wall, and the girls flattened themselves against it. When I put my hand on the door, nothing happened. It wasn't particularly hot or cold. It didn't vibrate, bulge, or do anything else that you might expect from a demonic factory door. When I turned the handle and pulled, it swung open soundlessly. Nothing jumped out. I edged inside, using all my senses in an effort to catch the demons before they pounced.

I shouldn't have bothered. They were out in plain sight. The door opened smack in the middle of a giant basement. The room was dominated by long rows of machines crusted in the same black stuff that ringed the door. It looked like a bunch of alien assembly lines, studded with wires and tubes and all kinds of stuff I didn't understand. A big iron vat loomed against the wall opposite us, and the right side of the room was obstructed by stacks of boxes that reached to the ceiling.

Those giant stacks seemed crazy high. I didn't see any forklifts around, but the demons obviously didn't need any. The worker demons didn't seem very familiar with this thing called *gravity*. They were giant spiderlike things about the size of tigers, with black glossy bodies and blurry-fast legs that defied my attempts to count them. The demons climbed up the sides of the machines and the wall of boxes; one hung upside down from the ceiling, its legs fiddling with a loose tube that dangled overhead.

There were more spiders than I could count. These were not the kind of odds that made me comfortable. I took a step into the room and started to swing the *kusari-fundo* in wide, lazy loops. Good thing I'd picked the one with the heavy weights; the light ones probably wouldn't have had the power to get through those hard outer shells.

But the demons didn't attack. They barely seemed to notice us. They scurried busily over the clanking and hissing machinery, packing boxes and making imperceptible adjustments to the various gauges and valves dotting the instrumentation. I glanced back. Darcy was still in the stairway, guarding our line of retreat, but Ruthanasia stood a couple of steps behind me, and she looked as confused as I felt. Didn't the demons care that we were here to destroy their soul-jar-bobblehead-machine thingies? Weren't they supposed to be trying to kill us?

This was way too easy. We crept toward the machines, the air getting hotter with every step. Sweat began dripping down my temple. I held a hand up to Ruthanasia, pointed to the machine, and indicated that she should back out of the way. Once she and Darcy were out of range, I reached toward a valve and twisted it.

The valve let off a huge blast of steam and nearly took my eyebrows off. That got their attention. A spider demon dropped to the floor a few feet away. I backed up hastily, letting the steam form a barrier between us.

The demon reared up onto its hind legs, towering over me. I twisted my arm, swinging the *kusari-fundo* at the chitinous belly of the creature, and the weapon crunched into the thing with a flash of white light. Greenish blood sprayed onto the floor. I spun, maintaining the momentum of my swing, and the free end of the chain wrapped around the demon's standing legs, the weight snapping one of them clean off.

The beast wavered and toppled to the ground, its balance destroyed and the remaining legs wiggling in the air. I stayed in a crouch, ready for the onslaught, but none of the other creatures attacked. They didn't seem to care if you killed their buddies, only if you dorked around with their stuff. Which meant we'd have to figure out how this machine worked and take it down strategically in one shot if we didn't want to fight them all. One at a time was doable, but I didn't think it would be so easy if they swarmed.

Where were the souls? Without them, this would have been just another bobblehead factory. All I had to do was free them, and we could get the heck out of here. I took a deep breath, ignoring the thick, nasty taste in the air, and felt for them. They were here; I just knew it. But I couldn't afford to guess where. I had to be right the first time.

My eyes were drawn to the vat opposite the stairway door. There was only one vat, compared to the twenty or so assembly-line machines, so was this it? It sat in the middle of a bristle of wires and was covered with a lid full of pressure dials and blinking lights, so I couldn't just look to see what was inside. But five spider demons crawled along its surface, compared to only one or two for the other machines. I didn't need any other proof to know that the vat was important.

"I need to check that out," I said to Ruthanasia, and pointed toward the vat. "Stay with Darcy and be ready to make a quick retreat."

Ruthanasia looked up at it. "Okay. I'll head for the doorway. We'll keep the exit open."

She backed away, but I was already focused on the task at hand. It was time to free some souls.

I stepped cautiously toward the vat. Cables crisscrossed the space; I stepped carefully over one and ducked under another, jerking the *kusari-fundo* up hastily when it almost connected with the cable on the floor. On the vat, one of the demons paused in its fussing to look at me with faceted, alien eyes, waiting to see if I'd make contact with its precious machine. The abrupt motion threw me off balance, and I wobbled dangerously close to one cable and then another. The spider thing drew closer, chittering to its fellows. A second one joined it, watching, waiting for me to put a hand down, to skim the black web of cords with my shoulder, to place a single foot wrong.

Slowly but surely I made my way to the vat. It was at least two stories tall and bigger around than our town house. That was what it felt like, anyway. I felt tiny and insignificant. No way would I ever manage to win this fight. I figured I should just give up and go home.

What the heck? I blinked, shaking my head, and my vision miraculously cleared. Sure, it was big, but not *that* big. More luxury-sized SUV than house. And there was no way I'd quit like that. I eyed the spider demons swinging from the cables as if the wires were a giant, mechanized web, and I said, "Get out of my head. I'm not giving up."

They watched me in twitching silence.

When I was only a few steps from the vat, I knew I was in the right place. I could hear the souls of the damned packed inside. Their cries for mercy hovered right at the edge of audible without quite crossing over. But I could feel them. It made my teeth hurt.

I didn't know how the souls had gotten there. Michael hadn't told me the mechanics, just that the demons tricked people into making a deal and then saved their souls to snack on later. I probably didn't want to know the rest. If these were the kinds of people who would make deals with demons, some of them had probably done some pretty horrible stuff. But they deserved a chance to make things right.

There was a pressure valve at right about eye level. A good whack from the *kusari-fundo* would take it right off. I took a quick look around, judging how much room I had to work with, and began to swing my weapon, steadily and deliberately building up momentum.

"Hey, guys?" I called to Darcy and Ruthanasia. "Get ready to move in a sec, okay?"

They didn't answer. I carefully stopped the swing before turning to look over my shoulder. They were talking to each other; Ruthanasia's back was to me, and I couldn't even see Darcy. What in the heck were they doing?

"Guys?" I asked, and then I heard this alien hum so strong that the walls vibrated. My teeth began to chatter. And somehow it felt off to me. The vibration of a Relic felt powerful, but it didn't hurt. This did—it felt like I was about to rattle into tiny little pieces and shatter all over the floor.

I took a half step toward Ruthanasia and Darcy, looking for the source of that horrific sound. It was Darcy. She opened her mouth, and blackness came out.

Calling them "flies" didn't do them justice. They were about as big as butterflies, black-winged, with stingers like toothpicks. I could see them clearly from about twenty feet away; they were that big. Their wings dripped muddy brown ooze that speckled Darcy's cheeks as they escaped from her mouth.

Ruthanasia scrambled backward as the swarm continued to erupt from Darcy's body, forming a cloud about head height. The hum grew, drowning out the teeth-gritting noise from the vat behind me. I would have been relieved if I hadn't been so scared.

Finally Darcy's body just . . . deflated. As if there had been nothing inside but a giant swarm of flies. No bones. Nothing human.

I kept expecting her to get up, grin, and yell, "Gotcha!" Because this had to be a joke. Darcy couldn't be a sack of bugs; she was my friend. Bugs do not force-feed you nachos and take you out shopping and make you have fun despite yourself.

But they might make you act funny. How many times had I thought she hadn't been herself lately? Michael *had* been wrong. Ruthanasia wasn't the demon. That demon attack in the bathroom had been intended to divert our suspicion *to* Ruthanasia, not away from her. It had worked. We'd never suspected Darcy.

I put my head into my hands and took an unsteady step

right onto one of the cables. One of the spider demons chattered nervously. I whipped my head around, expecting it to pounce on my head. It didn't. It backed away from the swarm of flies, its belly to the ground in a posture I could only describe as cringing. It was afraid.

"What the hell?" I murmured, my weapon hanging uselessly at my side. How was I supposed to fight *bugs*?

Ruthanasia looked up at the seething mass of demonic insects hovering over her.

"Are you nuts?" I shrieked, lurching in her direction, only to get my foot caught in the maze of wires. "Get out of here! Find Michael!"

Her face was taut with anger. "This is for Lauren," she said, totally ignoring me.

"Ruthanasia!" I tugged my foot free, which threw me off balance and made me stagger into one of the spider things. It took a halfhearted swipe at me, ripping my sleeve. I jabbed at one of its eyes, splattering myself with more goo, but I didn't even pause to wipe my fingers. I had to get to my friend before it was too late.

But it was. She dug into one of her pockets and came out with a derby brochure. Her knife was clutched in the other hand. I had no idea what she thought she was going to do with a knife and some paper against a swarm of bugs, but I felt pretty safe in assuming it wasn't going to work.

The swarm sank toward her. She didn't run, although I saw the fear on her face. Instead, I heard the unmistakable sound of a lighter being struck, and she lit the brochure on fire.

"Suck it," she said, and then she threw the flaming paper into the swarm.

Spots danced before my eyes, either from lack of oxygen or from the light show. The flies literally burst when the flames hit them. They made a popping sound that reminded me of those little bottles people always use on New Year's, the ones that you pull the string out of and a bunch of streamers come out the end.

Too bad there wasn't enough fire. The flames obliterated maybe a quarter of the swarm before they went out, and then the swarm engulfed Ruthanasia. She flailed and cursed as the bugs closed in over her.

"Casey!" she shrieked. "Do something!"

What was I supposed to do? I didn't have a giant fly-swatter, I didn't carry a lighter, and my *kusari-fundo* was useless against bugs. My eyes scanned the room frantically for something useful as I scrambled closer, tripping over random equipment.

"Get off her!" Michael flew through the door. His wings blazed with a pinkish light so bright that my eyes felt like they might melt.

"Michael!" I yelled. "Where have you been?"

"Chasing your butt all around town," he snarled. I took a step back, and his face cleared a little. "I had to track Ruthanasia's car; I can't sense you in here."

Then the swarm spoke. In the movies, bug beasts always took the form of a humanoid figure or maybe a face, so you could see their "mouths" move when they talked. But not this thing. It hovered in an amorphous blob, and all its insectile little mouths spoke at once. It sounded almost robotic. "Begone, Sentinel, lest you fall. You teeter on the edge," it said.

Michael's face tightened, his lips drawing down into a frustrated scowl. His eyes gleamed the same dull red that I remembered from the park.

"Michael!" I yelled. "Stay out of this! You don't want me to have to fight two demons, do you?"

And then Ruthanasia gasped, "Help me!"

"Get her out of here!" I cried.

He blinked in surprise when he saw her on the ground. But he recovered from the shock quickly. Faster than fast, he swooped down and picked Ruthanasia up. Her face was pale; she clutched her hand to her chest. It looked like a lump of melted wax. I wasn't sure if the damage was from the fire or the bugs, but either way, I couldn't bear to look at it. I felt like a coward, but I couldn't look at it any longer.

"I won't leave you, Casey," Michael said, his wings blazing brighter with his anger.

Ruthanasia began to convulse in his arms, foam dripping from her mouth. Her body shook uncontrollably, the movements so erratic that he almost dropped her.

"Please!" My voice rang out, stronger than I felt. I worried I might pee my pants, that's how scared I was. But I'd lost Darcy already. I wasn't about to let Ruthanasia fall too. And Michael looked like he was about to lose it. "If you don't go, she'll die."

Michael kicked the wall in frustration, punching a hole

into the brick. "Don't do anything stupid, Casey. I'll be right back."

The light from his wings blurred into a streak that climbed the stairs. It took a moment for my eyes to recover from the bright flash that accompanied his flight, but once they did, I saw that Michael and Ruthanasia were gone.

The swarm swiveled in the air to look at me. Thousands of faceted alien eyes evaluated me and found me lacking. I wanted to cower before the swarm, throw myself on the ground and beg for mercy. This was clearly a powerful demon. What did I think I could do against it? I was nothing.

That was when I felt it—the all-too-familiar thrum of defiance building inside me. The idea of quitting still pissed me off. Maybe these things were twisting my thoughts. But there was nothing they could threaten me with that I hadn't made peace with a long time ago. I wasn't afraid to die. I was afraid of not living. Before, my anger and fear had made me lash out at people I cared about, spinning me out of control. But now my anger felt focused. Now I had something really worth being angry about.

"Hunter." The swarm drifted closer, undulating above me. The hairs on my arms instantly stood on end. "Bow down before the Lord of the Flies."

I felt the black cloak of its will push down on me, buckling my knees. I staggered, grabbing one of the wires and tearing it out of its casing. The spider demons let out high-pitched, agonized screeches, but none of them dared come close. The swarm watched with glittering eyes as I struggled to stay upright. Heck, I couldn't even breathe, the pressure was so strong.

"Get out," I managed to say, but the words came out in a whisper.

The swarm darted toward me, buzzing hungrily. I felt the demon's will push me again, smothering my desire to fight back, urging me to lie down and die. It was so tempting. Anything to make the pain stop.

"Suck it, demon," I said, echoing Ruthanasia's words. And suddenly I knew what to do. I had no way to defeat a demon lord. But at my back were thousands of souls crying out for a second chance. Darcy deserved it; if she'd sold her soul, she was probably in there. And Little Casey's mom and Lauren, if that was what happened to them. If I could stand tall for just one moment despite the fact that I was scared shitless, I could give them that second chance.

I rose on quivering legs, stretching my arms toward the swarm as if to welcome it, and then I swung my *kusari-fundo* as hard as I could. Not toward the demon. Toward the vat. The chain wrapped around a pressure valve and tore it free.

The vat exploded. I threw my arms up to cover my face as pieces of metal rained down around me but miraculously failed to hit me. The dull murmur of the souls inside rose to a triumphant fever pitch. The demons had tricked them. Imprisoned them. Tortured them. And now they had a chance for vengeance.

They took it. The air filled with a bright, howling light. The buzzing voice of the Lord of the Flies turned into a howl of agony as the swarm was buffeted by flickering humanoid shapes. The air filled with lancelike streaks of light; the spider demons crouched in corners and shrieked in panic and pain. I heard a sound like rain and couldn't figure out what it was until I saw the flies pattering onto the ground, covering the cement floor.

"You!" The remaining flies turned to me, and I felt the anger of the demon within. Its fury hit me so hard that I slammed back against the machinery, and twisted metal punctured my skin in various places. Darting white lights kept striking the swarm, injuring the bugs, but there were still enough to take me down. I staggered, trying to flee, but there was nowhere to go.

The swarm darted toward me, and I screamed, falling to the ground and holding my arms overhead. White light streaked before my eyes, forming a barrier that the Lord of the Flies struck against, howling in anger. Empty insect hulls fell to the ground in a torrent, and the swarm still battered the wall before me, desperate to get to me.

The light of the barrier flickered. I could see the souls within growing dimmer and dimmer as the demon ground them down.

I swore I heard a whisper then, and a thin layer of light settled on me like a blanket. Or maybe a shield. "Get out, Casey."

Darcy. She'd been in that vat after all. I didn't know how the demon had gotten to her, and right then I didn't care. She was my friend. And friends don't abandon each other.

I thought about everything that had happened. Everything I'd lost—Darcy, and the kids with cancer who hadn't made it, and a year of dead time I'd never get back. I thought about Rachel and Kyle and my insane parents. Ruthanasia. Michael. I wanted my life back, and I was ready to fight for it.

My knees shook so hard, I could barely stand; my stomach heaved with terror. The pancakes stayed down through a sheer act of willpower. But I still stood. Before me, Darcy flickered one last time.

Her light went out.

The Lord of the Flies howled his triumph. The swarm that settled on me was maybe a tenth of its former size, but it was still enough to cover my skin. I felt the weight of monstrous insect bodies on my face. Their legs scrabbled at my lips, trying to work their way into my mouth. I felt them crawling in my clothes.

I felt a surge of panic. Any moment, they'd start eating me alive or something equally horrific.

But I'd won.

They'd thrown everything they could at me, and I'd been terrified every step of the way, and I'd stood up to them anyway. I—the poor damaged cancer girl—had faced repeated demon attacks and lived. And now I understood why I'd been chosen: I had nothing to lose and everything to gain.

Michael had said that one day I wouldn't need an object to make a Relic. That comment hadn't made sense to me at the time, but it did now.

"I'm ready," I said.

The flies scrabbled into my mouth. Their oily, rotten taste made me gag. I struggled against the urge to vomit, taking a deep breath. With the breath came that galloping rush of electric energy from the Between, the same white light that made up Michael's wings. But now it filled my entire body with life and motion and power. If I held on too long, it would wash me away, but now I knew how to ride it—like pain—how to let myself go and just allow the energy to pour into me, because the pain would be over soon, and if nothing else, I knew how to endure.

A glow filled the room, and it was me. My body hummed with power as I opened myself up fully to the Between. I didn't feel scared anymore. This was where I belonged.

The flies disintegrated. I could hear the frustrated howl of the Lord of the Flies as its body turned to ash and floated to the ground. And as the last insect fell, there was a clap like thunder as the Lord of the Flies popped out of existence, and the air consumed the empty space.

The room was still and silent. My body no longer hummed; I let the electric energy go back to where it had come from. The motionless flies were already starting to sink into the cement, leaving no evidence behind. The spider demons were gone, destroyed by the avenging souls, or maybe just hiding. At this point, I really didn't care.

The souls were gone, including Darcy. I felt bad that I hadn't gotten to thank her, or ask what had happened, but she had to be okay, right? I hadn't felt any cosmic stairway to heaven open up and carry them away to nirvana, or whatever was supposed to happen. But I hadn't felt them being sucked into a whirling vortex either. Hopefully, they'd gotten exactly what they deserved—a second chance. I wasn't sure what that would be—an afterlife, maybe? Or reincarnation? But whatever it was, it had to be better than ending up as a midafternoon demon snack.

I went upstairs and out the back door into the fresh nighttime air. I'd never been so happy to be alive. After everything I'd been through, that was saying a lot.

The bright lights of the convenience store were a shock after being in that dark basement for what had felt like hours. I pushed open the door, shielding my watery eyes with one hand. The clerk eyed me carefully from behind his shield of Plexiglas. I probably looked like the average pothead on a munchies run. I tried a smile and a wave, but he only scowled and dropped his hands out of sight under the counter, where I was sure he had a gun or an alarm. Maybe both.

Caffeine would make me feel less like a member of the zombie hordes. I grabbed a soda, paid for it, and immediately cracked it open and drained half the bottle in one long swallow. I burped. Then I fainted.

How embarrassing.

A few weeks later, I emerged into the alleyway behind the convention center, sweaty and elated and generally happy to be alive. The charity bout to raise money for Ruthanasia's reconstructive hand surgery after her tragic "fireworks accident" had been a lot of work to put together but totally worth it. We'd lost the bout, which was no surprise, given that Ruthanasia couldn't skate and poor Darcy was decorating milk cartons and Missing Children boards. I couldn't decide if I'd lost or won the battle with the Lord of the Flies, but I was still standing, and that felt momentous.

"Case!" Kyle sprinted out the doors with a huge handful of receipts clutched in front of him like a weird bouquet. "We made over fifteen thousand dollars tonight! Holla!"

"Woo!" I clenched my fist and pumped it. "Couldn't have done it without you, man."

"You're right." He grinned. "And totally my pleasure. I'm worming my way into Michael's good graces so he'll take me on as an assistant coach. Then you'll have to follow my every command. You know that, right?"

I snorted. "Fat chance."

He mock-grumbled at me. "Fine. See if I take you out for pizza."

"Did someone say the magic word?" came a voice behind us.

I whipped around to see Michael grinning at us from the

doorway. He'd been maniacally happy ever since he'd found me unconscious in the convenience store. Like the kind of happy that makes people wonder about your sanity and makes the cops question you at length about the disappearance of one of your skaters. But somehow his brother the computer genius had manufactured a pretty tight alibi for him, so the cops had been left with nothing but vague suspicions about Michael's weird behavior. We couldn't exactly tell them that he was elated to have racked up his first completed mission as a guardian of the universe.

"I dunno, dude. Is the magic word 'pizza'?" asked Kyle.

"Yep."

"Then I did."

"Cool." I was starting to feel a little invisible—and a little pouty over it—when Michael picked me up and swung me around in a dizzying circle. Then, with my skates dangling a good six inches off the ground, he kissed me. I couldn't figure out if my head was swimming from the spin or from the lip-lock. I didn't care.

"Ahem." Kyle cleared his throat loudly, and Michael and I reluctantly released each other.

Michael shot an apologetic glance at my best friend. "Sorry, dude."

"Next time, get a room," joked Kyle.

"How about I set you up with one of the girls and we get adjoining rooms? I think Ruthanasia is single."

They started toward the door without me, talking smack and dissecting the bout. They'd already begun to devise new and nefarious ways to torture us at practices. It was so cute that I couldn't even get mad.

"I'll just wait here, guys. Don't mind me," I called.

Michael raised a hand and waved without turning around. "We'll be back in a minute!" he replied.

The door closed behind them, and I huddled against the wall. The breeze was starting to feel a little overly cool as my body temp returned to normal after the workout I'd had. I'd skated in at least two thirds of the jams. It probably would have been wise for me to take off the skates, but that would have required effort.

The one minute turned into four, and they still weren't back. I would have worried, but Kyle texted me: MORE PAPER- WORK. WAIT LONGER. The guy even shouted in texts.

I rolled up and down the short alleyway in a belated attempt to give my muscles a cool-down so they didn't cramp later. And when the trio of demons appeared at the end of the alley wearing Apocalypsies tees and sporting enough teeth to drive an orthodontist to binge drink, I wasn't even surprised. I hadn't seen any demon activity since we'd emerged from the factory. I knew it could only be a matter of time.

"Hunter," said the middle one, and either they were cold too or I scared them, because his voice shook, and he took out a knife and held it up in front of him like he needed the reassurance of steel in his hand.

I rolled my eyes. "Spare me the ridiculous posturing and let's get on with it already. I know why you're here."

The metal door behind me slammed against the brick with

a hollow boom. It didn't feel like a threat, but I'd been wrong before, so I risked a glance. My teammates poured out— Ragnarocker, Barbageddon, Angel Pop, all of them.

"What's going on out here?" demanded Barbageddon, quickly assessing the situation. She was off the crutches now and ready for some action.

"Hey, Knifey Boy. You're not messing with my girl here, are you?" Ragnarocker asked, popping her knuckles and moving to flank me.

"Because that would totally suck," added Barbageddon.

The girls arrayed themselves around me, sweaty-faced, runny-mascaraed, bruised and dinged and totally fierce. Maybe they didn't know a demon from a doorknob, but if Ruthanasia was any indication, they had enough heart to stand against a horde of demons. The Sentinels seemed to know a lot of things about demons, but I knew hunting. And these girls had the heart to take a stand if only someone would show them how. I could be that someone.

The demons began exchanging nervous glances, backing uncertainly toward the dim mouth of the alleyway.

"I tell you what," I said. "I'm feeling nice today. We'll give you a two-second head start."

I felt the girls shift around me, tensing on their toe stops, muscles preparing to launch into motion. We must have been quite a sight, because one of the demons turned tail and ran.

"This," I declared, "is for Ruthanasia. And for Darcy."

"Yeah," Barbageddon echoed.

"Get them!" I shouted, and we charged forward as one,

the blockers leading the way like a battering ram, the jammers clustered on the inside, waiting for the right time to make a surprise strike. But we never got the chance. The remaining two demons took one look at the oncoming Apocalypsies and sprinted for safety. We stopped at the mouth of the alley, hurling taunts after them. It probably wasn't smart, but it felt so good to laugh in the face of danger again that I joined in.

"Wusses!" I yelled. "Go back to where you came from!"

"You fight like toddlers!" Barbageddon shouted.

I burst into giggles. Sure, I was still afraid. If I hadn't been a target before, I was one now. But I didn't have to face the forces of darkness alone. And I'd proven that I wasn't a poor little cancer girl anymore and never would be again.

Now I was a demon-fighting derby girl, and I wasn't going to back down. Because I had a life to live, and no demon was going to take it from me.

ACKNOWLEDGMENTS

I'm one heck of a lucky woman. I'm lucky to work with amazing people like Kate Schafer Testerman and Wendy Loggia, who have helped make me a better writer than I ever thought I could be. I'm especially lucky that they laugh at my jokes. And I'm lucky to be a part of terrific writers' groups like the Baconators (Stasia Kehoe, Jessi Kirby, Elana Johnson, and Gretchen McNeil) and the Screwtop Bottles (Sara Beitia, Josie Bloss, Julia Karr, and Rebecca Petruck). They laugh at my jokes too, which is a pretty terrific part of them.

I owe a special debt of gratitude to Aimée Carter, who urged me to put on my big-girl panties and tell this story even if it scared the bleep out of me. The best friends aren't afraid to kick you in the butt when you need it, and I love her for it.

And Kiki Hamilton and Keri Mikulski, who read the earliest version of this manuscript, are saints, plain and simple.

My kids, Connor, Lily, and Renee, are the awesomest of awesome people who make me awesome by association. Which is, quite frankly, *awesome.*

And then there's my husband, who can't be thanked enough. Back when we were just friends, Andy was diagnosed with leukemia. When we started dating, his hair was just starting to come back. He wasn't supposed to survive, but he did. We couldn't have a family, but we did. And then he topped off those miracles by becoming a pediatric oncologist. He works side by side with the doctors who saved his life. More than anyone else, he understands what his patients are going through. This book is my love letter to him, because he's proof that you can do more than survive after cancer. You can *thrive.* And then go on to save your future wife from killer bees—but that's another story entirely.

See what I mean? Lucky. Minus the bees, anyway.

A Q&A WITH

CARRIE HARRIS

Tell us the story behind the story. What made you want to write a book about cancer and evil bobbleheads? No offense, but that's a crazy combo.

It *is* a crazy combo, isn't it? I think that's part of what I like about it. Here's how it went down: I decided to write a book about a cancer survivor in honor of my husband, Andy. He's an awesome guy. One time, he cut a watermelon in half with a katana because I asked him to (and yes, I still giggle hysterically over that). I've also seen him catch a shuriken with his hands like an action movie hero, which is surprisingly attractive. In short: *awesome*. We've known each other for a long time—we played Ultimate Frisbee together back in my college days. But one day, he stopped showing up. He'd been diagnosed with acute myelogenous leukemia. He was nineteen years old.

The details aren't mine to tell; all I'll say about his experience is that the prognosis wasn't good. He wasn't expected to survive. It would have been easy to give up hope. He went through hell, but he survived through a combination of terrific medical care and sheer bullheaded will. More than one person called it a miracle.

We started dating just as his hair was growing back. I still have a lock of it from his first post-cancer haircut. There were a few setbacks and health scares. There was survivor's guilt. And sure, I did what I could to help with those things, but I always wished I could do more to show him how much I admired him for being the kind of man who doesn't give up regardless of the odds. In my mind, that kind of man won't let you down. That kind of man is a keeper.

He changed his major from engineering to premed. And then came miracle number two—the treatment had supposedly destroyed his chances of having children, but our son was born in 2003. (And let me tell you, the conversation where you tell the in-laws that their presumed-sterile son is your baby daddy? *Awkward.*) Our twins followed in 2006. (And the conversation was much less awkward that time, in case you were wondering.) He'd beaten the odds once again.

Then, as if all that wasn't astounding enough, he became a pediatric bone marrow transplant doctor. He works side by side with some of the physicians who saved his life. And more than anyone else, he knows what his patients are going through. Sometimes he's the only one who can reach them because he understands on a level that few others can. And true to form, he won't give up on them, no matter what.

With all this in mind, it's probably no surprise that I have a very strong emotional reaction to YA books about cancer. There are some great ones out there, but I've always wished there were more books about survivorship. There is life after cancer, and those are stories that deserve to be told. Finally, I decided to quit whining about that and write one myself.

I really wanted to pay tribute to Andy's experience. But even in the face of cancer, I can't stop making wisecracks, because I think laughter is one of the best weapons we have against the darkness. So I decided to combine his favorite things with mine. Reading this book should give you a pretty good idea of what life is like in the Harris household—minus the demons, of course. I put in cancer survivorship and ninjas for Andy, and he was kind enough to allow me to exploit both his personal experiences and his professional knowledge, so hopefully I've got the details right. (If not, we all know to blame me, right?) We watch a lot of *Ninja Warrior* together, so I added a dash of freerunning. (Get it? A *dash.* Har har.) I put in things that really crack me up, like roller derby and bobbleheads and Halloween. It was both the easiest and hardest book I've ever written, but I'm really proud of it in the end. Ultimately, it's a love letter to us and what we are together.

Roller derby is a big part of this book. Have you ever skated?

I've thought about it a lot; does that count? But seriously, I haven't tried out for a team because right now my kids have to take priority over hobbies. But I'm a huge fan of the Detroit Derby Girls and make an idiotic fangirl out of myself over Racer McChaseHer, who is a jammer for our travel team. One of the things I really love about the derby is that teams are volunteer-run, and then on top of that? They adopt charities. This is not the kind of sport you do because you want to be rich. It's one you pick because you love it and you want to make the world a little more awesome. I really love that, and it fit with what I wanted for Casey.

I hope to skate someday. I think I'm going to call myself Carrie Carrie Quite Contrary, like the nursery rhyme, only my garden will grow with kick-assery.

Casey's story is inspirational. What can readers do to make a difference, short of joining their own derby team and fighting demons?

This is an excellent question! If this book—or any other, for that matter—makes you feel strongly, take that passion out into the world and use it to make a difference! Sadly, not every patient has a happy ending like Casey and my husband, and I think we could be doing a lot more to make that happen. Each year, 175,000 kids are diagnosed with cancer worldwide. Cancer is the number one disease killer of kids in the United States and Canada, but at the time I'm writing this, only about 2 percent of the National Cancer Institute's research dollars are devoted to children's cancers. That statistic gives me the angry eyebrows every time I read it.

But there are a lot of things you can do that make a difference. Big or small, they add up. Here are some ideas of how you can take action to help kids survive to fight the demons.

➤ If you're old enough, donate blood! Kids with cancers and blood disorders need it! And don't forget to register as a bone marrow donor if you're eighteen or older. It's easy to do, and it doesn't hurt. All you need to do is swab the inside of your cheek. Not eighteen yet? You can still help organize a donor drive; check out marrow.org for details.

- Donate to your local children's hospital. Make hats for cancer patients, donate pillowcases to make their rooms comfortable, or send books to the hospital library. Most hospitals have a wish list on their websites.

- Become a St. Baldrick's Shavee. St. Baldrick's (stbaldricks.org) is an organization that funds childhood cancer research. Being a shavee is just what it sounds like—you collect money to shave your head. You can even organize an official shavee event. They say it's just like a walkathon, only without the blisters. That cracks me up.

- Organize a lemonade stand or sell paper lemons through Alex's Lemonade Stand, another organization that funds research. Check out their website (alexslemonade.org) to learn about the four-year-old cancer patient who started the whole thing.

- Host a bake sale through Cookies for Kids' Cancer (cookiesforkids cancer.org). You can either bake your own or order through their site and make it an official event.

- Get your school to participate in a Pennies for Patients drive for the Leukemia & Lymphoma Society (lls.org), volunteer at a Light the Night Walk, or walk or run in a Team in Training event.

If you undertake any of these things, drop me a note at carrie@carrieharris books.com. I want to hear about it and put you on the list of People Who Are Awesome and thank you for being a Person Who Is Awesome. Which is a little redundant, but hopefully you know what I mean. We might not fight demons in alleyways, but there's a little hero in all of us.